FROZEN ECHO

Linda Kay Silva

Bella BOOKS

2012

Copyright © 2012 by Linda Kay Silva

Bella Books, Inc.
P.O. Box 10543
Tallahassee, FL 32302

All rights reserved. No part of this book may be reproduced or transmitted in any form or by any means, electronic or mechanical, including photocopying, without permission in writing from the publisher.

Printed in the United States of America on acid-free paper
First published 2012

Editor: Katherine V. Forrest
Cover Designer: Linda Callaghan

ISBN 13: 978-1-59493-302-8

PUBLISHER'S NOTE

The scanning, uploading, and distribution of this book via the Internet or via any other means without the permission of the publisher is illegal and punishable by law. Please purchase only authorized electronic editions, and do not participate in or encourage electronic piracy of copyrighted materials. Your support of the author's rights is appreciated.

Other Bella Books by Linda K. Silva

More Than an Echo

Echo Location

When an Echo Returns

Spinsters Ink titles by Linda Kay Silva

Across Time

Second Time Around

Third Time's A Charm

Dedication

This one is dedicated to Team Storm…those incredible individuals who help shape, mold, edit, and whip into shape my words, paragraphs. and occasionally even me.

Billie—for your technological know-how, your gorgeous cover mock ups, your typing skills, and your ability to find anything and fix everything.

Sandi—for the fastest fingers in the West, your inline comments, and your critical insight of my manuscripts.

Linda Callaghan—for your gorgeous cover art and ability to capture the essence of every book.

Katherine V Forrest—for the liberal use of your blue pencil. You make every page better.

Jessie at Bella—for helping me keep track of what is what and just making a really hard job look easy.

And of course, Lori—for giving me the time and space to do what I love most. Thank you for your complete acceptance.

About The Author

Linda Kay is still happily teaching various literature courses at a military university. She teaches everything from World Literature to Sci-fi/Fantasy and Women's Literature. In 2011 she garnered the Excellence in Teaching and Learning Award at her university as well as a Golden Crown Award for *More Than an Echo*. Linda Kay resides in California with her amazing partner of 15 years, her lovable dog of 6 years, and a menagerie of turtles and tortoises she has rescued. When not writing, teaching, playing tennis, or riding her Harley, Lucky, she can be found trotting the globe to such phenomenal places as Swaziland and Jamaica. Linda Kay is currently working on the eighth book for both series and apparently has lost her mind and started another series. Linda Kay is convinced she has more than 24 hours in her day. Maybe she does. After all, her life is filled with the supernatural, right?

"I have an inoperable brain tumor."

Those six words were like the whip of a cat-o'-nine tails against my heart, and I kept hearing them over and over again. My mentor, Melika, was dying, and it felt like a piece of me was now dying right alongside her. I wasn't ready when she told me and all this time, I still wasn't. I never would be.

I'd known something was wrong…something I couldn't put my finger on at the time…something elusive that kept skirting around my thoughts like a shadow in my peripheral vision. I had even tried to read her, but even in her weakened state, she'd been able to keep me out.

The night before I was to leave the bayou after cleaning up after Katrina hit, she and I sat out by the firepit like we had done so many times before. When she reached for my hand and looked into my eyes, I knew whatever was coming would hit hard. I had no idea just how hard.

My heart broke then and there and I sobbed into her shoulder for what felt like hours. This woman, who had been like a mother to me, was dying, and all the supernatural power in the world couldn't help her.

When I finally stopped bawling, she told me it was time—time for me to step into her shoes and do for others what she had done for me. And she had done more than mentor me—Melika had saved my life. She had stepped in to care for a scared little girl and taught me how to function in a world that would not have accepted what I was. But she was more than just my teacher. She had also been my friend, and the only mother I had ever known. The thought of this world without her was as foreign a concept to me as rushing off to the Alaskan frontier to bring Tiponi Redhawk back, and that was precisely what I was doing.

And make no mistake about it, Alaska was still a frontier. There were bathrooms in San Francisco larger than some Alaskan towns, and the idea that there were places that really have thirty days of night scared the crap out of me. If it had been anyone else in trouble, I wouldn't have gone at a time like this, but it was Tip, and for her, I'd do anything…even hustle to the frozen tundra of the largest state in the union to extract her and the youngsters she had gone to retrieve.

Tip.

She did not yet know that the woman to whom she had pledged more than three quarters of her life to was dying. I was the first Mel had told. She needed to know whether or not I would accept the mantle of leadership she must pass on. She needed to look into my eyes, lower her own shields, and read me to make sure that I was prepared for this enormous responsibility. Before I had the chance to say yes, Tip had gone missing and Melika's powers had become too erratic for her to be able to communicate telepathically with us. It was as if I had left one crushed world and stepped into another all in a span of a few days.

Whoever said no rest for the weary knew what they were talking about. I'd barely caught my breath from dealing with the heartsickening aftermath of Hurricane Katrina that left my gorgeous and unique home of New Orleans a disaster zone, when I found myself on a private jet soaring to the white wilderness of Alaska. The two states couldn't have been more different. The good news was I could do little but sit and reflect back on the crazy events of the last couple of weeks, glad I was still alive. Well…alive enough to put my head down and keep working, so that's what I did…or at least tried to.

I am an award-winning journalist by trade. Recently, I'd left my position at the *San Francisco Chronicle* to pursue freelance work. So far, I'd done pretty nicely for myself, especially with my inside view on the disaster in New Orleans. Now, I was trying to figure out what subject I could write about that didn't include Sarah Palin or the Iditarod.

Closing my eyes, I tried to just relax. Quite frankly, I hadn't sat still for…well…longer than I can remember. I'd been running nonstop since well before Katrina hit, and once she landed, I was knee-deep in debris, detritus and death. Closing my eyes, I laid my head back against the comfortable seat and headrest of the expensive Lear. Private jets were the only way to go in these times of long security lines and overcrowded planes, and I was touched that my best friend, Danica Johnson, had sprung to rent the finest and fastest for me.

"Dani's rich, huh?" a young voice penetrated my thoughts, interrupting my semicomatose state.

Opening my eyes, I looked across the aisle at my charge, twelve-year-old Cinder. She looked as tired as I felt and I wondered if maybe I should have left her at home with Melika. Then I had to remind myself that Melika was sick, and my heart felt heavy again.

"Very," I said out loud, following her gaze as it caressed the butter leather upholstery all around us. The butterscotch color was warm and inviting, and if my mind hadn't been racing, I might have fallen fast asleep.

"Nice ride she gave us."

I nodded. Cinder did not talk. No one was sure why, but she communicated telepathically with me and a few others. Telepathy is not *my* primary paranormal power, though she had somehow managed to reach into my mind whenever she wanted.

I am an empath.

I have the ability to feel the emotions of those near me. Sometimes, this is a good thing—if I want to know if someone is lying, or dangerous, or just needs a hug because they are sad and depressed. Most of the time my power is annoying because I don't *want* to feel what everyone else is feeling. That's a heavy burden to always know the truth about someone's emotional state. Unexpressed emotions should be private, but they aren't to an empath unless, like me, one has exceptionally strong psychic shields. So I learned long ago how to build mental shields to keep those unwanted emotions at bay. Without shields and other defense mechanisms, all those other emotions would drive me mad. Years ago, I had seen firsthand an empath without shields and it wasn't pretty. She was a drooling ball of flesh rocking back and forth on the dirty floor of a psych unit. Since then, I had seen her face at least twice a month in a nightmare of some sort. She never left me, though I suspected she'd left the planet long ago and probably by her own hand.

"You're right. It was nice of her to rent one for us. Danica has been very generous with her millions."

"She is the best friend in the world and always takes care of us, huh?"

"Yes, she is and yes, she does."

"Like Tiponi. She would take a bullet for you."

I studied her blue eyes and puffy lips that bordered on pouty. Why was it kids thought that bullet sentiment romantic? "Maybe at one time she would have. People change." I shrugged.

Boy wasn't that the truth? I was the perfect example. Fourteen years ago, I had made my way to the Louisiana bayou from an orphanage so that I could be trained by Melika. Today, I was preparing to take her place, only instead of teaching my charges on the bayou, where it was safe from prying eyes, I would be moving my school to a vineyard chateau in Marin, California, built for me as a surprise by Danica.

Upon returning from Louisiana after Katrina, Danica drove me to a one-hundred-and-seventy-acre vineyard complete with a refurbished French chateau that had been overhauled and modernized to protect my students from the trespassing eyes of the outside world. It had been her gift to me for all the years of our friendship. It was almost too much.

Almost.

I'd gone from student to college student, to investigative reporter, to mentor, and none was as scary the transition as the last one. That particular hat was not one I could wear alone, and I knew Dani would never have followed me out to the bayou. She was all city, that girl, and if I wanted her to be part of my life, she knew she would have to build a school for me near her home in San Francisco. And that's precisely what she did, and I loved her all the more for it.

The responsibility of caring for young supernaturals in need of training scared the hell out of me, and Dani knew it, so she'd built the most elaborate and secure mansion money could buy. I needed to train these youngsters in quiet, secluded safety because their powers were volatile and uncontrollable. The preteen sitting across from me was no exception.

Cinder was a firestarter, the rarest of all supernaturals. She has the power to harness molecules and change their energy into fire that she could only sometimes control. She needed training desperately, but it just seemed like we never had the opportunity to get down to it. Melika had been working with her, and Cinder had managed to go from throwing huge fireballs to accurately guiding laser-like streams of flames at a target. It was progress, but it was just the tip of the iceberg.

Most firestarters died before they hit their teens usually by spontaneously combusting before anyone even knew what they were. Fortunately, we got to Cinder in time to train her and keep her from burning herself up in a fit of everyday childhood rage. Rage and fear were two triggers capable of setting a firestarter off. Too young to control their emotions, they were incredibly dangerous when they were scared or afraid. I know. I'd seen what happened to Cinder when that happened.

"You worried you haven't heard from Tip, huh?"

Turning, I looked out the window at the passing clouds. Tiponi Redhawk, my ex, had traveled to Russia to collect triplet paranormals who needed out of the country and into our new school. They would be among my first students, along with Cinder and a couple others. *If* Tip could get them to the states safely. That was a big if. It wasn't easy collecting supernaturals and keeping them safe from those who would exploit them, and triplets were quite a hat trick for anyone who could get them to the states. That someone was Tip.

Since she had left, our communication had been spotty. I assumed it was because she was giving me space to work on my relationship with police officer Marist Finn. It was so like Tip to bow out gracefully instead of digging down deep and fighting. But after a couple of days of no communication, I was beginning to think otherwise. Tip never let this much time go by without communicating with me. She always let me know when she'd made it safely back from a collection. She hadn't said a word to me, and that could only mean that something was seriously wrong.

"There are dead areas in Russia and Alaska where our psionic energies are dampened and cell phone bars are at zero. My guess is she's moving in and out of those zones trying to shake any possible tails."

"Genesys?" Cinder asked, tilting her head in question.

I turned back to her. "Among others."

She rubbed her chin, too pensive for a kid her age. She had seen her fair share of tragedy far too soon. *"S.T.O.P?"* S.T.O.P stood for Save The Other Paranormals. It was a group my sister belonged to that acted much in the same way we did, only they pulled no punches—and they punched hard.

"I wouldn't put anything past them. A set of supernatural triplets are a rare breed. There are a lot of people out there who would love to get their hands on them. We had to prevent that from happening, so Mel sent Tip."

"Do you think something happened to Tip? Is that why we haven't heard from her?"

"If anything happens to Tip, I'll know. Wherever she is, she's safe for now."

Cinder returned her attention to her Nintendo DS, and left me to my many thoughts, the first of which was Finn.

My on-again, off-again girlfriend, Officer Marist Finn, did not yet know the extent of my special abilities. I'd been struggling with the notion of sharing my deepest secret with her. Not until her life was in danger had I realized that *my* life was better with her in it. I had decided when I got on the jet that when I returned from Alaska, we'd sit down for the *big talk*. I was actually looking forward to it. My many secrets were really beginning to weigh heavily on my shoulders and drive a wedge, as secrets will do, between us. It was impossible to have a real relationship with those I kept from her.

And I wanted a real relationship. I wanted Finn.

Officer Finn was an amazing person. She was bright, beautiful and an exceptional cop. She had these incredible eyes that felt like they were gazing into the fiber of my soul, and when she laughed, the entire room became brighter. Everything about her spoke of her integrity and discipline. I admired so much about her—which was one reason why being so dishonest with her was becoming harder and harder.

Just as my eyelids began getting heavy, my vidbook vibrated. Popping it open, I saw my best friend's warm face smiling back at me.

"Hi Dani."

Danica grinned, showing perfect rows of white teeth against her caramel-colored skin. "Morning, Clark. How's the flight?" For the last decade, she's called me Clark, as in Clark Kent, because I have powers and am a reporter. She's goofy enough to still think it's funny.

"Smooth sailing so far. I can't thank you enough for arranging this for me...for us."

"Commercial flights suck these days. I prefer the extra legroom. Is Firefly behaving herself?"

I looked over at Cinder, who held up the okay sign, her three extended fingers glowing.

"She loves a good adventure, that girl. How's the chateau coming along?"

"The final inspection is today at noon, and if we get the green light, the chateau will be ready to rumble when you get back. We're putting all the final touches on the security system this weekend. Hopefully, you'll be back for that."

"And when is our first student scheduled to arrive?"

"William is picking him up this afternoon. Don't you worry about a thing, Clark. Everything on our end is copacetic. All we need is for you to get home safely. I wish you would have let me come with you. Have Glock, will travel, you know?"

Danica had killed a man with that traveling Glock, protecting me and Cinder. Since that day, she never left home without it. I wasn't so sure that was a good thing. She had an itchy trigger finger when protecting me and Cinder.

"Because you know as well as I do that we need you there. I told you. It's too hard passing permit muster from so far away. This is simply a safety escort for Tip to get her and the triplets out of Alaska."

Danica laughed, and when she laughed, so did her eyes. She was a beautiful woman with smooth skin and Beyonce-like hair that hung down her back in waves. She was grace personified when she moved, and her voice was liquid velvet. In a word, she was incredible inside and out, and had an astronomical number of bedmates in her life to show for it. However, to me, she was my rock, my touchstone. She was also the glue in all my worlds.

"Oh, would that anything in your life was simple, Clark."

Truer words have never been spoken. My life had been a tilt-a-whirl ever since I could remember…in and out of one foster home after another, not knowing until only recently why my parents had abandoned me at the steps of an orphanage when I was five. All those years of wondering and then when I found out why, I realized that knowing hadn't made anything any easier.

"I would have felt better if you'd have let me, or even Sal, come along. You never know when you might need some muscle, even if it's natural muscle."

Sal was our head of security. A natural was what supernaturals call ordinary humans—and recently—I'd hired some of the best naturals to take care of our security. To date, most naturals thought our kind only existed on television and in the movies. Only Danica and my small cadre of naturals knew about me and my paranormal family. For how long, I wasn't sure. The world was changing and supernaturals like me needed to change with it.

"You need Sal there with you, Dani. You guys take care of the newbie and keep your eyes on Finn. See if she saw what we think she saw. Feel her out and see if she knows anything."

"She still hasn't recovered from the trip, has she?"

I shook my head. Who had? When we left New Orleans, we

were one man less and battered and bruised both physically and emotionally. "No, and we've yet to discuss it. Just...be there in case there's any post-traumatic stress, okay? Spin any tale you need to, but try to get a sense about whether or not she saw us. I'll talk to her about...it...when we get back."

"Of course. Being here for you is what I do, and I am incredibly cheap. Cup of coffee here, a doughnut there. Anything else you need?"

I thought for a second and then shook my head. "I don't want any more disruptions out there for you. You've done so much already. Just kick back and enjoy yourself when you get the green light. Go on a date. Prowl the city. One of us needs to be having a good time, you know?"

Dani paused as she studied me. "I always have a good time. Hey, Sal said she knows a couple of ex-military guys out there in your winter wonderland who will lend a hand if you need it."

"Tell her thanks, but I think we have this covered."

She nodded. "I've got all the Vid's GPS systems online... except for Tip's. She must have gone to ground because her book is offline. Be sure to keep the book powered up. Yours *and* Firefly's." She paused and leaned closer to the monitor. "I know that look, Clark. What's going on?"

The vidbook was a checkbook-size computer/cell phone/webcam Danica's company started developing a couple of years ago. It was almost obsolete now, as her boys were working on something so far into the future, I couldn't really wrap my mind around it. The vidbook ran via satellite and had a powerful GPS system. All of us had them, and they had saved our bacon more than once. It bothered me to know that Tip's was not online. She had never been that incommunicado with me...ever.

"Don't worry. I'm not looking at a head-to-head battle with Genesys right now, Dani. We're not ready. I just want to collect my people and come home."

"I'm aware of that, Clark, which is why armed men isn't such a bad idea. Like it or not, we've got your back even from Marin. Just say the word and we can send some no-neck guys with high-powered rifles out to help."

I knew it was useless arguing with her, so I didn't. Danica

had been watching over me since I was fourteen. Half black, half white, she, like me, never fit in anywhere in the ghetto of Oakland, so we were a perfect match. We'd been best friends for more than half my life, and I suspect would be for the next half.

"I appreciate that Dani. Thank you, but we're hoping for a simple extraction. Bailey and Taylor have scouted everything out in Nome and it looks like all we need to do is get to Tip and then get the hell out of Dodge."

"Getting her would be simple if you knew where she was. The boys and I will do everything we can from here to try to locate her."

"Thank you."

"Thank me when you get home. You know I never sleep well when you're out being a superhero. Touch base often. And tell Firefly to toast anyone who gets in your way."

"You know how I feel about that."

Dani laughed. "Yes, I do. Oops! Gotta jam. Will is flagging me down and it looks like he has one of the city guys with him. See you soon."

With that, she logged out. While I had the vidbook open, I decided to check on Finn.

Looking at the screen with a photo of Finn on it, my heart warmed. Marist Finn was one of life's good guys: an honest cop, a decent person, a giving partner, she was worth protecting... worth a second chance. She was everything I wanted in a partner, and I wanted the chance to make this relationship work.

My life had been filled with an array of second chances, and I knew firsthand what it meant to never give up, to never lose hope. I would never lose hope of having a normal relationship with someone who knew the truth about who and what I was, but I'd never found the courage to tell Finn the truth. I needed to find that courage. She deserved that much from me.

When she didn't answer her vidbook, I left a brief message about missing her and thinking of her and for her to be careful on the mean streets of San Francisco. My eyes lingered on her grin before I logged off. She was quite a catch, and I felt incredibly lucky.

Looking over at a now sleeping Cinder, I felt a maternal

desire to give something back—something Melika and Tip had once given me long ago on the banks of the bayou. I knew, firsthand, how scary the world was when no one wanted you, when you were too different or too weird to love. I knew the fear, the gut-wrenching horror the first time your powers kicked in and you had no idea what the hell was happening to you. I knew the loneliness that comes with being something the world would fear if it knew what you could do.

I knew.

I also knew the joy of being accepted by others like me, of having friends. I knew the incredible feeling of success when you finally mastered a component of your powers. I knew the wonderful bond of being with those who were like you and how quickly they would become your family. How easy it was to be with those who did not judge you.

I knew.

I had a family: a very large, extended family that embraced me for all of my idiosyncracies. It was made up of telepaths (thinkers), telekinetics (movers), empaths (feelers), and a host of other supernaturals who trained out on the bayou with me fourteen years ago. And though we had all grown up and gone our separate ways, we would always be family, and a true family takes care of its own.

I would soon be the head of that family. I thought I might have time to get used to the idea, but I didn't. After Katrina, everything had changed. I barely had the time to catch my breath after the mess she made before Melika delivered the news that rocked my world. Now, I was no longer a student. I was the teacher. Now, I would be the one giving second chances, and to be honest, I wasn't at all sure I was ready.

We landed in Nome in the early afternoon, and Cinder was excited as all get out. She loved traveling and new experiences, and I was glad Melika made me take her.

When Cinder kept staring out the window, it took me a minute to realize she had never seen snow.

"It's so white. Like it's so bright, there are hardly any other colors."

She was right, and I zipped up the brand-new parka I'd bought for the trip. We had no need for parkas, boots or gloves in California or Louisiana, so Danica had sent one of her minions to buy up some winter clothes for the two of us. We were both bundled like two little kids who could barely move.

"Do I have to wear all these clothes?"

I looked at my rapidly maturing charge with her flaming red hair and piercing blue eyes and nodded. She was growing up so fast. "Yes. Once we step out of this plane, you'll be glad you have them."

"You know I don't need them, right?"

"Pretty sure everyone would stare at someone who wasn't wearing a jacket in this freezing temperature, don't you?"

Cinder nodded and zipped her new parka all the way up to her chin.

I thanked the pilot for his time. He told me his orders were to stay until the trip home. I was glad of that. Exit strategies were vital in our line of work, and if Tip had a tail, we would need a getaway vehicle and someone to drive it.

When the jet's door opened, the biting cold hit me in the face like a frozen hammer. "Jesus." It was so cold, it took my breath away.

"Boy, Echo, you weren't kidding. It's cold even for me. People really live here? Ick."

"It's not like home, is it?" As I started down the metal stairs, I saw two familiar, equally bundled figures waiting near the tarmac.

"Right on time, boss," Bailey said, wrapping her arms around me. "It's good to see you."

Her cheek against mine was very warm, as creatures tended to run warmer. That's what Bailey was—a creature. Her ability to read and often communicate with the natural world made her an incredibly powerful supernatural. I had been witness to that power in the bayou when she set a wild boar after a man. The boar gored him and ate him alive. You can't buy that kind of loyalty or power. It was as amazing as it was frightening.

Stepping back, I shook Taylor's hand while Bailey swept Cinder up in her arms. "I appreciate you coming, Taylor."

She nodded and smiled softly, a grin that lit up all five feet of her. "You never know when you'll need someone to slip into a tight space. I only hope it's warmer in those spots. It's fucking freezing here!"

Taylor was a natural, and had once been a professional thief wanted by Interpol and just about every federal agency in the United States. In all her years as a thief, she'd never been caught. Well…not officially. Once she'd met Delta Storm Stevens, Taylor had turned in her thieving tools and joined up with the good guys. I'd liked her right away. Straight shooter. Honest. Loyal. Good people…and now, she was Bailey's lover.

"Let's hope you're just here for the sights," I told her.

Taylor laughed, running one hand through her pixie cut. "Oh, Echo, the only other person I know who's more of a trouble magnet than you is Storm. So, forgive me if I don't hold my breath on us merely *sightseeing* here in the frozen tundra."

Glancing around, I was amazed at just how frozen this tundra was. There was so little color in this place, and the air was so damn cold, it hurt my throat to breathe with my mouth open. If the sun was out, it must have been hiding behind a snowdrift or something. Everywhere I looked, I saw gray, gray, and a lot of white. That was about it. The buildings were almost too hard to make out against the gray of the sky. They looked like stalagmites popping up from the ground.

We hopped into a warm cab and headed to our hotel room to drop off our luggage before going to a diner on the edge of the city.

Nome is an interesting city with incredibly cold climate and an average snowfall of over four feet. The temperature gauge outside a bar read nineteen degrees below zero. I involuntarily shivered.

"Is that sign broken?"

I felt Cinder warm up the car as we sat close together. We'd barely scratched the surface of her capabilities, which had saved my life more than once. As Dani put it, she threw a mean fireball. Still, that was merely one of her weapons. It was now my job to find and develop her other skills—her other weapons—for Cinder was, by the very nature of her powers, a killer.

"We're not used to this kind of cold, are we?" I said, putting my arm around her. "We're sunshine and humidity kind of gals."

Bailey did the same, and together, the four of us chatted amiably as the cab made its way over the frozen ground. I was most amazed by how many people roamed the streets in this weather regardless of how bundled up they were. Who on earth could live here?

"Jackrabbit Run is one of the best diners in town," our cabbie said. "Order an elk filet and you won't be sorry."

I cut a look over to Bailey, who pinched the bridge of her nose and ground her teeth. As a creature, the killing of wild animals for food never sat well with her. I didn't blame her.

We paid the cab driver and ran into the diner. Once seated, we ordered pasta and pizza, and when the waitress left, we made our plan.

"What have you found out?" I asked, leaning closer to Bailey, who laid a map on the table and pressed the wrinkles out. Bailey was a beautiful blonde with blue eyes that often changed colors. She was different from the rest of us in that she was training to be a shaman—a healer. I'd seen her put homemade salve on gunshot wounds that looked four days old in less than eight hours. She was that good.

"Tip and the triplets made it out of Russia intact. That much we do know." She looked up from the map, her eyes a steel blue. "And we know she's here in Alaska...somewhere. They were seen coming off a boat. It's hard to miss identical triplets."

I looked from Bailey to Taylor, and back to Bailey. They both looked somewhat cowed. "What do you mean...*somewhere?*"

They exchanged glances like two siblings who were about to get in trouble.

"Oh God, you lost her."

"More like she lost us," Taylor said. "We don't know what happened, E. One minute, we had her. She was right in the palm of our hands, and the next, she was off the grid."

Bailey set her vidbook on the table. "Her GPS has been turned off."

I nodded. "Dani confirmed that this morning. I was just hoping maybe you guys had a visual."

"Wish we had better news for you, E."

"I can't imagine Tip would ever turn hers off unless she had a good reason. So she's either in trouble or she must be in a dead zone. I hear there are tons of those out here. The boys were saying something about some horror movie called *Thirty Days of Night* or something. Roger is sending me IMs saying there are all sorts of dead zones there because of the electromagnetic fields."

"There are, but for whatever reason, she's turned the GPS off and isn't responding to cell calls."

Taylor nodded. "We're hoping she's gone to ground or is protecting the whereabouts of the triplets, but if she doesn't turn that damn thing back on soon, she's the proverbial needle times three."

Pulling out my vidbook, I called Dani, who answered on one ring. The three possible pictures-in-picture boxes also popped up, showing the faces of Roger, Carl and Franklin, three Berkeley grads with a combined IQ of fifty million. Danica had hired them as a package deal when she first started her incredibly successful business called Savvy Software. Hiring those three had paid off brilliantly for her. They were worth every penny she paid them.

"Yo, Princess, nice Gortex parka. I think I see your breath." Roger laughed, as he always did, at his own geekiness.

"She's off the grid," Danica said, before I asked. "Completely."

"I got that. I thought you said she turned it off. Could it just be a dead spot?"

"The boys traced the silence back to the moment she crossed into Alaska. Her last GPS is about ten clicks outside of a town called Wales."

"Wales, Alaska? I've never heard of it." I looked at the map where Bailey was pointing. It was the town way up north, seemingly only a stone's throw from Russia. "Okay. I see where it is."

"Roger?" Bailey turned the floor over to him.

"Okay, Princess, here's what little we know about the village called Wales. The good news is it has an airport. It may be small, but it has a runway that will do the trick. So getting you from Nome to Wales won't be a problem."

"That's the good news?"

He nodded, pushing his black-framed glasses up the bridge of his nose. "Less than five hundred people live there, but it's hard to say since there are folks living on the outskirts of every town or village in Alaska. All population numbers are relatively close, but who knows for sure?"

I bowed my head, and my stomach began twisting as I thought of Tip out there alone.

Roger continued. "The only reason Wales is on the map is a burial mound from the Birnirk culture was discovered near there, so now it's a national landmark."

I held my hand up. "Wait. Tell me about the Birnirks."

Roger flipped through his notes on a monitor next to the one he used for the vidbook. "Let's see...prehistoric Inuit civilization from about five hundred to nine hundred AD, disappearing around one thousand AD. Researchers found this burial mound in Wales, and a dozen more in Barrow, further north. There's not much more to Wales or the culture of the Birnirks. We'll keep digging...pardon the pun."

Danica came back on. "I don't know why she would turn off her vidbook, Clark, do you?"

I shook my head. "Any possibilities besides dead zones?"

Carl's face moved closer to the screen. His hair was pulled back into its typical ponytail and the indentations of where his glasses had sat were fresh. He was always misplacing them on the top of his head. "Electrical displacement occurs at several places in and around Alaska, not to mention all of the paranormal sightings and activity reported every year. Superstitions abound anytime there are burial grounds near a town or city. You need to be careful around those. The natives, and by that I mean the locals, are particular about who goes snooping around them."

"Not to mention all of the other weird activity since that stupid alien abduction movie came out," Roger added.

I waved that away. "Tell me more about the Inuits."

Roger consulted his notes again. "Well, they are really called Yupik, and they believe everything has a spirit. And an Angekok was a Yupik person who could talk to the spirits or heal people. They had men's communal houses, where they would teach the boys hunting. A shaman was usually present. They often had women's houses which were often connected by a tunnel, presumably so the shaman could go back and forth." He looked up. "Shall I go on?"

"Just one question. Were these lodges underground?" I watched as Roger looked down, his fingers flying across the keyboard.

Looking up, he replied, "Some were. Most weren't. They were often built in berms or openings that looked a little like this." He clicked on the screen and an image popped up. A hillside with a doorway built into it appeared onto the screen.

Bailey and Taylor were now looking over my shoulder. "You don't think..." Bailey whispered in my left ear.

"Anything else about Wales we should know?"

Roger and Carl shook their heads before Danica ejected their pictures from the screen. "You warm enough?"

I nodded. "We're good. Thank you for talking me into bringing Cinder. She's like a portable electric blanket."

"You needed firepower, Clark, and if it wasn't going to be me, she's the next best thing."

"Ahem," came Bailey's voice from behind me.

"Hey Bailey. I have to say, you're good, but my money will always be on Firefly."

Cinder hopped up and waved to Danica.

"There she is! Hey you. You take good care of those three lovely ladies, you hear me?"

Cinder nodded rapidly. She was beaming.

"Okay, Clark. We'll let you know the second the Big Indian's GPS is back online. I wouldn't be too concerned yet. There's all sorts of weird shit going on in Alaska. It could be anything."

I nodded. Only problem with that notion was the question of why hadn't Tip gotten hold of me telepathically? When we were lovers, I couldn't ever get her out of my head. She was the strongest telepath I knew and she was always barging in on my thoughts. It had been a bone of contention during all our years together. Now that I needed to know what was going on, I couldn't manage to hear even a whisper.

It was beginning to worry me.

"You all stay in touch. We've got a bead on all four vidbooks. Should we lose one signal, for whatever reason, I'll let the rest of you know."

"Thank you."

"Be safe. Take care of each other."

I signed off and returned my attention to the map. "So, what have you two found out?"

"We've arranged for a plane to take us to Wales tomorrow morning. Taylor got her hands on a flight log between Nome and Wales, and there's no one matching the four of them having flown in or out of Wales."

I nodded, staring at the map.

"E?"

I'd been waiting for this. "No, Bailey, Tip hasn't contacted me. I haven't heard from her since Mel asked her to leave me be."

"Oh God. Then she still doesn't know—"

"That Melika is dying? No. She doesn't. And she won't learn of it here, either."

I looked each of them in the eye. "I mean that. Once we get the triplets back to California, I'll go back home with Tip. She'll need me there when Mel tells her."

Bailey and Taylor exchanged glances once more.

"What?"

"E, I hate to state the obvious here, but if you're really going to try to make it work with Officer Hunky Pants, then being Tip's go-to girl has to end. Now. Today. You can't keep holding each other's hands during tough times. You have to let someone else do that. You have to let her go."

Taylor was nodding. To my surprise, so was Cinder.

"Do you have any idea, any *at all*, how much this is going to devastate Tip? Finn or no Finn, I won't let Tip go through that kind of pain alone, and I won't tell her when she is so far out of her element. No way."

Bailey laid her hand on top of mine. It was still very warm even in this climate. "We all understand that, E, but what if Finn doesn't? Are you willing to risk your fledgling relationship to hold Tip's hand again?"

"I'll cross that bridge when I get there. Right now, we need to eat and get some sleep. Tomorrow might be a really long day."

Taylor and Bailey both chuckled. "Knowing you, *might* is an understatement."

The cab driver had been right; the food at the diner was delicious, with lumberjack-size portions that none of us could make a dent in. By the time we made it back to the hotel, Cinder was asleep and my eyelids felt like sandpaper had been glued to the insides.

But the moment we stepped out of the cab and into the snow, my mental alarms went off. So did Bailey's, and we both laid a hand on Cinder's shoulders as we watched a tall, thin woman approach us wearing a very expensive London Fog jacket, leather gloves and earmuffs. She was not bundled up nearly enough for this cold, and the accessories she wore were strictly for show.

She was one of us.

"Echo Branson," the woman said, almost tenderly. Her red hair was thick and hung just below her shoulders; too long, I thought, for a woman almost forty. Her deep green eyes did not leave mine, as she ignored everyone else in my group. She had her shields up and I could not read her intent. I was pretty certain by the looks of her that they weren't good.

I felt Cinder's body get warm even with my gloves on. I barely squeezed her shoulder and spoke to her telepathically. *"Too many people around, Cinder. Not here. Not now. You must show discipline here."*

"She's bad."

"We don't know that. You just cool your jets. Unless she fires on us, keep your flames to yourself. Do not fire on her unless we are in danger." As I watched the woman, I wasn't the least bit surprised to see five husky-like sled dogs sitting on five different sides of

the intersection, called, no doubt, by Bailey. That was her special ability. She was part of nature and could call any creature within paranormal distance.

"And you are?"

"Sonja, and it's a...pleasure to meet the next great mentor of supernaturals around the world."

To my surprise, Taylor stepped up, toe-to-toe with her. Well, their toes met, but Taylor was barely over five feet. "Look, lady, whatever it is you came to say, say it and then piss off."

Sonja looked over Taylor's head and said, "Call off your dogs, Miss Branson. I assure you, I am not alone and I have no compunction about using my powers in public."

I glanced beyond her and saw the dogs were walking toward us now, about forty feet away. "She's not the dog you should be worried about."

Sonja chuffed. "Oh, come now, Miss Branson. Surely you do not wish to get into a pissing contest right here in the middle of the street. What good would that serve, except to out us all?"

"Then I suggest you deliver whatever message you were sent here to deliver and be on your way." I had a feeling I knew who she worked for. "It's okay, Taylor, step away. She's just a messenger."

Reluctantly, Taylor stepped back. I could feel Cinder getting warmer. I told her, *Even if she does something, you are* not *to retaliate unless we are in danger.*

"Why not?"

"You know why not. Too public. Too risky. That's why she met us out here. She doesn't want a fight...yet. We've got this. Trust me."

"This is a courtesy call to you, Miss Branson. We know why you're here and we've come to offer you a deal of sorts."

"No deal," Bailey said. "Now fuck off."

The dogs were now within twenty feet of Sonja. She didn't even seem to notice.

"We want those triplets Tiponi Redhawk stole from us in Russia. If—"

Bailey suddenly burst out laughing.

Sonja cut her a look. "I'm glad you're amused, Bailey, but the loss of those triplets has set us back over ten million dollars.

Since we cannot recoup the money, then we'll take the triplets off your hands in exchange for letting you leave here alive."

"I haven't heard a deal yet," Taylor said.

Sonja ignored her, superiority oozing from her paranormal skin. "We have a pretty good idea where Redhawk and the triplets are on. Stay out of our way and we'll let her live. Get in our way and she will be the first casualty in this war you've started, followed by all of your little friends here. It's your call. What'll it be?"

I stared at her a moment, then I looked at Bailey, looked at Cinder, and back to Sonja. "Wow. Hmm. So you think you can accost me and my people in the street, threaten our lives, and then just walk away? Well, you can tell your boss—" and with that, I sent out an energy blast that lifted Sonja off her feet and pushed her fifteen feet away, where she landed on her back, surrounded now by the five snarling dogs.

"To go fuck himself." Walking up to her, I could feel Bailey's and Cinder's energy behind me, poised to strike. Sonja was completely winded staring up at me with fire in her eyes.

Leaning over her, I fairly growled. "You tell your *boss* that I will *never* deal with him. I will *never* turn another supernatural over to him, and if *he* gets in *my* way, I'll have Cinder turn him into a goddamned crispy critter. *Capisce*?"

Her chest heaved as she nodded and pushed herself up to her elbows. "Big...mistake."

"We'll see whose mistake it is." Turning on my heel, I led *my* people into the hotel, leaving the dogs to guard Sonja as she hurled multiple threats at our backs.

"Shit, Echo, what in the hell was that?" Taylor asked when we got inside.

Turning to Taylor, I bit my lower lip as I considered the most concise answer. "It's a long story and I have to figure out where all the chips lie on this one. Can it wait?"

She nodded. "Old Sonja out there works for *them*, doesn't she?"

I nodded. "Genesys. And it looks like they are playing for keeps this time."

In our moose-enhanced hotel room, the four of us regrouped and let home base know what had gone down with Sonja. I'd given Danica and the boys from the Bat Cave a couple of jobs to do since we now had proof Genesys had been tracking Tip and were now probably trailing us.

"The good news, if there's any to be had," Bailey said, as she sprinkled some powder into a cup of mint tea before handing it to Cinder, "is that we know they don't have her, nor have they done anything to her. There's still time for us to reel them in."

Cinder took the tea, sipped it, and then made a face.

"It will help you sleep, Heatwave. I know you got all amped up to fry her Jimmy Cho's off, but we need you well rested tomorrow. Looks like things are going to heat up around here with or without you." Bailey winked at Cinder, who still pulled a face.

I concurred. "Could be a long day, Cinder. Bailey's right. Drink up."

Nodding, Cinder drank the tea in one gulp, the heat of it not bothering her at all. *"I am kind of tired. Fill me in in the morning? I don't want you guys treating me like a little kid anymore."*

"Of course. And you're still a kid."

"To you, maybe, but I can cook someone with the best of them." A slight grin played at the corners of her mouth as she left the room.

I had no words to reply, so I just watched her go into our bedroom. When the door closed, the three of us returned our attention to the map Bailey was smoothing out.

"Here's my thinking," Bailey said softly, pointing to the map. "Genesys knew you were here. They are expecting you to lead them to Tip and the triplets. The message wasn't really to get you to back off, but to press forward. Reverse psychology, as it were."

Taylor nodded. "Otherwise, why would they still be in Nome? They were waiting for the one person they knew can lead them to her." She turned to me and tilted her head. "And though I am pretty sure she didn't slip fifteen feet away, I'd love to know exactly what happened out there. Delta said you guys were special. I'm thinking super-duper special."

I nodded and shrugged. "That's one way of looking at it. Okay. So they only know as much as we do about Tip, maybe less. They know she made it to Alaska. They know she has the kids with her. Other than that?"

"They don't have shit. From the sounds of it, E, Tip didn't just get them out of Russia. Sounds like she tore them right out of the hands of Genesys and that's why they are so pissed."

"I agree," Taylor added. "Sonja's approach wasn't to scare us off. Quite the contrary."

I thought back to the way Sonja acted, the manner in which she came at us. "You guys are right. She meant to scare us enough that we would hightail it to Tip with them right on our heels." This would explain why Tip had shut down completely…so she couldn't be tracked.

They both nodded.

"And they probably know we hired a plane. They'll be waiting for us to beat a quick retreat out of here."

"Which we aren't going to do. They have underestimated us once again."

"The biggest problem we have," Taylor said, pacing across the room, "is not knowing their numbers. It's going to be much harder to make a move one way or the other without knowing what we're up against."

"Then we need to split their forces up."

Bailey shook her head. "I don't know, E. Splitting them up means splitting us up, and I'm not so sure that's such a good idea here in the freezer."

I nodded, thinking I was glad I'd sent Bailey and Taylor ahead. "We can't take them to Tip, even if we knew where she was, and we can't stay together or that's precisely what will happen."

"I agree with Echo on this one, Bailey," Taylor said. "Once we split up, we'll get a better idea of how many they sent. Staying together out of fear is a bad idea."

"Besides, Genesys has unlimited funds," I added. "So my guess is, they've spared no expense outfitting their people on the ground as well as in the air." I studied the map. "One main road from Nome to Wales leaves us really vulnerable to being followed. I don't like that at all."

Bailey studied the map quietly before turning to me. "Then we don't take a road."

"We have the choice of air or land, and you think we shouldn't take the road?"

She smirked almost wickedly. "Nope. We take a dogsled."

Taylor sat back down. "That's brilliant."

I stared at them both. "Are you insane? It's what? A hundred miles? A hundred degrees below? That's crazy talk."

"Eighty-one, as the crow flies, but the main road only goes into Brevig Mission, which is only thirty-four miles from Wales. Think about it, E. They'll never see it coming and following us on sled will be so much harder than by car."

I had to admit she was right. It was a solid plan. "Okay, then we need to completely split up. One on the plane, one on the road, two on a sled."

Bailey nodded. "Me and Cinder on the sled."

"No way."

"Look, this is fucking scary wilderness, E, with ice and wolves, bears and snow. I'm the obvious choice. No animal will attack us as long as I am around. Don't be pigheaded about this."

Taylor held her hand up. "I don't mean to sound dense here, but won't Red Sonja know it's us leaving? I mean…she has some sort of powers like you, right?" The moment she finished the sentence, Taylor knew she'd blown it.

I looked at Taylor and then to Bailey, who shrugged and then nodded slightly. "Yeah. I told her about my abilities, but I didn't mention anyone else's. I'm sorry, E, but—"

Taylor smiled softly and whispered. "Your secrets are safe with me, Echo. With all of us. Sal, Delta, Connie, the whole nine. We understand everything is on a need-to-know basis. We get that. We really do. Trust me when I tell you, you couldn't have chosen a better group of normal people to put your faith in. We'll never tell a soul." She looked at me and chuckled. "Though I have to say, normal is soooo not a word that has ever applied to Delta Stevens."

I believed her. Delta's people were almost as good as mine. Almost. "I know that, Taylor. I have no issues with you knowing..." I paused. "Just what is it you know?"

Taylor lowered her head and her voice along with it. "You guys are...special. We all knew that after the first time we faced Genesys together. I asked Bailey right after, but she was mum about it."

"But then we got...close, and it was time. I've seen you struggle, Echo, and I just don't have the discipline you do around not telling. I didn't divulge anything else. I swear."

"What does she know?"

Taylor answered. "Bailey is Dr. Doolittle, Cinder is the Human Torch, and you're some kinda Megamind. I only know about Cinder because of the way she heated that taxi up. She was all toasty."

Bailey shook her head. "You watch too many movies, and I so did not say that."

Taylor locked eyes with me. "I got the gist of it, Echo. Bottom line is, you guys come with your own arsenal. Does that about sum it up?"

I nodded. "Quite well. I don't have to tell you what will happen if we're found out."

"No kidding. Look, Delta may not have your innate skills, but she's supernatural nonetheless. My lips are sealed."

"Perfect. Make sure they stay that way. So, to answer your question, Sonja and her people will definitely know if we get on that plane, yeah."

"Then we need to make her think we're getting in a car *and* in the plane," Bailey added. "She won't be able to focus on both. While they have their attention diverted, we'll take a dogsled out of Dodge."

"Who gets on the plane?"

Taylor raised a hand. "Me. I'll fly into Brevig Mission and find my way to Wales."

I studied the map. "Thirty-five miles, Taylor?"

"Cake, Echo. Don't forget who I am or what I used to do for a living. Only one person ever caught me, and she's not a cop anymore. I can do this."

Bailey and Taylor held hands, and I warmed thinking of the last time Finn and I held hands.

"Trailing Taylor will take their best, and their best isn't good enough against her."

Taylor nodded. "I got me some superpowers of my own. Now, I think Bailey ought to take the car first just to throw them off. You can meet her there with an empty sled."

I looked at Taylor, surprised. "Why take the car first?"

Bailey answered instead. "Because I can block the road long enough for the dogs to get to me, jump out, and send the car in the opposite direction of Wales. Following me isn't enough. We need to send them on a goose chase so I can make it back to you guys."

"Brilliant. So Cinder and I will be busting a line to Wales on a dogsled. How do we get sleds?"

"I'll handle it," Bailey said. "Taylor and I already checked them out when we first got here. I know exactly where to go to get sled drivers. Those things are a lot harder to drive than they look. We'll need a pro."

"What time is our flight?"

"Ten. I'll go make some calls. Anything else?"

I cocked my head at her. I'd not gone to school on the bayou with Bailey. We'd met when Melika summoned us all down to help after Katrina. We weren't friends at first sight, but I'd grown to like her and trusted her with my life.

"Yeah. Thank you both. I knew sending you two up here was the right call."

While Bailey stepped aside to make her calls, and Taylor went in to check on Cinder, I called home. Danica answered on the half ring.

"Hey, Clark. You okay?"

Before I'd finished telling her about our plan, she'd pulled up a topographical map and zoomed in. With a special pen, she drew a line from Nome to Wales up and around the topography, explaining what to look for, how to lean on the sled, and to listen to the driver. "Did you know the Iditarod started because a disease broke out and there was no other way to get the serum out except by sled? That's what the Iditarod was about, so I think you're in a great place for an expert sledder. Trust them. Listen to them, and you'll be fine."

I nodded. "Nice map. How's Finn?"

"Getting stronger every day. You not talking to her or what?"

"I've called twice, but both times she didn't pick up. I'm a little worried."

"Clark? Is there something you're not telling me? You and Finn are okay, right? I mean, nothing's happened between you, has it?"

"We're as good as we can be, given what she saw in New Orleans. I managed to talk to Delta before we came. She said Finn sleeps a lot and has been really quiet. There are conversations we need to have, but I don't want to do it over the phone, you know?"

"She's a little freaked out about her NOLA experience. I think she's having problems drinking it all in. It's not easy thinking she saw what she did. You may need to give her some time."

"I appreciate you keeping an eye out on her."

"It's what we do. You need to decide what you're going to do about telling her."

I thought about Bailey and how quickly she had told Taylor. I was not that revealing and never would be. I weighed my choices more carefully than that and often paid the price for doing so. "I know. As soon as we get home. "Did we pass inspection on the chateau?"

"All but one. The final final one is tomorrow. I thought we were done today, but you know how those guys are. He's bringing in the big gun. That'll be the toughest."

"You worried?"

"Not at all. Connie is a genius and Sal has electronic skills like I've never seen. I had the geek squad double-check all our IT equipment. They were really impressed. We'll be fine."

"Good. It looks awesome. I still can't believe you bought a vineyard."

"It's already making a profit."

"Of course it is. You're Lady Midas."

"Or something. What time you starting off?"

"Ten."

Danica typed this into the computer. "Okay. We'll be here."

"One more thing. I am going to be doing a series of stories on life in Alaska. Can you email me all of the newspaper names in Alaska? I might want to do a story on the sledders and that berm and I think there are any number of magazines that will be interested."

"Absolutely. We'll send that forthwith. Anything else?"

"Don't come up here, Dani. I know you want to, but please don't. This state is unlike anyplace I have ever been, and once we leave Nome, finding us would be nigh impossible. Promise me you won't come to Alaska."

"I can't promise. You know I can't. I'll do what needs to be done here, but don't ask me to make promises you know I can't keep."

I nodded. "Point taken. I'll keep you posted."

"You damn well better."

We hung up, and I looked over at Bailey, who gave me a thumbs-up. It looked like we were going on our own personal Iditarod.

The freezing weather chilled the marrow of my bones, and at nine o'clock in the morning it was a pitiful twelve degrees below zero. I'd never been in this kind of cold, having spent most of my life either on the bayou or in San Francisco, where cold weather was an anomaly. It was so cold, even our breath looked solid. I felt like an Otter Pop.

Pulling Cinder closer to me, I felt her natural heat radiating from her and knew she wasn't experiencing this cold at all.

"Plane's all set," Taylor said, flipping her collar up as we stood in the lobby of the hotel whose decorator, I was pretty certain, was into moose kitsch.

I hated that we were sending her off by herself, but she assured me that flying solo was how she'd never been caught… well…almost never, but that was her story to tell.

"I'll be fine, Echo. I'm no threat to them. And should they attempt to grab-and-run with me, they'll be in for a rude awakening. I got this wired. Trust me."

Trust was something supernaturals ration out in tiny bits to normals. It is never easy trusting anyone after what most of us have been through on our paranormal walk through normal life. It was easier for me to trust more than most since I can detect a lie a mile away and underwater. My red flags wave whenever I feel someone being disingenuous. Taylor passed muster on all counts.

We hugged Taylor goodbye and set out for the car rental where we finally managed to rent a four-wheel drive Jeep with a driver.

"Ten miles," Bailey said. "There's an area here," she pointed to the GPS on her vidbook, "with a caribou ranch. That's where I'll stop them. Caribou will be perfect for stopping a freight train. Then we'll take this frontage road and you'll meet me here. Patterson Pass. The driver will stay there for thirty minutes before heading back to town the long way. I'll drop a Ben on him to keep his mouth shut if anyone should ask."

"Sounds like we have it covered," I said. "We'll meet you with the sleds at Patterson Pass. Be careful, Bailey. If Genesys managed to recruit a Sonja, who knows what else they have. My guess is they are arming for a war we can't afford to wage right now. The kids are far from ready and we're…well…we're still regrouping after Jacob Marley…"

Bailey rubbed my shoulder. "I know, E. It so sucks." Bailey smelled the air like a dog. "I couldn't pick up Sonja's scent. Just *what* is she?"

I glanced down at Cinder. "If I'm not mistaken, she's a firestarter."

"Oh shit."

I didn't take my eyes off of Cinder's. There were times when I could have sworn I saw flames dancing in them. "I'd heard there are quite a few supers here in Alaska, but I never thought Genesys would wrangle a pyro into the group."

"I imagine we've only scratched the surface of these fuckers, E. They want more than to collect and experiment on us. You know they want to figure out how to create us, and that, my friend, would turn the world against us in a nano."

"Yes, it would. But as much as I would love to take them down once and for all, it will have to wait. We have more personal agenda items to take care of first. Sonja's going to have to find someone else to fight for now."

Bailey nodded as she tied her long blond hair back in a ponytail. "She made it sound like they had actually collected the triplets and that Tip somehow Snuffy Smithed them away."

"Well, that's not unlikely, knowing Tip. Just stay safe, okay? An adult pyro isn't someone to mess around with."

Cinder made a disparaging sound in her throat.

"You're good too, Cin, but Sonja...well...she's probably had plenty of practice and years of experience."

We left Bailey at the rental place and wound our way through town on foot, where it was harder for them to follow. Unless they had an empath who could feel our psionic energy, it would be difficult to tail us for long.

At the White Wolf Sledding Company, I met Rick, the owner, who introduced us to two Inuit sledders; Suka, a tall, thin Indian with intense dark eyes, and Maniitok, a shorter, warm little man with laughing eyes and a warmth that more than made up for Suka's dour personality.

I read them both, of course, and found Suka to be bitter, having to waste his time with two women tourists he felt would last less than ten minutes before turning back to the town. Maniitok was completely the opposite. Jovial, light and chatty, he loved his job and had a special bond with the two front sled dogs. He didn't seem to mind either the cold weather or his colder partner.

"Suka and Maniitok are two of my best, but I explained to your friend I would have to charge you for the overnight stay in Wales and the trip back."

I nodded. "Not a problem."

"It's quite a distance, you realize. Eighty miles straight away, but over a hundred via dog. That's long even for people who live here. You sure this is something you want to do?"

Handing him my credit card, I nodded. "Positive. We're tougher than we look."

Taking my card, Rick shook his head. "Alrighty then. Have a seat while Suka finishes harnessing the dogs."

I sat in an overly warm waiting area, while Cinder stood at the window watching the dogs get harnessed. Her eyes never left the lead dog.

Opening my vidbook, I called Melika. It would be early in the bayou, but she was an early riser.

"Echo! Good to see you, my dear. I take it you're in Alaska?"

Before the brain tumor, Melika would have already known that. Now, she had shut down much of her power to conserve her energy for healing.

"We are. We're on the move this morning to locate Tip and her recoveries, but we ran into a super named Sonja. What can you tell me about her?"

Melika's eyes narrowed, her right eyebrow raising. "Sonja Satre is in Alaska? Hired by Genesys, no doubt."

By the look in Melika's eyes, I knew Sonja meant trouble.

"Sonja is one of a handful of PKs in the world to have survived puberty. Trained in Canada, she hires herself out as a mercenary of sorts, helping anyone who can pay her to do whatever needs to be done. The last I heard of her, she was responsible for that subway fire in Tokyo. Well-traveled, well-connected, Sonja Satre is a dangerous woman, Echo. Be very careful with her."

"When you say mercenary, you mean that in the literal sense?"

Cinder turned and looked at me.

"Yes. The Others have a file a foot thick on her. She'll do anything for a price. She's torched mansions, blown up cars, even started a forest fire once. Meet her price and she'll do it. There never was a Ben Franklin she didn't like, and she has liked plenty."

The Others were our version of a government by committee. They were the retired supers who watched over the paranormal world making sure things got cleaned up before anyone could know we really existed. They kept a close eye on mentors, on students, on all of us.

"Genesys has hired her then. She came bearing a thinly

veiled threat." I explained our impromptu meeting in front of our hotel. As I relayed the series of events, I noticed how thin and wan Melika looked, and decided then and there that I would not keep checking in with her. I would lead on my own and do what I thought she would do, but I needed to let her rest. It was time I stepped up once and for all.

"I see. My guess is she's their local connection, but doesn't work for them. Sonja isn't the kind of person to have a boss of any kind. She'll take directives, but not orders."

"How powerful is she?"

"Very. If she had wanted to, she could have killed you all before you ever saw it coming."

I cringed. "Good to know. How do we stop her?"

"You don't. Unless you can knock her out, she's tough to reach when using her powers. She has all the fiery weapons at her disposal: balls of flame, flame thrower, sparks, super novas. Power beyond anything Cinder has harnessed yet. She is not one you want to mess with."

I nodded and Cinder returned her attention to the dogs.

"How are you feeling, Mel?"

"Neither better nor worse, I'm happy to say, though my brother's constant twitterings about finding some way to save me are about to drive me mad."

Her twin brother, Malecon, had actually tried killing her not too long ago, and I thought I had killed him. I had not, and he resurfaced the moment he knew Melika was dying. No one trusted him, of course, but Mel did and asked the rest of us to trust her judgment.

That was much easier said than done, but so far, Malecon's presence in her life appeared to be a good thing, and I wasn't going to argue with that. I could tell by the sound of her voice that she was happy for the company. It was a twin thing, I was sure, and her forgiveness of him was more than commendable… it was saintly. "So he hasn't tried to poison you or smother you in your sleep?"

She chuckled, a sound I hadn't heard in ages. "Oh heavens, no, my dear. He prattles on about new techniques in the Orient, new procedures in Switzerland. He truly has returned to care for his sister. He has been as pleasant as he was when we were children."

"You're a better man than I, Gunga Din. Not so sure I could ever forgive anyone who tried to kill me. What does Bishop say about all this?"

Bishop was their mother, whom Malecon had once wanted to kill as well while under the influence of the chaos factor…a genetic abnormality that drove him to the brink of insanity. Bishop was now retired and living with the Others.

"Oh, she's old school, that woman. Never forgives, never forgets. She was partial to Jacob Marley, you know, and since my brother was responsible for that poor boy's death, I'm afraid forgiveness won't be forthcoming. Ever." She waved it away. "She's safe, happy and enjoying herself with the Others. Under the circumstances, all of us are doing very well."

"So she's no longer in seclusion?"

"She is not. She hasn't been since you saw her. She's been, well, quite busy."

"Doing what? What does a newly retired supernatural *do* in retirement?"

Melika appeared pained. "Well, most take a few months to settle into life on the island, but not my mother. She has been going to bat for you with the Grand Council, among other things."

I blinked. "What?"

"She believes in you, Echo. She always has. Besides me and Danica, she is your biggest fan. She wants them to be as well."

"I don't need them."

"Yes, you do. Well…you don't, but life would be easier if you had their backing. I know you all got off on the wrong foot, and I can't say I blame you. I raised you to think for yourself, and you've done that. They are, of course, not at all happy with how you thumb your nose at them. They exist for a reason, Echo, and you keep skirting around their rules. Bishop's been trying to smooth things over in the event you decide to work with them."

"I don't know if I should be glad or not. If they aren't going to join us in the twenty-first century, and understand that we need to take on Genesys to survive, then I am not sure that's a club I want to belong to."

She barely grinned. "Having their backing could prove very useful. Give it time, my dear. In the meantime, what of your communication with Tip? I cannot tell you how detached I feel not being able to contact all of you telepathically. It is most disconcerting, not to mention lonely. I am so used to hearing you all."

"I'm sure. We have the general vicinity where they might be, but in an area the size of Alaska, that vicinity is pretty large."

"Not a word?"

"Not one. Her vidbook is off the grid as well."

Melika nodded and I could practically feel her energy being depleted. "Gone to ground then. Good."

"Good?"

She leaned closer to the screen. "Echo, while I realize you have chosen Finn, you are still intimately tied to Tiponi. If anything were to happen to her, you would know on the deepest depth a level of pain you've never experienced. It would incapacitate you. As long as you never feel that, you can rest assured she is alive."

I nodded, remembering how I felt when Jacob Marley died. I couldn't imagine Tip's death. Couldn't and wouldn't. "I understand."

"Good."

"What can you tell me about these triplets?"

She pinched the bridge of her nose. She was tiring.

"Last question, I promise."

"Alexie is a thinker. Boris is a mover. Nika, their sister, says little and we have not determined what her powers are."

"Got it."

"That's not all. Genesys wants them because the rumors are when all three are physically united, they have the ability to bilocate."

My jaw dropped. "Are you kidding me?"

She shook her head. "You can imagine why Genesys desperately wants them. The ability to bilocate means they could find paranormals all over the world without ever leaving the Genesys compound."

"Oh God." My hand went to my mouth. "That would be catastrophic."

She nodded. "Indeed. They had them. Genesys had them in their grasp, but somehow Tiponi spirited them away, got them out of Russia. You know the rest."

"Wow. I wasn't even sure bilocation was possible."

"Everything is possible, my dear, but those three children, they are exactly what Kip Reynolds at Genesys has been searching for all these years; the perfect bloodhounds."

"Jesus."

"I don't know the specifics of Tip's collection, but I do know that Genesys will bring in their big guns to collect those kids. You did well in choosing Bailey to go with you."

"You think the three of us are enough firepower?"

"Yes, I do. Find Tip and do whatever you need to around Genesys, but be careful."

I peered hard into the monitor, wishing I could read her now. "This will move us from the battle to an all-out war. You know that, right?"

"My dear, this became a war when you intervened the first time. You flicked that first domino the moment you got in their way over rescuing Cooper from them. Now, they are all clacking together. The time has come..." She closed her eyes and suddenly, Malecon's face replaced hers. He was the exact image of his sister, only in male form.

Haitian by birth, both twins had hazel eyes that often appeared yellow. Their skin held a reddish hue and both still had much of their jet black hair. Some would call Malecon handsome. I considered him deadly.

"She's weak, Echo. Time to finish up here."

"What *time* was Mel talking about?"

Malecon looked away from the screen and then back to me. "Time for you to finish what you started. It's time, dear Echo, to destroy Genesys."

Cinder was enamored with the dogs as they nipped and played with each other. Two sleds of eight dogs each pulled up, loaded with blankets, a food warmer and emergency supplies.

I had no idea so many things were needed for a hundred-mile trip.

Suka stepped off the sled and came into the warm office, his parka completely unzipped. I couldn't believe he could actually be warm in this weather. "We're all set. There are blankets, thermoses of coffee, food for lunch, snacks and sixteen beautiful dogs." He knelt down next to Cinder. "I see the way you look at the dogs. They are beautiful creatures, no?"

She nodded and smiled.

"She doesn't talk," I said softly.

He never took his eyes from her face. "That's all right. There are plenty of women I wish would follow suit." He rose and chuckled. "Maniitok will give you the lowdown of how to be a good passenger and what to expect. Please pay close attention as these are working dogs and not pets."

Cinder shot out of there toward the brown-and-white husky leading the pack, her arms open.

"Wait!" Suka said, but it was too late. Cinder had her arms around the animal's neck and was burying her face in the fur. "Well, I'll be damned."

"I'm sorry. I'll get—"

"No, no. It's cool. It's just that Panik never lets kids that close to her. She distrusts people she doesn't know. Cinder must be special."

"You have no idea."

I joined Cinder out in the biting cold and took my place under a bunch of blankets on the sled. She was still petting Panik when Maniitok hopped on the back and grabbed the handles.

"Her name is Panik," he explained. "It means daughter. She is the daughter of the pack leader, Amagug, which means wolf." He pointed to a gray-and-white husky that looked just like a wolf.

Suka introduced Cinder to all of the dogs, but she was clearly smitten with Panik, whose tail thumped against the side of the sled as she looked at Cinder. Clearly it was love at first sight.

"Ready everyone?" Suka said after Maniitok gave us the rundown on the dos and don'ts of Dog Sledding 101.

I looked over at Cinder. *"You're going to love this."*

She was beaming. *"I already do, but...how is Mel?"*

"She's good. She's...resting, which is more than I can say for us. Ready?"

She smiled so brightly, I almost forgot this wasn't a fun tourist ride.

"Hold on, ladies. We're looking at five, maybe six hours, depending on the weather."

"What do you mean *the weather*?"

Suka looked up, his face open to the heavens. "Feels like snow. That would slow us down quite a bit."

Turning to him, I whispered, "There's more in it if you can get us there faster."

He leaned forward and whispered back, "Money or not, the dogs can only go so fast, ma'am."

"I understand. And thank you."

"Thank me once we arrive in Wales." Standing on the back of the sled, he grabbed the reins and said, *"Hike!"* and away we went.

At first, the wind felt like it was burning my face, but after a while I relaxed and enjoyed the sounds of the dogs crunching through the snow and the shooshing sound of the sled as we whisked along. Let me tell you, those sleds really move, too. I was slightly surprised by how fast we were moving and how much distance we covered in such a short time.

"You sure you want to head to Patterson Pass?" Suka asked, raising his voice above the shooshing sound. "There's a better route than that."

"Yes, we're picking up my friend."

"Alrighty then."

Burrowing down into the blankets, I watched as the beautiful scenery flew by. Tall, snow-laden pine branches bending toward the ground. They looked like a painted postcard. Alaska was prettier than any postcard, but even a picture couldn't capture the cold as it seeped like ice water through the blankets and my new parka. I'd never felt such cold and was pretty sure I never wanted to again.

As if reading my mind, Suka said, "There's hot coffee in the gray thermos and cocoa in the red one if you get too cold. I understand you are from California. Californians don't typically like our kind of cold."

"Thank you. I'm good." I couldn't tell him I didn't want to have to stop and pee. We were deep in the wilds of the wilderness and I knew there would be only one choice of bathroom. No thanks. No coffee for me.

I don't know if I dozed off or if I had just zoned out during the peaceful ride, but it felt like only minutes had passed when we arrived at Patterson Pass. We shooshed on up to the tiny dot of a town and found Bailey waiting exactly where she'd pointed to on the map.

"Hurry," she said, hopping onto Maniitok's sled without any introductions.

"It would be easier if the girl came with us," Suka said. "Weight-wise."

Cinder hopped out and jumped under the covers with me. I was really glad she did because her warm little body heated those blankets almost instantly.

"Go, go, go," Bailey said, once she was sitting down.

I looked over at her. "We okay?"

She nodded. "Oh hell yes. Caribou for miles, but we need to get a move on."

And we did.

For several miles, I just enjoyed the gorgeous white blanket of wilderness that covered everything from poles to leaves to rocks. I'd never seen so much white. I wondered about the difficulty of living so far off the grid. I mean we were really far north. How did people live day in and day out in this cold? In this almost colorless region of the world? I could not even imagine.

Suddenly, Maniitok's sled slowed down to a stop, and we pulled up next to him.

"Got a limper," he said. "KoKo's foot." Hopping out, he tended to the dog, who yelped when he picked her foot up.

I exchanged a glance with Bailey. She wanted to help, and I saw no harm in it. Before she could get out of the sled, all sixteen dogs started going wild; barking whining, a few even howled.

"What's going on?" I asked Suka. He seemed to be listening

to something beyond the dogs. Then I looked over at Bailey, who was doing the same thing.

It was Bailey who answered. "Bear family," she said succinctly, her gaze never leaving the woods just outside of where we stopped. The hackles on the back of my neck stood on end. We were in trouble.

Suka and Maniitok both grabbed their rifles. "Could be wolves," Suka said, jamming one into the chamber with an ominous click.

Cinder pulled her hands out from under the blanket, but I shook my head. *Do not make a move, missy. Bailey's got this covered.*

"Not wolves," Bailey said, getting out of the sled. "Bears. Big ones."

Suka and Maniitok looked at each other. "Beg to differ with you, ma'am, but I think we know our dogs a bit better than—"

Bailey turned to him. "I'm sure you do, gentlemen, but now is not the time for a pissing contest. You're just going to have to believe me when I tell you that it's a bear family out there, with mama in charge, and I don't need to explain what that means."

Suka glanced over to Maniitok and shrugged. "I'll just untie KoKo and we can carry her until—"

"Too late!" Bailey cried, whipping around to make eye contact with me. I knew what that look meant: keep my eyes on Cinder.

I did more than that. I pulled her to me with one arm and prepared to throw up a defensive shield with the other.

Before either man could set his rifle on his shoulder, the loudest crashing sound I'd ever heard came rumbling through the bushes. It was the biggest bear I'd ever seen. Actually, it was the first I'd ever seen, but it was still enormous and rumbling toward us with hostile intent.

"Fuck! It *is* a bear!" Suka cried, putting his eye on the sight.

"I got it!" Maniitok said, taking aim. But before he could squeeze off a round, Bailey knocked the rifle from his hands.

"No!"

"What the fu—"

"Do *not* shoot that animal," Bailey commanded, standing

with her hand on top of Panik's head. Every dog silenced and sat down, all eyes on her. This was her power. This was what she did better than any animal whisperer alive. Bailey commanded nature, and it listened to her.

For my part, I laid my hand on Suka's leg and shook my head. "She knows what she is doing. You are going to have to trust us."

He lowered his weapon, not because of my touch, but because he was stunned by the silence of his dogs and the way they sat there staring at her—waiting for her command.

The bear, a big brown thing, was about forty feet away. It stood on all fours for a minute, then rose on its hind legs, sniffed the air. When came back down, it locked eyes with Bailey, and for the longest time, the two of them just stared at each other in this eerie silent vacuum created by the silenced dogs. When the bear turned and looked at us over its shoulder, it made a snarfling sound before returning to the cover of the woods as if called.

Maniitok and Suka stared at each other in disbelief.

"Now," Bailey said, kneeling to examine KoKo's paw. "Let's see what we have here."

"She doesn't let—"

"Hush, Maniitok," Suka said. "Didn't you see?"

Bailey pulled something from between KoKo's pads. Then, she went to her backpack and pulled out a small canister of the same green goo she'd once applied to a gunshot wound on Tip.

"This will help."

Maniitok stared, slack-jawed, as the dog let Bailey tend to her wound, his rifle hanging limply from his shoulder.

"It was a stick wedged between her pads. That unguent will speed the healing."

"I'll take her off the line."

Bailey shook her head. "No need. She's no longer in pain and would prefer to be working."

Suka set his rifle down and walked over to look at KoKo's foot. Then he and Maniitok stared at each other for a long time. It was as if they were having a conversation much like Cinder and I do.

"You are..." Suka struggled with all he'd just seen. "You are not what you seem."

"I am just a woman who has spent a lot of time with shamans," she said, returning to the sled and putting her green goo back in her sack.

Suka shook his head. "No. It is more than that. You were not afraid of the bear. The bear was not afraid of you."

"A bear, even a mother, is loathe to take on sixteen huskies," she said.

Maniitok said softly, "Ask her."

"No. They are tourists."

"Don't be so stubborn. *Ask her*!"

Bailey tilted her head. "Ask me what?"

Suka bowed his head slightly, his voice soft. "I know you are in a hurry to reach Wales, but our shaman, Atka, has been sick for a week now, and we fear she may die. She is too weak to bring to a doctor, not that she would go see one. Would you—"

Bailey looked at me, her eyes pleading. I did not want a side trip. I wanted to get to Wales and to Tip as soon as possible. I knew we should help. I knew there was nothing wrong with one small detour, but I wanted to get the hell out of this cold.

In the end, it was Cinder who decided for us all.

"Yes." Cinder's voice was clear and commanding.

Suka, Bailey and I all stared at her.

She looked at me, almost shaming me with those eyes. *"We help people, Echo. It's what you've always taught me to do. They need us."*

From the mouths of babes. "How far out of the way is it?"

"Not far. We can get in and out in less than forty minutes."

"You're outvoted, E," Bailey said quickly. "Okay, fellas. Mush!"

And mush they did.

The Inuit reminded me of some of the Native Americans I'd met in my life, only they had flatter faces and were less red in skin tone. What they all had in common was a warmth of spirit I always felt whenever they were around, and I found their smiles and laughter contagious.

The "village" was a small cluster of square boxes for houses, where each house had a dog run with at least two dogs. There were sleds out front, a couple of snowmobiles, and an area I assumed was for livestock.

"Snowmobiles? Why didn't we take one of those?" I asked to no one in particular.

"For this distance, in this weather, you would never take a vehicle that could break down or run out of gas," Suka explained. "These dogs? Never slow down. They love sledding and do not need gasoline."

I nodded, getting a sudden chill at the thought of breaking down in such hostile terrain with no big, furry, warm dogs to keep me alive. The very thought of being lost out here scared the crap out of me.

"Do you have family here?" I asked. I could see Bailey chatting Maniitok up ahead of us. She was, as always, comfortable no matter where she was. I don't think I had ever met another person so comfortable in their own skin.

"My grandmother lives here, yes. I will go see her when we drop you off at Ana's place."

I didn't like the idea of the drop off. We had someplace to be, and I wanted to help and then get moving.

As we passed a cluster of small wooden homes, all with gray smoke curling from the chimneys, I was reminded of the tin shacks perched on the bayou, and marveled at how anyone could live in such a place with the hard, cold ground surrounding them. The ground was frozen hard, snow clung to everything, and the climate made everything feel so gray and bleak. It was as if no color could survive here.

Suddenly, color in the form of a bunch of children burst from one of the houses and came running our way, laughing and yelling and having fun, apparently oblivious to the cold.

"School," Suka said, slowing the sled down some. "The children heard the dogs. They love visitors."

The sled came to a slow, if not loud stop as the dogs seemed to be as excited as the children.

Leaping off the sleds, both Maniitok and Suka were surrounded by a swarm of laughing Inuit children, all of whom seemed to have a story to tell. They were all chattering at once.

"Come on, E. The shaman's house is the last one in the village." Bailey helped me and Cinder out from our covers, and the moment the kids saw Cinder and her flaming red locks, they turned and stared.

"They don't see many white girls out here," Suka explained. "And probably none with that color hair." He pointed to Cinder.

Cinder was as awestruck with them as they were with her, so I nudged her toward them. "Go on. Make a snowman or something. Bailey and I will be right back."

It had taken me a while to stop seeing Cinder as a helpless little girl and to start treating her as someone who could take care of herself. This was one of those times I needed to trust that.

"Last house. Have fun."

She ran into the group of kids, swallowed whole. It warmed my heart to see it and I made a mental note to make sure she had more kid time now that we lived in Marin.

Following Bailey and Suka to the house, I felt the cold seeping onto my jacket…not through my jacket, but on it…as if it were settling in for the ride.

"Don't start busting my chops about that bear, E. It was a mama bear with two cubs in the bush. She could very well have come after those dogs, and the guys would have been forced to kill her."

"I wasn't going to bust your chops…at least, not about that."

She turned to me. "Since when do we not help people, E? I know you're itchin' to get Tip out of Dodge. So am I. But—"

I held my hand up to stop her, feeling guilty about my narrow agenda. "I just wish you would have talked to me before telling Taylor. It's really important we're all on the same page."

"We are. But when it comes to relationships, I let no one, not you, not Mel, not the Goddess herself tell me what I can and can't tell my lover. I'm sorry if that pissed you off, but it's still my life. I may do these things and help others, but in the end, all life decisions will be made by yours truly."

I nodded. "I understand."

"Do you? E, you've waited so long to tell Finn, it may already be too late."

I opened my mouth to disagree, but I knew better. She was right. "Let's hope not."

When Suka stopped at the front door, he said, "I will go in and speak to the Ngekok first. I will explain who you are and that you might be able to help." With that, he disappeared into the square house with a peeling blue door.

"I've never met an Alaskan shaman," Bailey whispered. "This is very exciting."

Bailey had been taught by a shaman in the Amazon as well as in Australia and Peru. I'd seen her handiwork myself and knew she was no slouch as a healer, herbalist and animist.

The front door opened and Suka beckoned us in.

As we entered the small home, I was immediately struck by its warmth and coziness. There were a couple of logs on the fire, and an overstuffed couch in front of it with a colorful woven blanket laying across the back. Something yummy was on the stove, two more dogs were asleep near the hearth and didn't give us so much as a glance. To my surprise, the Ngekok was a woman.

Bailey seemed taken aback as well.

"Atka," Suka said to her before speaking his native tongue. As he spoke, the old woman opened her eyes and looked at us. She wasn't as old as I thought she would be for a shaman, but her eyes and emotions told the story of a woman who didn't feel well. I didn't need to lower my shields to know she felt horrible. I read the pain in her eyes, then I read the rest of her emotions.

"It's her chest," I whispered to Bailey. "Her lungs."

Bailey nodded. "Good enough." Peering into her backpack, she rummaged through it, pulling out various small canisters filled with powders, leaves, mosses and any number of organic materials known by shamans to have healing properties.

"What can I do?" Suka asked.

"Can you get me some hot water and a second glass of cold water for her to drink?"

"Yeah, sure."

Atka said something to him, so he looked up at me and then answered her.

"What did she say?"

Suka looked at me. "She has a fever."

I read right through his little fib. "What did she *say*, Suka?"

He shook his head and looked down. "She said you were the one she's been waiting for."

My eyebrows rose. "Me?"

"No." He jutted his chin out to Bailey. "Her."

Bailey smiled slightly at me before returning to her powders.

When Suka went into the kitchen, I knelt down next to Bailey as she mixed two colorful powders together. "What's wrong with her?"

Bailey closed her eyes and laid her hands on Atka's chest, where she breathed in and out with the shaman for several moments, the only sounds the crackling from the fire and the slight snoring of the dogs.

I estimated Atka to be somewhere in her fifties. Her face was slightly wrinkled, her long hair only sprinkled with gray. She was a handsome woman, even as ill as she felt, and she was definitely not feeling well. Her chest hurt, she was short of breath, and it was a good thing we'd come. I would not imagine that she could have lasted too many more days.

Atka spoke to Bailey in her native tongue, and Bailey did not move her hands from the woman's chest. When Suka returned, Bailey took the glass and poured some greenish-yellow powder into it. "I need a warm, damp washcloth as well."

"Bailey?"

She hushed me with a look. When Atka began a slow chant, Bailey joined in as if she knew the language. I stepped back in awe. Together, Suka and I watched in silence as Bailey and the shaman finished whatever prayer they'd been chanting. Bailey rubbed something into the woman's chest before carefully laying the washcloth on it. Lifting her head, Bailey held her up as she sipped the water.

"This will help her sleep, and clear the fluid in her lungs. Expect her to sleep a good twelve to sixteen hours. Keep the house filled with steam." She pointed to the fire. "Put a pot of water over the fire with these herbs in it." Bailey handed a baggie full of herbs to Suka, who nodded.

"If she can breathe these in for at least ten hours, it should clear her lungs up pretty quickly."

Atka drank all of the water and then lay her head back down and closed her eyes. Her labored breathing calmed a bit.

"Let her rest, but keep that water heated."

Suka nodded.

As Bailey packed her bag, the old woman opened her eyes, said something to Suka, and then turned to Bailey. "Come back to see me. I have much to teach you and you will need to learn what I know." She looked over at me. "To be able to save her."

I look at Bailey. "Me?"

Atka nodded. "You. That is…all I can say." Then she closed her eyes and laid her head back once more.

Bailey nodded and respectfully we said our goodbyes.

Outside, Suka spoke to a young woman before handing her the bag of herbs. She took it and headed into the house.

"She will see to it your directions are followed." Suka blinked hard, fighting back tears. "Thank you. Atka is a well-loved and cherished member of our tribal community…the spirit of the village. Saving her means everything to us."

"Glad I could help. I don't know that I saved her, but she will rest more comfortably now."

"Are there no other doctors or shamans who could have helped?" I asked.

Suka stared at me. "Of course there are. Did you not hear Atka? She was waiting for Bailey."

I looked at Bailey, who nodded. "It's true. She knew we were coming. She is…very powerful. She should be fine now, but you'll need to keep an eye on her. The herbs and steam should clear her up."

Laying a hand on Bailey's shoulder, I gave it a quick squeeze. "You're wonderful, you know that?"

"I'll bet you say that to all the girls."

Arm-in-arm, we made our way to where all the children, including Cinder, were playing.

"She's never really had kids to play with," I whispered to Bailey.

"You'll have to do something about that when you get home. She hasn't had much of a childhood, and now we find out she's not going to be one very much longer."

When Cinder first came to us, we estimated her age to be around ten because she was so small. We were wrong. It took Dani's boys less than an hour to track down her birth certificate. Cinder was twelve.

I nodded, watching Cinder laughing for the first time since I'd collected her. Something happened then…a moment of complete clarity; something that settled in my heart and whispered to me that we were going to be all right. That with or without the Others, I would be a damn good mentor who made sure my charges had as normal an upbringing as possible. Cinder deserved that and I would move mountains to make sure she got it.

When Cinder looked up and saw us, her play came to an abrupt stop, as if we'd caught her doing something wrong.

"Did you need me?"

As much as I hated to do it, I waved her over. I would have liked to let her play for a while, but we were burning daylight. "We're done here. Back in the saddle, Cin."

Nodding, she ran over to the circle of children, said her goodbyes, hugged Panik, and then hopped in the sled, her energy lighter than I'd ever felt it.

"That was so much fun!"

"I'm glad you had a good time."

"They're super nice, Echo. I'm glad we came."

"Thank you isn't enough," Maniitok said as he prepared his sled. "Atka is an important figure in our community, and the salt of the earth. We would be lost without her."

Bailey climbed in and stuffed her backpack between her knees. "We have someone like that in our lives as well. Glad we could help."

Suka got on back and waited while Cinder and I bundled up. "We will not be charging you for the return trip. It is the least we can do."

As we pulled out of the small village, I put my arm around

Cinder and pulled her to me. "You looked like you were having a great time out there."

"*I was. They were the nicest kids I ever met...*"

"*But?*"

She frowned. "*I don't know how, but...I could...I could understand them.*"

I turned to her. "What? What do you mean?"

"*I mean...I understood their language. In here.*" She tapped her temple. "*It was weird...and cool...but more weird.*"

I'd heard of supers who had no language barriers, but this was quite unexpected, but then, the unexpected happened in my life all the time.

"We'll have to look into that when we get home. I've heard of some supers who can do that."

She beamed and snuggled up next to me. "*I kinda liked it.*"

How ironic for our little mute to suddenly become a lingopath. Would I ever have a moment's respite from all I never knew?

Looking at my charge, I grinned. I seriously doubted it.

The temperature, I was certain, dropped ten degrees once we were back out on the sleds. Cinder managed to keep us warm beneath the blankets, but my face felt like a frozen mask. I had to tuck it in the blankets to keep it from freezing off.

Just as I was getting ready to nod off, my vidbook vibrated and buzzed. When I opened it, there was Taylor's face.

"Yo, Echo! Your face looks frozen!"

My mouth barely moved. "It is. What's going on?"

"Okay, the shit's hitting the fan in bumfuck Egypt out here." Her voice was barely above a whisper, and my alarms started ringing. I was wide awake now.

"You okay?"

"For now." Taylor looked both ways and lowered her voice even more. "Genesys showed up right after I landed. I managed to lose them, but those bastards were persistent. Tailed me for nearly a mile before I shook 'em."

"How many?"

"Three. All men, no necks. Wearing lumberjack clothes from Old Navy. Look, Wales is a postage stamp. There's no place to stay in town that would be safe, but that is not my issue at the moment."

"I'm afraid to ask. What's your issue?"

"I need to put the brakes on these guys. They're big, bad and ugly. They're turning every place inside out. They're pissed I got away from them and have called in reinforcements. I heard one of them on a cell while I was escaping into the brush."

"What's your game plan?" I could tell by the look in her eyes something was up. I hadn't known Taylor long, but she had many tells, and that twinkle in her eyes was one of them.

"I need to take them out of the game, quietly, *that's* my game plan."

I nodded. "Be careful, Taylor. They're playing for keeps."

"So am I. Echo, I can tell these people are serious. These aren't collectors. These jokers are killers. Trust me. They aren't here to scoop up your triplets as much as they're here to take you and Tiponi out. Big and beefy and well-armed."

I inhaled deeply, the cold air burning my lungs. Then I looked back at Taylor and nodded. "Do what you think best, but leave no trail and stay out of harm's way. Storm will kill us if anything happens to you."

"Yes, she will, but it's me you're talking to, Echo. Look, we need to be able to move around out here without these jack-offs threatening us or following us, or—"

"Killing us."

She nodded. "Heavy artillery, James Bond shit. They're not here to do anything but terminate anyone who stands in their way. Don't worry. I won't let them even get off the ground. Just don't come all the way into Wales. There's not a damn place to hide. When I take care of these yahoos, I'll try to secure arrangements on the outskirts of town…someplace we can get away from quickly if we have to. I have a call in to my peeps to see if they have any connections out here."

"That's perfect. You sure you're going to be okay?"

"Me? Oh hell yeah. This is cake. You guys be careful out there. There's a storm coming."

"Hard to tell, it's so damn cold here."

"No shitter! My marrow has icicles. Remember, Echo, don't come into this burg. Wait on the outskirts a few miles unless you hear from me before that. Until then, circle the village and wait."

I nodded. "Taylor?"

"Yeah?"

"Please be careful."

"Hey, I'm no Delta Stevens, but I can hold my own against these chumps. Trust me. They're soft and I'm hot."

I started to close the vidbook, but decided against it. Instead, I called home.

"Echo!"

"Hi Delta."

"Damn, girl, you look cold all bundled up like that. Looking at you is making me *feel* cold."

"Cold is an understatement. How do people live in this?"

"No clue. Connie has you on GPS. Looks like a storm is coming your way. Everything all right?"

"It's Taylor. She seems to think she can take out three of Genesys' men, and I am a little worried she might be in over her head."

"Yeah?"

"Can she?"

Delta laughed. "She's one of the best. Unlike some of us, though, she'll handle it without killing anyone. Taylor's no killer, but she has mad skills. She'll get in their space without anyone knowing. You know how Ninjas get in and out without being heard? Taylor could teach the Ninjas a thing or two. Don't you worry about her. As long as she has us in her back pocket, she's never alone. She knows that."

"Did you suspect something like this when she accompanied Bailey?"

"Echo, you know you're a trouble-magnet. I can count on anything happening around you and Danica. Why do you think Taylor is so prepared?"

"Is she?"

"Like a goddamned Girl Scout."

Delta Stevens had emerald green eyes, unlike anything I have ever seen, yet it wasn't their greenness that riveted me to them, it was an intensity that reached through the screen and grabbed me. When Delta Stevens spoke, you listened. "Look," she told me now. "We may not have your special abilities, but we've got talents you've never dreamed of. I'd never put any of my people in danger they couldn't handle. Taylor can handle this." She paused and lowered her voice. "You want me and Connie to come out there?"

"No, no. We'll be fine." I turned away from the monitor. Light snow began falling. "Thank you, though."

"And Echo? As long as we take a breath, you're never alone, either. We take care of our own."

"I appreciate that. See you soon." Closing the vidbook, I sank back into the blankets.

The snow was beginning to fall hard, and I wondered how in the hell Suka or the dogs could see where they were going.

"It's just a little snow, Echo. The dogs have no problem with—" Suka cocked his head and listened.

Cinder and I exchanged glances. We'd heard this sound before. Suddenly, Cinder pulled her hand out from under the blanket. It was glowing like it did prior to her shooting a fireball.

"Bailey?" I could tell she was feeling or hearing something neither Cinder nor I could.

She turned around and looked up in the sky. "I hear it! Bird in the air!"

"Split up!" I yelled. She turned back around, said something to Maniitok, who shook his head.

I looked up at Suka. "Choppers! And they are after us! We have to get out of here!"

Suka's eyes registered part fear, part disbelief. "Are you wanted by the police?"

"It's not the police that's after us. We need to split up, and now!"

"*Hike! Gee!*" Our sled suddenly veered off to the right and away from Maniitok's sled. The dogs were hauling now, as the sound of the chopper blades whipped closer and closer, whipping the snow into a frenzy. I felt like I was in a vanilla shake.

Looking ahead, I saw the tree line of the forest Suka was heading toward. Glancing back at the chopper, now visible against the white backdrop, I wasn't at all sure we'd make the forest before they could, before they might—

And there it was...the awful thunking sound of bullets embedding in tree trunks—another sound we'd all heard before—a sound you never forget hearing.

"*Bailey!*" Cinder cried in my head. She wasn't afraid. She wanted to act, and I couldn't let her. Not now. Not yet.

"*She is safer separated from us. Hang on!*"

Cinder nodded and we ducked lower under the covers as the sled started hitting bumps and making us airborne. Tree limbs lashed out at us as the dogs continued pulling us deeper into the woods and further from the sound of the chopper and that horrific sound of lead smacking wood. As we crashed through the underbrush I was sure had never seen man's footprints, the dogs slowed down. I turned to Suka to tell him to keep going, but he was gone.

Gone?

"Oh no. No, no, no." Frantically pushing the covers off, I carefully made my way to the driver's section behind where he had been standing. He was gone.

Cinder was also up and out of the covers now. "*Where is he?*"

"I have no idea!" I yelled, unnecessarily loudly. Taking the reins, I said, "Easy...easy." The dogs slowed considerably before finally coming to a stop in a small clearing. Evergreens rose all around us as the snow fell harder, landing on the already snow-laden branches. I could not see ten feet in front of us, but I didn't need to see to know we were in trouble. No one but Genesys would have a chopper out in these conditions.

I lowered my shields to see if I could feel Suka, but I knew the weather, the heavy snowfall, would make it difficult to read anything.

"*Echo?*"

"I'm trying, Cinder."

"*Use Panik.*"

"What?"

"*The dog. Use the dog. She'll find him.*"

Feeling the chill like a freezing cold shower, I made my way to the front dogs and looked for a way to unharness Panik.

Cinder's warmer fingers worked better than mine and she had Panik free before attaching a rope to the dog's harness.

"Fire," I said to Cinder, my teeth beginning to chatter. "Stay with the dogs. Don't—"

"*Go, Echo. I am not cold, but Suka will be. You need to go…now!*"

Taking Panik, we ran back the direction we came. Already, our tracks were filling with snow, and my heart filled with dread the further I got from Cinder. At least I couldn't hear the choppers anymore.

We must have gone a hundred yards or so when Panik found Suka and let out a howl that was colder than the snowfall. She knew before I did what we were going to find. Kneeling next to Suka and the dog, I did not need to feel his pulse to know he was still alive. He had a head wound, but I couldn't tell if it was from a bullet or if one of the branches had knocked him out. All I knew was that he was unconscious and freezing. I needed to get him back to the fire and the other dogs before the hostile climate came for him.

I tied the rope around his ankles so both Panik and I could drag him back. I could think of no other way to get him back, and wondered if Cinder was scared. My telepathy with her was limited by distance, so I couldn't communicate with her unless we were near each other…and I needed her nearby. It was taking everything I could do not to panic, but panic was taking a comfortable seat on my chest, reminding me of the fragility of life.

"*Hike!*" I commanded Panik, picking up my leaden-weighted legs. My God, I had no idea walking in snow was so difficult, or that people could still sweat while so very cold. Every muscle in my body was screaming at me as I pulled dead weight through the snow like a plow.

The snow fell harder now, but I could see an orange light in the distance. Cinder must have built a roaring fire I couldn't wait to get next to. My nose felt frozen, my cheeks hurt, and I was sure my toes were getting frostbite. I needed that fire.

As I neared it I realized I had guessed incorrectly. Cinder hadn't built the fire...she *was* the fire. One huge glowing orb of fire.

I stopped dead, my chin on my chest. I had never seen...never known...her power like this. There she stood, as if the nucleus of this flaming cell, an orange and bright yellow cloud of flames surrounding her like some macabre halo. It was one of the most amazing things I had ever seen.

The dogs were laying behind her, oblivious to the spectacle that made me stop and stare.

"I wanted to make sure you made your way back. It's snowing really hard."

"It's perfect...um...whatever it is."

"Suka alive?"

"So far, yeah." I continued walking, pulling Suka's heavy weight along. When we reached Cinder, she extinguished whatever that aura was and helped me pull him under the makeshift cover she had constructed under the overturned sled. How she managed to get it turned over was beyond me. Those things were heavy.

"I made a little shelter using the sled. It's not much, but it'll keep the snow off us."

Cinder undid the rope from Panik and helped me get Suka under the propped up sled she had leaned against a tree, so there was just enough room for the three of us to huddle together without letting the snow fall on us.

Once we were covered up and made warm by Cinder's body heat, I examined Suka's head wound.

"Damn it."

"Bad?"

"Bullet wound. Looks like it just grazed him, but was probably enough to knock him off the sled." Reaching into my bag, I pulled out a long-sleeved T-shirt and wrapped it around his head. "Keep your hand pressed against it."

Cinder looked at me funny, then slowly unwrapped the shirt before laying her hand on the still bleeding wound. Her eyes were locked on mine as her hand became hotter and hotter. *"Heat caught...court..."*

"Cauterizes."

"*Yes.*"

Cinder had only been out of my care and hanging on the bayou with Melika for a few months, yet she had learned so much. How could I even come close to teaching her about her potential when I had no idea she could do *this*?

"*Mel taught me that. She calls it Uriel. Angel of light or flame of God.*"

"I like that. It suits you, but I have to say—"

"*Pretty impressive, huh?*"

"I'll say. Can you make it hotter?"

"*Oh yes. I can control it now. We worked a long time on that. Mel says it's the skill that kills most of us, and she wants to make sure I know how to control it.*"

"Is it different than the supernova?"

"*Yes. Very. I can do this with or without heat, with or without light.*"

"Well, right now we could use a little of both." I gazed outside at the whiteout conditions and wondered how something so white could be so dark. I shuddered at the thought of being in it. I also shuddered at the thought that Bailey was out in it without a Cinder.

Cinder removed her hand and I could smell the slight odor of burnt flesh. Holding her hand over his head, she produced a light so I could look more closely at his now cauterized wound.

"Good job."

"*Don't worry about the cold, Echo. I can keep us warm until—*"

"We have to get out of here as soon as the snow stops falling. Suka needs help and that chopper is surely just waiting for us on the other side."

"*Until then, stay under the covers.*" Cinder grabbed a blanket and made a flap in order to keep the heat in. Then she got between me and Suka and turned on the heat. It was incredibly welcome.

"*Will the dogs be okay?*"

"They'll be fine. Those thick coats of theirs protect them from the elements. You really like Panik, don't you?"

"*I like them all. I've never had a pet.*"

I nodded. Few of us ever did. I wondered why. Opening my

vidbook, I wanted to see Bailey's face and make sure she was all right. When nothing happened, I checked the power. It was fine. "Come on!" I said, trying it again. "Damn it! Must be one of those dead spots."

"Bailey might have escaped. And if she didn't, someone's gonna get eaten by a bear or wolf or something."

"I'm sure she's fine. Danica, however, will call out the National Guard if she doesn't hear from us in a couple of hours."

Cinder glanced down at Suka. *"Can he make it that long?"*

"I'm monitoring him. If he gets too weak, we're going to have to brave the damned snow and make a go of it with or without choppers on our tail."

Cinder nodded. *"I'm ready when you are. Just say the word."*

I looked over at her, amazed at how quickly she had grown and changed. "You're quite a super, but when did you get so old?"

She returned my sentiments and that was when I realized what a young lady she was turning out to be. *"Old soul is what Melika says."*

"Then that's probably true."

"I'm not a little kid anymore, Echo. I know something's going on with Melika. She's sick, isn't she?"

What could I say? I'd never lied to her and wasn't about to start now. She was right. She wasn't a little girl. Death and destruction makes one grow up rather quickly, and we had suffered enough on both counts. "She's very sick, Cin. The kind of sick you don't get over."

"Cancer?"

"Brain tumor."

Cinder choked back her sadness and turned away. I didn't need to read her to know she was crying. Reaching over, I held her warm hand in mine.

"Is she scared?"

I tilted my head at her. It was such a sensitive question from a kid who, like the rest of us, was going to lose the only mother she knew...or at least...the only one who loved her unconditionally.

"No, she's not. You know Mel. She's more concerned for us than she is for herself."

"How long?"

"She doesn't know."

"I can't believe Tip isn't there with her."

"She doesn't know."

Cinder whipped her head around. *"What?"*

"I haven't told her. She's not in a place to deal with that loss. When we get out of this mess, I'll tell her, but not before. She is going to need time, and she ought to be with Mel when she finds out or she's likely to go around the bend."

"Good thinking."

I squeezed her hand. "It's okay to feel sad. I'm really sad about it."

"And that's why you're taking on the mentoring so soon, huh?"

I nodded, and I thought I felt the small space heat up. "Cinder?"

"I'm trying not to start bawling. So much is changing."

"I know, but love, that's okay. Life is about changing. Successful people are those who go with those changes and make something even better. We will be successful, Cinder. I promise you that."

Cinder peeked out from the blanket. The snowfall wasn't letting up. *"What are we going to do?"*

"Now? I think we need to wait this snowfall out. He feels stable for now, but rattling around on the sled, lost in the snow, seems like a really bad plan."

"I can keep us warm, but I need to go and beef up a fire for the dogs, and in case there's a rescue team or something."

"If rescuers can see us, so can Genesys."

She turned and studied me a moment. *"Yes, but I won't turn rescuers into burnt animal crackers, Echo."*

Before I could say anything, Cinder was gone. I tried my vidbook again, but there was nothing. If I was going to make it work, I'd need to get away from where we were.

Watching Cinder toss logs onto the fire, my heart warmed. She was growing up so fast. I shuddered at the thought of what Bailey could be going through without her. Were they okay? Had they gotten away or had Genesys gotten to them?

This was the second time Genesys had tried to take my life,

and I was getting pretty damned tired of it. It was time to go on the offensive. They had put me and the people I loved in grave danger for the last time. When Cinder and I got out of this, we would take them out, one by one, until there were no more in my way to Tip.

I was done playing nice.

What had Danica said to me once? *"Killing some people is nothing more than taking out the trash."* Well, somebody needed to bring out the big Dumpster because the garbage man was on her way.

Pulling the blanket back, I watched Cinder petting Panik. The girl was in love, for sure. The fire was raging, due in part to Cinder's flaming fingers. I had no real clue how she could do what she did without getting burned up, and made a mental note to learn more about pyrokinetics. Surely there was no other being more special than they.

When Cinder came back in, she was perfectly dry, another gift of her powers.

"Snow isn't letting up."

I nodded.

"Dani will really worry."

"Got any suggestions?"

"Let me take two of the dogs out and see if I can get a signal long enough to—"

"No way. There are bears and—" I caught her staring at me with a 'so what?' look on her face. The truth was, even a bear couldn't live through one or two of Cinder's fireballs. The cold wouldn't get her, and if she took the dogs, they could bring her back here safely. It wasn't a half-bad idea.

"Fine."

Her eyes grew wide. *"Really?"*

"Like you said, I have to stop treating you like a little girl, Cinder, and recognize you for the strong young woman you are. Can you use a compass?"

She nodded.

"There's an app on there that will at least keep you from getting lost. Take two dogs, and be on the lookout for bears or cougars or wolverines."

"*Gotcha.*"

"If you don't get a signal after ten minutes of walking, come back. If you aren't back in thirty, I will die of worry. If you come back after thirty, I will so kick your ass."

She nodded once before laying on the blankets. Suddenly, I felt so warm, the blankets felt like electric blankets on high. "Please be careful."

Nodding, she took Panik and another gray-and-white dog, and disappeared into the whiteout, leaving me to experience the longest thirty minutes of my life.

It was time to meditate.

Closing my eyes, I reached out to Tip once more. How was it our connection had been broken? How could a place so cut us off from each other that she couldn't reach me?

"Tip, please. I need you now. I need to know you're okay. I need you." I breathed calmly, opening my mind to her, waiting, as I had never waited before, to hear her thoughts, to hear anything from her.

Nothing came.

I had learned long ago that my telepathic connections were a result of my emotional impulses toward those sending. I am not a telepath by any stretch of the imagination, but I have a sort of selective telepathy. It's a little like selective hearing. I can communicate with the three supers I loved; Tip, Cinder and Melika.

And that was when it hit me.

Maybe it wasn't Alaska preventing Tip from hearing me. Maybe it was me. Maybe she couldn't hear my thoughts anymore because I was in love with someone else. Or was I? I was, wasn't I? Or maybe I was just heading in that direction with Finn. My stomach suddenly churned and gurgled. That was it, wasn't it? My new love had deafened her to my calls. I was, for the first time in fourteen years, truly without her.

And it was the most disconcerting feeling I'd ever experienced.

Opening my eyes, I checked my watch. It was a little before noon. How long had we been immobile? Cinder had only been gone five minutes. It took everything I had to keep panic at bay.

In my head, I knew she could take care of herself better than anyone, maybe even better than Tip. I had watched Cinder kill two men as easily as striking a match. She held no remorse for their deaths, probably because, at the time, they wanted to harm me. Still, it had taken me a long time to get used to the notion that Cinder was a killer. Her skill enabled her to do so easily and quickly, and I had seen her powers enough to know she was nearly unstoppable as a killing machine. Very little can stop fire. I'd seen that as well. In my heart I knew Cinder would be fine. It was my head that wasn't so sure.

Suka moved slightly under the blanket and groaned. The blankets had become cold in Cinder's absence, but the fire outside still burned brightly. We would not freeze to death in the next thirty minutes, that was for sure.

Five minutes turned into ten, ten into twenty, and my heart was banging madly against my chest as if trying to get out. Had I just made the first monumental error as a mentor? Had I just sent our youngest student to her death?

Twenty into twenty-five.

"Come on, Cinder. Where are you?" I tried meditating, but I couldn't focus.

Pulling the blanket back and peering outside, I stared at a second blanket of white so dense I couldn't see anything. Not the fire ten feet away, not the dogs, nothing but a sheet of freezing white.

That was when panic hit me hard. I felt a claustrophobia of some sort as everywhere I looked nothing but a curtain of cold whiteness greeted me. Dropping the flap, I closed my eyes and breathed deeply. I had to believe in her. I simply had to. I could not afford to let doubt creep in. Cinder was a smart girl. She was with the dogs. She had her powers. She would be fine.

Twenty-five into thirty.

My eyes came open, and I foolishly considered, for just a nano, flipping this sled over and making a run for it...see if the dogs couldn't find each other. That was when the blanket was pulled back, and there she was, with the two dogs on either side of her. She was still bone dry.

"Thank God!" I said, pulling her to me. She immediately

warmed me and the air around me, heating up our shelter. I'd never been so grateful in my life to have her back. "Are you okay?"

Cinder pulled away to lay across the blankets to warm Suka. *"I went as far out as you told me, but it flickered on for half a second, then nothing. I didn't get completely out of the woods, but I'm not sure that would have mattered."*

I agreed. We were probably in a dead zone for a lot of things. Some paranormal researchers believed it was due to unstable energy created by the aurora borealis.

"Well, I've decided we're going to wait this out. We can't go anywhere until the snow stops."

"Nighttime is going to be really cold."

"I know. I'm worried about Suka. I'm not sure he'll be okay overnight." I had checked his wound, and Cinder had stopped the bleeding, but that didn't mean he was out of danger. He should have come to by now. As I was feeling his head, my left hand felt an egg-sized bump on the back of his head. "Oh shit. He really hit his head when he fell. Damn it."

"Can't see out there, Echo."

"Then we wait."

So we waited it out, sharing the thermos of coffee and eating a package of crackers. I tried not to think about Bailey, about Tip, about anything negative, so I thought about my mother, a woman I had only recently met.

Trish was a nice enough woman. She'd been so happy to see me after twenty-eight years of wondering what happened to the daughter she left behind. I had been pleasantly surprised by how much I liked her. She was sincere and honest, and emitted a warm, welcoming aura about her. Thinking about her seemed to calm me some and brought out the maternal instincts in me.

"Get some rest, Cinder. We're going to need your heat tonight."

"I'll throw more on the fire first."

Day slowly turned to night as we huddled together for warmth. Cinder brought the dogs around the sled for extra heat, but it was cold. Freezing cold. I half expected the dogs to freeze to death, but I had to believe they'd be okay. Huddled under the blanket, I thought about all the movies I'd seen where they say don't fall asleep or you never wake up.

So, I didn't.

All night long, I sat there, waking Cinder up when we needed more heat, thinking about all I needed to do to crush Genesys and everyone involved with it. And I needed to crush them. I needed to do more than stop them for the moment. I needed an all out, go crazy ass nuts on them and their entire operation. I was done pussyfooting around with them, and it was time to plant the seeds of their destruction. My kids may not be ready for the war against them, but I sure as hell was.

As soon as I saw the first light, I pulled the blanket back from the shelter and heaved a sigh of relief. It had stopped snowing, the dogs weren't frozen, and the sun was actually coming up.

Looking back in the shelter, I saw Suka move. He blinked slowly, bringing his hand to his head and gingerly feeling around.

"What...where—?"

I explained what had happened, and as I did, he looked around, puzzled. "We should be frozen." He looked around at the shelter. "Good shelter. Smart girls." He tried sitting up, but closed his eyes and moaned softly. "So, bad people are after you. I can't say you're the first people who have come to Alaska to get away from someone."

"I apologize for bringing you into this, Suka. I never meant to involve you guys."

He nodded slowly and winced. "One cannot always second-guess what Fate has in store for us, Echo."

"Does it hurt?"

He nodded. "Nauseous, but I can get us out of here." He looked around slowly. "How is it so warm in here?"

"Oh. We had the dogs in here all night."

He nodded, his skin clammy and pale. "Very good. If I could have something to drink?"

"We saved you some coffee. Take your time. We've made it through the night. A few more minutes won't kill us."

Cinder nodded, and scooted over to me so Suka wouldn't feel how warm she was.

When Suka was ready, we flipped the sled back over and followed his instructions for reattaching the dogs. Once we were ready, we repacked the sled and I tucked Cinder in before moving back to where Suka stood.

"What are you doing?" Suka asked.

"I am standing with you. In case you get dizzy or feel faint."

He nodded. "Come. Let's see where we are and get our bearings."

I was never happier than when that sled started pulling us out of the woods. I could see the clearing where the helicopter had seen us about a hundred yards ahead. As we neared the clearing, I heard the sound of engines whining. It wasn't a helicopter this time. It was worse.

They were snowmobiles and they were heading straight toward us.

Suka heard them, too.

"Stop the dogs, please," I told him.

"I can get us—"

"No, Suka. I won't put you in any more danger. This isn't your battle, and I won't put you in harm's way again. Please. Stop the dogs."

"I'm not leaving you to face whoever that is."

"That, my friend, is death to your dogs if you go out of the woods. Please. It would wreck Cinder if she watched Panik get killed."

Suka glanced down at his dogs and weighed his options.

"Believe it or not, we'll be fine. Please."

The sled came to a slow stop about fifty yards from the edge of the woods.

"You sure?" Suka looked at Cinder, torn between saving himself and leaving us at the hands of the snowmobilers.

I nodded, no longer cold, even though it hadn't warmed up much from the night. My adrenaline had kicked in. I was ready to face whoever was foolish enough to come after us. "Positive. Once you hear the snowmobiles rev three times, you'll know we won and can come out. If you don't hear that, assume the worst and get out of here. Don't look back, don't come to see if we are okay. Just go."

He nodded, pulling an enormous bowie knife from a sheath strapped to his leg and handing it to me. "I have a feeling you'd have no issue using this."

Taking the knife, I nodded. "Good read."

"Echo, I don't know how you not only survived the night in a blizzard, but built a fire that size. You two won't go down without grizzly bear fight in you."

Cinder and I stepped off the sled. "Thank you. For everything."

Reaching up, he touched his head. "I'm thinking I need to be thanking you."

The sounds grew nearer, and Cinder and I stepped away. Cinder then ran to Panik and embraced the husky before returning to my side.

"Ready."

Together, Cinder and I walked out of the woods shoulder to shoulder. Coming right for us were two snowmobiles; a yellow one and a red one, one hundred yards away. Raising her hands, Cinder nodded. She was ready. On my go, she would melt both machines and riders into two balls of molten metal.

As I raised mine, I lowered my shields to get a read of what was coming. I suddenly stopped and placed one on her shoulder. "Wait."

"They're almost here."

"They're not hostile."

Cinder half looked up at me. "You sure?"

I was tired and run-down. When that happens to an empath, it's hard to make accurate reads, so her question was a valid one.

So I read again and watched as the two snowmobiles stopped a good thirty yards from us.

"Echo?"

I squeezed her shoulder. "Same. Hold your fire."

"Echo Branson? Danica and Sal sent us!" came a male voice from the yellow snowmobile.

Cinder and I looked at each other.

"Danica said you'd doubt us!" he called out, cupping his hands around his mouth. "She told us to say that Clark better get her ass on the vidbook or some mulatto girl was going ghetto."

A smile crossed my face and Cinder's as well. It was the cavalry.

"Do you need medical attention?" the man on the red snowmobile asked.

"Stay ready," I said to Cinder. "They are telling the truth about Danica, but we need to be on our toes. They could have been followed."

"Always ready."

"Off the snowmobiles, please, and keep your hands laced behind your head. One suspicious move and you'll die where you stand."

Together, we tromped through the snow as both men dismounted their snowmobiles and did as I demanded.

"There's a chopper to the east of here," the taller one said. "So if they're looking for you, we need to DD out of here before we all show up on any radar panel."

"Where did you guys come from anyway?"

"Brevig Mission. You're about twelve miles outside of it. We live there."

"You *live* there?"

The shorter one on the yellow snowmobile lifted his goggles and nodded. "Sal and us go way back, ma'am. She's had us on standby watch for two days."

"You're kidding."

"Ma'am, I hate to be a buzz kill, but that chopper's gonna swing by this way in the next fifteen minutes, and we need to be outta here. We'll get you to Wales, but you have to trust us."

"Would you do me a favor and rev your engines three times?"

He did so and, shortly after, Suka emerged, mushing his dogs.

"Everything okay here?" Suka asked, eyeing the two men suspiciously.

I nodded. "They'll get us to Wales."

Suka reminded me of a big dog sniffing at two dogs who had walked into his territory.

"We'll be fine, Suka. You need to get your head looked at and we need to get the hell out of the open."

"We have a doctor friend outside of Brevig Mission," the shorter one said. They were too bundled up in camo for me to tell anything else about them other than their size.

Suka nodded. "Me and the dogs will follow."

I had a feeling he would have anyway.

As I approached the yellow snowmobile, the guy extended his hand. "Pitt. That's Loco. We were in the military with a friend of hers. Josh. When he died, we all stepped up to make sure Sal was taken care of. That little gal has a lot of big brothers, and any friend of hers is a friend of ours."

I nodded, grateful for that. "Nice meeting you. That's Cinder, and he's Suka."

"Come on, Pitt. We gotta get a move on."

Cinder looked at me and I nodded. We both got on back of the snowmobiles and held on for dear life as Pitt and Loco flew out of there and skipped along the snow like a rock across water. It felt like my fillings were being jarred from my head.

"I need to check for a cell signal!" I yelled above the whine of the engines. I had no idea how loud those things were.

"Not here! I'll stop when we get out of the dead zone!"

Nodding, I buried my face against his shoulder blade and held on.

The trip was faster than I realized, and suddenly we were in the tiny burg of Brevig Mission. Did I say tiny? I meant miniscule. This was not really a town, by definition, but was more of a settlement. Looked like it had a church and a store. That was about it.

The snowmobiles came to a slow stop, and Pitt turned to me. "Try it now."

I slid off the snowmobile and opened the vidbook. Danica answered on one ring and I saw Sal's and Connie's faces in the background. All looked relieved to see mine.

"Where the fuck have you been?" Danica asked.

"Snowstorm. Genesys. Bears. Helicopters. You name it. We're fine now. Thank you for your foresight in arranging this backup. It came at the perfect time."

"You think I'd let you go off to bumfuck Egypt without backup? How well do you know me?"

I grinned. "Not as well as you know me, apparently. Good call on the soldiers."

"The boys were on standby from Sal, who seems to have a sailor in every port. When I hadn't heard from you, and the GPS went bonkers, we waited and waited until there was one slight moment when the GPS kicked in. It was barely a second, but Carl caught it. Earned himself a bonus for that one."

Cinder.

"We nailed the location and sent them after you. Where's Firefly?"

"She's right here. We're fine. Genesys took a couple of shots at us. Grazed our driver, but the snowstorm prevented them from doing any more damage." I looked up in time to see Suka and the dogs roll up. He looked really pale.

Pitt leaned over and whispered, "The doctor's retired, but Loco will show you the way."

I returned my attention to Danica, who was talking to someone else off screen. "Dani, they've started something I want to end here and now, but first, where's Bailey? We got separated during the snowstorm."

Danica shook her head. "Off the grid. Wish I had better news. She's not with you?"

"Shit."

"Don't panic. You and Firefly made it out okay. The boys are all over the GPS. The moment she makes it out of the dead zone, we'll have a bead on her."

Panic began welling up in my chest. "Okay. Okay. We'll check around here for Maniitok and Bailey. I can—"

Suddenly, Sal's face was on the screen. "Echo, listen to me. Don't panic. I can hear it in your voice. Send Pitt and Loco out to find her. Tracking is what they do, and no one in the state is better at it than they are. You and Cinder need to get something to eat, get your wits back, and take time to breathe. Let the guys do what they do best."

I nodded and looked behind me at Suka. He was barely able to stand.

"Echo!" Sal called out.

I returned my attention back to the screen. I hadn't realized how tired I was. I wasn't focusing very well.

"We're putting a picture up of Bailey for you to show Pitt and Loco."

Nodding, I handed the vidbook to Pitt. "That's Bailey. That's what she looks like only in a big, fat, puffy parka."

"I'll ask around town," Suka said. "Strangers are easy to spot here. They are usually wearing big, fat, puffy parkas."

Pitt shook his head. "No, dude. You need to get that head looked at. It's not looking so good." Pitt peered at it closely. "Looks like it's burnt or something."

Suka started to disagree, but I shook my head. "Uh-uh. Pitt's right. You need that looked at."

"Look. Loco will take you to our doctor friend on the outskirts of town. I'll check around and see if Bailey and—"

"Maniitok. Short Inuit guy about ye tall," Suka answered, holding his hand parallel to the ground.

"If Bailey and Maniitok are here in town. Maybe they haven't come in yet. First, I'm going to take Echo and Cinder where they can rest and recoup. Spending a night in the cold takes everything out of you."

Sal nodded. "Roger that. Get them food, warmth, and a change of clothes. Then find Bailey."

"Ten-four, Salamander," Loco said, saluting. "We'll give you a holler when we locate her."

Another photo of a glowing Bailey came on the screen and both Pitt and Loco peered at it. "Wow."

"Yeah. She's a looker. Find her, fellas, and I'll double your fee."

Pitt and Loco looked at each other and laughed before handing me the vidbook. "No need. We're doing this 'cause Salamander asked us to. Don't you gals worry none. We'll find your Bailey."

I looked at the vidbook and Danica was back on.

"Okay, Clark, I *know* you want to charge on out there to find her, but Pitt and Loco know that area better than almost anyone. You get some rest. You need to be able to focus if you plan on going after Genesys. Trust us, Clark. You've got a team in place. You need to gather yourself, rest, and we'll get started tomorrow. It's not a request."

I felt Cinder's warm hand in mind. *"She's right. I'm so tired."*

Looking down at Cinder, I nodded. "You're right, Dani. Thank you for sending the boys to get us."

"All we needed was one beep. One blip. One light. We got that and away they went. Go on now. We're here. We're always here. Get some rest and start fresh in the morning."

I mouthed, "Thank you." Closing the vidbook, I turned to Pitt and nodded.

"We've got just the place. Loco will take Suka to the doctor and I'll take you two to our R.C."

"R.C.?"

"Rehab Center. It has a nice shower. You'll see."

Twenty minutes outside of town, Pitt pulled up to a small, square cabin with a plume of gray smoke coming from the chimney. It looked like something out of a fairy tale.

"Here?"

"Yeah. This is a safe place."

The front door opened and was immediately filled by one of the largest men I had ever seen.

"Safe?"

Pitt laughed. "Him? Hell no. But he's on our side."

Looking at the giant, I forced a grin. "Thank God."

Jumping off the snowmobile, Pitt ran up to the door and right up to the big guy. "The fuck you doing? Trying to scare the girls? Get on out of the doorway you big lug."

Cinder stared at me, eyes wide with questions I had no answers to.

"Trust, Cinder. We need to go with the flow here. I'm beat. So are you. He's just a big guy."

Pitt ran back to us. "I'm sorry about that. It's been awhile since we had any visitors and I wanted to make sure the place was…you know…kid friendly." I studied him and realized that he really did look like Brad Pitt. "Come on in."

We followed him into the cabin, where the giant was stoking the fire in a huge rock fireplace surrounded by three very worn leather couches in the shape of a U. The large great room had a wall of windows overlooking a frozen lake. The house was larger than it looked from the outside, but this room was very homey and inviting.

"This is our Rehab Center," Pitt said, showing us to a decent-sized bedroom with twin beds, a small lamp, and a window overlooking the woods. "This is where veterans come to beat whatever addiction they are slave to."

I blinked. "Excuse me?"

"These guys get jacked up on all sorts of shit over there. In Vietnam it was LSD and marijuana. In the Gulf War, cocaine, and lately, oxycodone and other prescription drugs. They need to get away from their lives and come here to recover and get away from those who use."

"To detox?"

He nodded. "There are five smaller units out back. Gar is the only resident right now, so he stays in the Big House. The doc is out doing his daily medical runs for the people in the area. He's not really a doctor, more like a medic."

"So who owns this?"

"Doc does. When he was in Iraq, he decided to do something for all the vets he saw getting juiced on drugs, so he turned a family vacation spot into this."

"*Vacation?*"

"*Hush.*" I laid my hand on Cinder's shoulder. "What a nice thing to do."

Pitt nodded, and looked at me with misty blue eyes. I realized Pitt probably wasn't his name. He looked a lot like an older Brad Pitt with a scruffy five-o'clock shadow and blond hair. "It was bad over there, ma'am. Way worse than anything you were probably told stateside."

"So Gar is detoxing?" I already knew the answer, having read him when he stood in the doorway.

"Oxy. But his isn't my story to tell. You'll be safe here. There's chow in the kitchen. Gar's a pretty good cook. Get some rest. I'll wake you as soon as we find your friend."

"You sound pretty confident of that."

He grinned boyishly. "Oh, I am. We're trackers, like Sal said. We could find a piece of dandruff in a snowbank. That's not a proud boast, ma'am. We're pretty damn good. Pardon my French."

I thanked him and sat on the bed, opening the vidbook. "Change your clothes, Cinder, and then hop on in for a little rest."

Nodding, she disappeared into the bathroom.

The vidbook rang and Finn's face appeared in one screen-filling grin. "There you are! I've been missing you."

Her eyes danced and I realized how much I was really missing her. I asked, "How you feeling? You look great." She did, too. The sparkle was back in her eyes and the dark circles were gone. It looked like her experience in New Orleans was finally becoming a distant memory.

"Getting back into the swing of things tomorrow. My head has healed and the knot has finally gone down."

"Oh good. And then what will you be doing?"

"Then I have to meet with Internal Affairs. Everyone is scrambling around about a case that's gone south. They want to know if I know anything. I don't, of course."

"Sounds like a drag."

"Oh it is. IA is a pain in my ass." Finn peered into the screen as if trying to get a better look. "How are you? You look tired."

"I am. All this jet lag has caught up with me. I'm getting ready to take a nap."

She frowned. "It's still morning."

"Yeah, well I didn't get much sleep."

"And much more, I'm sure. Trouble has a way of finding you, sweet cheeks. And even with all of that, I still think you hung the moon. When you get back, and we have time, I'd like to lay all our cards on the table. I know you have secrets, and I don't need to know them if they don't affect us. A girl's gotta have some privacy, right?"

"Oh Finn, you have no idea how happy that makes me."

She waved it off. "Full disclosure isn't necessary or needed, Echo. I'm a cop—not one of those women who needs her partner to tell her everything she's thinking. It's unhealthy. You are you and I'm me, and together, we can create an us."

"I would love that. I really would."

"Good." Her eyes went to the door of her room. "My sister is here to bug me again, so I gotta go. When will you be home?"

"Soon. A couple of days maybe. It's hard to say."

"Keep in touch."

"I will."

"And stay safe. I'm really kinda liking you."

"Oh really?"

"Yeah. Really."

I then called Melika. There was no answer, so I left her a message letting her know we were okay. I did not tell her we'd separated from Bailey. The last thing Melika needed was more worry.

When Cinder came out of the bathroom, she was wearing flannel pajamas far too big for her.

"Where on earth—"

"There's a closet full of them. They're cozy." Hopping up on the bed, she dug under the covers like a little kid.

I moved over and sat on the edge of her bed. I had little to no maternal instincts except where Cinder was concerned. "You saved our lives last night," I said, caressing her hair. "I am really proud of you."

Closing her eyes, she sighed softly. *"Protecting you is my job."*

I looked down at her. "Is that what Melika told you?"

"Yes. She's been teaching me a lot of different powers— most, she said, are to protect you. That you were going to need me really soon."

"As usual, she was right."

She opened her eyes and stared into mine. *"You're my family now, Echo, and protecting you and the new school is what I was born to do."*

"And you're okay with that?"

She closed her eyes again and nodded. *"It gives my powers a purpose. That's what Mel told me. She said everyone needs a purpose and few pyros ever find one. I'm luckier than most. I have, and I accept it."*

I could feel her energy waning, so I stopped talking and waited until she was asleep before gently extricating myself from her and going out to the great room where the giant was standing at the kitchen counter. He had made a roast beef sandwich and slid the plate over to me.

"Eat," he said.

When I say huge, I mean gigantic. His shoulders had to be three or four feet wide, and his whole being was rectangular. His waist was as thick as his chest, and he towered over me at what had to be six and a half feet tall. When he slid the plate to me, his hand was as big as the plate, with what looked like burn marks on the back.

"Thank you," I said, biting into the sandwich. "I'm starving."

"What about her?" He motioned to the bedroom with his head. His eyes were light blue and he sported a cleft chin beneath a few days' growth. A boxer's nose sat like putty between two intense eyes, and a scar cut his forehead nearly in half. He reminded me of a statue I'd once seen in Florence.

"She's already asleep." I ate more of the sandwich while he sipped coffee out of a mug that looked like a thimble in his enormous hands.

"I'll let you eat in peace. If you need anything, just holler. They call me Gar."

I reached out to shake his hand. "Echo."

Tilting his head, his eyes held unasked questions. "Welcome aboard." Lumbering over to the fireplace, he grabbed a thick book and stood by the fire reading.

I finished the sandwich and put the plate in the sink before joining him in the great room. "That was delicious. I've never had roast beef that was so tender."

"Not roast beef."

"Oh."

He looked up from his book, a classic Steinbeck. I don't know why, but I was surprised.

"Elk. The natives bring it by whenever they have some extra."

"Well, it was delicious, thank you. I won't keep you."

Gar lowered the book and motioned at the sofa. "No bother. I haven't talked to a woman in two months. Nice change from guys."

To be polite, I sat down. I read nothing threatening about him—just a man who had suffered too many losses and held too much pain.

"East of Eden, huh?"

He nodded. "We don't get a lot of choices out here, so I prefer the longer ones. What brings you to this wilderness?"

"I...uh...am here to bring home triplets who crossed over the border from Russia."

He nodded, but said nothing.

"So you're here—"

"Cleaning out my system. Seems death and me didn't agree in that shithole of a desert. I held my girlfriend's blown-up body in my arms as she died from a roadside bomb. She was military, too. Fucking cowards. Don't remember much after that. Just started taking oxy to dull the pain."

His pain was still raw. "Nothing can dull that kind of pain but time," I said, feeling my own pain fresh from Jacob Marley's death.

"You know."

I nodded. "I do."

"That bomb took out six people I cared about. Guess it almost got me too. I suppose, in a way it did. Killed the guy I used to be, so when I got out, I came here. I'm not gonna let that war dictate who I become."

"What a great attitude. How much longer will you stay here?"

"A couple more months, then home to Los Angeles. I'm not ready to be back in the world."

I nodded, my eyes getting heavier.

"You look tired. Get some rest. You're safe here."

I rose, thanked him again for the sandwich, and then passed out the moment my head hit the pillow.

When I woke up, it was dark out the window and the smell of white wine and garlic wafted through the air, prompting my eyes to pop open and my stomach to growl.

Rubbing my eyes, I looked over to Cinder's bed to find it empty. Alarm gripped my heart in a vise as I jumped out of bed and ran into the great room where I found Bailey and Cinder sitting at the counter bar while Gar cooked something in a huge cast iron skillet.

"Bailey!"

She slid off the stool and ran to me, squeezing the air out of me. "Echo. My God is it good to see you!"

Stepping out of the embrace, I looked her over. She looked none the worse for wear. A few scratches here and there, but other than that, she looked well. "When did you get here?"

"Noonish. You were sleeping so hard I decided to let you continue. Cinder's been up about two hours. We've been enjoying Gar's cooking and war stories."

I looked at Cinder, who was rested, happy and hungry. *"Sleep well?"*

"Like a baby."

"How is she?"

"That's rude," Bailey said. "I'm fine. Maniitok took us to a hunting shelter just as the snow started falling harder. We had to dig our way out, which is what took us so long."

She held out her vidbook. "Tried everything to get this thing to work. What in the hell is wrong with this place?"

Gar chuckled, a sound that reminded me of gravel being crushed beneath the wheels of a truck. "Dead zone," he said to no one in particular. "They're all over Alaska."

"Did you let—"

"Yes, *Mom*, I made all the calls. Everyone knows we're safe, with all our body parts intact." Bailey smiled. "Hungry?"

I felt my empty belly. "Yes."

"Good. My man Gar here is whipping up some fettuccini Alfredo that's making my mouth water."

I hiked my butt onto the stool between Cinder and Bailey. The fettuccini aroma filled the whole room, and I suddenly felt like myself again.

"Where's Suka and Maniitok?"

"With their people, in town."

"Pitt and Loco are doing a recon of the area. They'll be back around five thirty. Before dark. Where in the hell did Sal find those guys?"

"No idea, but they're intense."

"Trackers," Gar muttered.

"What about them?"

Gar turned, spatula in hand. "Trackers are intense. Serious. Always in their heads."

And this from a guy who was super stoic?

"Anything from Taylor yet?" I asked. "We should have heard from her by now."

Bailey nodded. "She's outside of Wales. Took her a while to get out of the dead zone, but she's there in one piece."

"Her tail?"

Bailey laughed. "Dani called the local sheriff and said they were carrying drugs. They never got off the plane. Well, maybe not never, but they were stalled long enough to give her a good head start. My guess is all the weapons they had made the sheriff nervous."

"Excellent." I blew out a loud breath. "So we're all accounted for except Tip."

Bailey nodded. "Taylor didn't ask around. She felt too exposed. Too obvious. She's given us her coordinates and Pitt and Loco will gather her up in the morning. I figured you'd rather we all be together."

"Yes. Good idea, thank you."

Gar turned to us, holding two plates of the best-looking fettuccini I'd ever seen. "Smart girl. Small town. She'd draw attention to herself."

Taking a plate, I closed my eyes and inhaled the aroma "Oh my..."

"He's been cooking forever," Bailey announced, handing her plate to Cinder. "Let's eat and then sit down for a strategy session."

We ate in relative silence, while Gar cleaned up the kitchen. When he finished, he went back to the fireplace, threw in more logs, and then turned his back to it and stood without moving.

Bailey leaned over and lowered her voice. "You haven't...you know...heard anything?"

I shook my head. "Silence."

"Weird. So not like her."

Cinder came over and sat down next to me. It was almost dark out now and I wondered where the guys were.

"Okay," I said softly. "We're out of here in the morning at first light. We'll go by snowmobile so we—"

"Sleds are better."

Bailey and I looked at Gar.

"Snowmobiles announce your arrival. Everyone will know you've come. These people know the sounds of each other's snowmobiles. They'll know you're not one of them, so it's too risky."

Bailey nodded. "He's right."

"I sincerely doubt we can get Maniitok to take us to—"

"He'll go." Again, Gar.

"How do you know?"

"Indian way. They shot his buddy. Retribution is his responsibility. He'll go."

"Good. Then we get Taylor, find Tip, and get the hell off this iceberg."

Bailey drew her finger over the map. "We'll avoid actually going into Wales if we can. If we stay on the outskirts, I might be able to utilize my...knowledge."

Looking out the corner of my eye at Gar, I wondered how he could stand so still. "Gar?"

"Yes?"

"Bailey told you why we're here and what happened?"

"Yes."

"Your thoughts?"

"Mine?"

"Yeah. You're a vet. What are your thoughts about a plan of action?"

He stood still for so long, I wasn't sure he heard me. "You ladies think like guys. That's good."

"But?"

He shrugged. "You wait like women."

Bailey and I looked at each other. "Wait like women?"

He nodded. "Wait to react. Wait to go on the defensive when you need to go on the offensive. Men like to attack. You don't. Women avoid it more." He shrugged. "Just an observation."

I sat with Gar's observation for a long time, until Pitt arrived with Maniitok in tow, just like Gar had said. Everyone agreed the sled into Wales was the smarter choice. Pitt and Loco would accompany us halfway there, just as backup. Then, Bailey, Cinder and I could ride with Maniitok into the perimeter of Wales.

"Chopper was cruising up and down the coast," Pitt said, tapping his finger on the map. "Has to be their guys. Black chopper, no markings, clearly looking for someone."

"Why the coast?" Bailey asked.

"They may be expecting you to use the water to travel."

Gar's words kept banging around in my head. Is that what I'd been doing? Waiting? Reacting instead of acting? Acting like a woman and not a leader?

It was almost ten when we decided to hit the sack, though I was no longer tired. The guys fueled up the snowmobiles, Maniitok fed the dogs, Bailey called in to let Dani know our game plan, and I...I bundled up and stepped out into the cold, out into nature, out where I might possibly be able to reach Tip.

I needed to reach her. I'd never gone this long without touching base with her and I felt her absence like a gaping wound.

Watching my breath puff from my mouth, I stepped gingerly out by the dogs, knowing I was safe as long as they were near. Closing my eyes, I concentrated on my breathing. In. Out. In. Out. Clearing my mind of all thought. Opening it up, allowing her in, beckoning, as it were, for her to talk to me.

I waited a long time to hear her, but only the sound of the wind tickling the pine trees reached me. When I could stand it no longer, I concentrated all my energy on my thoughts. *"Tip! God damn it, where are you?"*

I waited forever to hear her voice and fought the edges of dread threatening to creep into my heart. I could not afford that emotion. It had no place in my world, so I took a few calming breaths and continued. *"Okay. I'm going to assume the energy displacement that causes cell phone dead zones is why you can't hear me. Or talk to me. I guess I just need to talk to you. To let you know we're coming. You're not alone. You're never alone."* Suddenly, tears came to my eyes and I impatiently wiped them away. *"I miss you, Tip. I miss being on the bayou with you and Jacob and Zack. God, I just miss the sun and the heat. This place feels like another planet. I know you hate it, too. The cold, I mean. I just...I need you to know I'm coming. We're coming. Just hang on. Please. God knows I can't do this without you. I...I really can't."*

Suddenly, I felt someone else nearby, and slammed the psychic door before turning around. Not hostile energy at all. Curious. Questioning.

"How long have you been standing there?" I asked Gar, who stood motionless in the shadows.

"Ever since you walked out here. Dangerous thing to do. Wolves, bears, all sorts of critters."

Walking back to the house, I moved past him. I would never have seen him had I relied on any of my five senses.

"Echo?"

I stopped at the door. "Yes, Gar?"

"You really want to find your buddy, you ought to be straight up with Pitt and Loco."

"Straight up?"

He chuckled that gravelly laugh once more. "The truth about why you're here. Why they're after you, and why two women and a child would come to the hinterlands of Alaska alone. It's almost insulting that you aren't being honest."

I cocked my head. "You mean alone as in without a man?"

He stepped out of the shadows. "I mean alone as in without any weapons. You're going up against shooters without any firepower. It's a fool's mission and you're dragging other people into it without giving them the whole story." Gar reached into his army jacket and withdrew a semiautomatic machine gun I'd only seen in movies. "Ever fire one of these?"

"Never."

"Can you?"

I shook my head. "No."

"What about this?" He reached into his waistband and pulled out a Glock similar to Danica's.

I tried not to grin. I had, in fact, fired one before. "I've fired one of those, yeah."

He handed it to me, butt first. "Good. Take it, then. I'll feel much better knowing you have some sort of protection."

Taking the gun, I shoved it in my waistband like I'd seen Danica do on more than one occasion. "Thank you. And thank you so much for your hospitality. I have to say...I don't get the addict vibe from you."

He nodded and opened the front door for me. "I'm over the worst of it. Just not ready for prime time." He smiled his first grin and looked years younger in that moment. "Can I ask you something?"

"You can try."

"How come Cinder doesn't talk?"

"Childhood trauma. Why?"

"I was like that for a while when I was a kid. Sometimes, it seems like I was happier when I didn't talk."

We both made a beeline for the fireplace and stood next to each other with our hands behind our backs.

"Really?"

"Yeah. Same reason. Trauma."

"How'd you get over it?"

"Time. Suddenly, I just found my voice. She will, too."

"I sure hope so."

"She's a smart one, that little girl. You can see it in her eyes."

We stood silently for a few moments before he stepped away from the fire. "Remember what I said, Echo. Straight up, and those boys'll find her in no time."

"I never told you Tip's gender."

"Didn't have to. I picked up a vibe myself."

I grinned. "Oh really?"

"Spent a lot of time with female soldiers. Not to be stereotypical, of course."

"Of course."

"Makes no difference to me. Just be straight up. They can help you better then."

I watched Gar lumber down the hall to his room, leaving me alone with my thoughts.

My Tip-less thoughts. My emptiness. My solitude.

It was time to follow Gar's suggestion. Time to stop waiting.

It was time to go on the offensive.

Morning came after a sleepless night filled with images of Tip and ice and endless white landscape. Cinder was up already and I could hear Bailey chatting amiably with Gar. Then, the smell of bacon wafted up my nose and I catapulted from the bed. Was there anything that couldn't be made better by the scent of bacon cooking?

When Bailey saw me, she laughed. "Gar calls bacon sizzling an aromatic alarm clock."

"No kidding." I looked over at the fire. "Where's Cinder?"

"Helping Maniitok with the dogs. You gotta get that girl a pet, E. She's in love with those dogs."

I peered out the frosted window to see her petting two at once. "You don't think—"

"That she's an animist like me? It's slightly possible. Secondary, tertiary, perhaps. Only time will tell."

"Good morning, Gar. Breakfast smells fabulous."

Gar turned and cocked his head. He had been in desperate need of a shave yesterday, but this morning he was clean-shaven and smelled of Old Spice. "Hungry?"

On cue, my stomach rumbled. This cold climate seemed to pump up my appetite. "Apparently."

"Good. Breakfast is in fifteen."

Going outside, I opened the vidbook and called Zack to check up on him. He'd returned to Atlanta to the Braves baseball organization he worked for as a scout. I didn't want to pull him into this battle. He had a wife and a baby on the way. Besides, he was still mourning the loss of Jacob Marley. Weren't we all? He needed a break from it, and I would give him all the time he needed, but that didn't mean I couldn't check up on him. Zack was like my brother, and I knew all too well of the yawning vacant spot in his heart.

Zack wasn't answering, so I left an upbeat message telling him to call when he got the chance. I was just checking in. No sooner had I hung up, than Danica called.

"What's the plan, Clark?"

"Good morning to you, too."

She shook her head. "It'll be good when you guys are safely ensconced here. You feel so far away. You might as well be on the moon."

"It's a whole different world out here, that's for sure. Foreign and freezing."

"So, how are we getting you out of there? Delta says you never go into anything like this without an exit strategy. So, what's ours?"

I liked her choice of pronouns. "We don't really have one yet because we don't know where they are. Does Delta have an answer for that?"

Danica shook her head. "No, but she will. She's taking us all out to the firing range this afternoon. I can't wait."

Danica had a sick love affair with that Glock of hers. Me? Guns made me nervous, but I could see their usefulness especially in times like these.

Knowing she needed a better visual of what I was doing and who I was involved with here, I told her that Pitt and Loco were awesome and that Gar had suggested I be more forthcoming.

She laughed and said, "Good luck with that. Do whatever you have to in order to bring your crew and yourself home."

"You'll see our GPS coming and going as we move through dead zones. Just don't panic if you see we're gone for a bit, okay? Those things are all over the place."

She nodded and looked away for a second to nod at one of the boys. "The boys have spent all night locating those goddamn black holes."

"What have you told them about…you know?"

"Honestly? They've not asked. I think they just dig the cloak-and-dagger shit." She waved one of them on before returning her attention back to me. "I still don't get why the Big Indian hasn't at least contacted you. That is so not like her."

"The way I see it, she either can't or thinks it's not safe."

"Not crazy about either scenario."

I nodded. "Tip knows what she's doing. I have to have faith in her."

"When are you leaving?"

"We're eating and then getting on the road. Or path. There are hardly any roads here."

"I know it's your call about how much to tell, but Alaska is a big place, Clark. Give them something to go on. Maybe listen to that Gar guy."

"Will do. Try not to worry. I'll be sporting one of these." I held up the Glock and she squealed with delight.

"Do me a favor and take off the safety. I'd hate for you to need to use it and not be able to."

I nodded and did as she asked even though it made me seriously nervous.

"You stay in touch...as much as you can, that is. You need anything? Anything we can get you?" She looked hard into the monitor. "You okay?"

I stepped further away from the cabin. "Dani...I can't do it this way anymore."

"Do what what way?"

"Wait around. Be one step behind Genesys. Always one step behind. I'm sick of it. I feel like they are the puppeteer and are always calling the shots. We're always on defense. It's time we upped the ante. I need them gone, Dani, and I mean really gone."

"Oh shit, Clark. You're serious. You've had that look in your eyes once before." Danica shook her head. "But not there and not without me...without us. Do what you went there to do, then come home and lay solid plans with the people who can help our side win." Danica peered into the screen. "We have *good* people, Clark. Experts. Don't do anything foolish until we can all be foolish together, okay?"

I laughed. She was, hands down, the best friend anyone could ask for. "Okay. You make good sense, but I better go. Breakfast is getting cold."

"Be safe."

I went back in and scarfed my delicious breakfast, packed my backpack, checked with Cinder and Bailey, and pulled Pitt and Loco aside. Neither had shaved and both had that musky man smell about them.

"I hear you two can find a piece of dandruff in the snow. I really need you to find my friend, Tip." Pulling out a photo I carried in my wallet, I handed it to Pitt. "She'll be with three kids."

Pitt took it but held his hand up. "This is what we figure. You're after something or someone this Genesys also wants. It's a race. They've got guns and wings. We've got dogs and..." He shrugged.

"And girls? We're not afraid, Pitt, and we're not your average single white female. We can get dirty with the best of them."

"That's not always a good thing. Fear has its place, Echo, and out here, there is a lot to be afraid of."

I nodded. "I know there is, but we don't have time to be afraid. I need to find Tip before Genesys does."

Pitt waited and I realized what Danica and Gar had once told me was right. Without letting people know what game they were playing you can't put them in danger. "Genesys is a subversive underground agency funded by our government to find and experiment on people who are…differently abled."

Pitt laughed. "That's a new one on me. You mean people who are extraordinary. We've seen their little subgroups here in Alaska before. They were called Exppro back in the day when the government had their hands in the alien cookie jar and other paranormal activities."

"Exppro?"

"Extraordinary People Project. Back in the fifties, the government did everything they could to discover the magic and mystique of this here state. They sent out all sorts of expeditions to see if it was the Inuit, what the Alaskans ate, the electromagnetic nature of the area or what. The Alaskans ran them out when they began rooting around burial grounds and shit. So, yeah, I know exactly what your Genesys is all about, and I'm glad Gar gave you that gun. You're going to need it. If they are anything like Exppro, they'll shoot first and never ask questions."

"They are very much like that, Pitt, but you need to know, we aren't helpless women, and we do not want you to pull any heroic stunt thinking we need saving. We don't. We need trackers, not saviors."

He looked dubious. "We'll do what we can to help. We'll take the lead into Wales, scout around, see what we can see. You and the dogs wait outside of Wales. We'll let you know if there is anything hinkey going on, but you need wings to get out of here. We can get us a chopper or a small plane, but it sounds like you're going to be carrying a full flight."

I nodded. "I think I know where I can get something large enough to carry us all."

Pitt grinned. "Of course you do. Come on, Echo. We're burning daylight."

In ten minutes, we were sled-bound once more. Maniitok made a final check on Suka, who was doing much better, and they exchanged dogs, making sure the strongest eight were pulling. Panik was one of the leads, much to Cinder's delight. Every chance she got, she was mauling that poor dog. Panik, for her part, seemed equally as smitten.

As the dogs mushed quickly along the newly fallen snow, the snowmobile whined in the far distance ahead of us until they were too far afield to be heard. Bailey was on the back of the snowmobile with Pitt, while Cinder and I were with Maniitok and the dogs. The ride was peaceful even though where we were headed promised to be anything but. I had a newfound respect for the wilderness, and wanted nothing more than to get out of this cold.

I turned to Cinder. *"How you feeling?"*
Cinder squeezed my hand. *"Ready."*
"Ready?"
"For them, I'm ready for them."
I nodded and squeezed her hand back. *"Good, because we're really going to need you."*

The ride wasn't nearly as long as the previous one. As we traveled through a landscape of ice and mountainous snowdrifts, and passed some incredible scenery, a few wolves, a family of bears fishing, and bald eagles overhead; it was gorgeous in a feral sort of way. The way the sun bounced off the snow lit everything up, and even the air seemed warmer. When we met up with Pitt and Loco, we were a few miles outside of Wales.

"Okay," Pitt said, adjusting his sunglasses. "We're going to run a five-mile perimeter around town, corkscrewing our way in. Do you have *any* idea where Tip would go?"

I thought of my dream last night. "Someplace icy. I saw like… a doorway leading to ice…or some sort of iced mound in the middle of a field. Wherever she is, there is a lot of ice and a mound."

Pitt and Loco looked at each other. "Well, that's not much to go on here. We'll keep in touch as we can." He held out his iPhone and we all bumped phones to exchange information such as cell numbers and contact info. "Want us to get Taylor first or after?"

"We'll get her."

Bailey looked at me.

"I want us together. Pitt and Loco need to attend to the recon. We need to gather our forces first and figure out what our next plan is."

Bailey hopped off the snowmobile and onto the sled. "Then let's get a mushin'!"

Pitt and Loco took off toward the coast while Maniitok and the three of us headed toward the coordinates Taylor had given. We were at the small cabin in less than fifteen minutes, where Bailey and Taylor embraced for a long time before pulling away and gazing into each other's faces. A part of me ached for Tip at that moment.

Tip?

Did I say Tip? I meant Finn. A part of me ached for Finn. Shit.

"I was beginning to wonder," Taylor said, breaking the eye contact and mussing Cinder's hair. "I don't know how these folks function with such spotty service. I thought the satellite hookup on this thing meant no dead spots."

"There are many of those," Maniitok said quietly. "But people who live out here are not the kind of people who wish to talk on the phone."

After the introductions, we filled Taylor in on our very loose plan.

"'Bout damn time we started taking the damn gloves off," she offered. "Taking potshots at you? Oh *hell* no! It's time to open a can of whup ass on someone."

"Okay, down Taylor. What do you know?"

Taylor laid her hand on Bailey's knee as she spoke. "This place isn't a town. It's barely a village. It's only claim to fame is some Indian burial ground that became a national park. They are very proud and quite protective of that, but it's really all there is."

Bailey and I looked at each other. Turning to Maniitok, I asked, "Is that here? In Wales?"

He nodded. "The burial mound of the Birnirk people I told you about was discovered just outside of Wales, not too far from here."

I stepped closer to him. "Tell me more about them."

He shrugged. "Don't know much. Some more were found in Barrow, but just that one in Wales."

"Have you seen it?"

"Seen what?"

"Seen the burial area?"

He shrugged. "Once or twice. It's no big d—"

"Does it look like this?" I took out a piece of paper and drew the doorway I'd seen in my dream.

Maniitok squinted at the doorframe leading to what looked like a small mound.

"Yeah. That could be it."

Glancing over at Bailey, I nodded. "Gotcha. Maniitok, this is where we want to go."

"Then let's go."

I shook my head. "Not this time, Maniitok."

"What about Pitt and Loco?"

I zipped up my parka and pulled on my gloves. "Not their fight."

"I can't just let you—"

"Not your fight, either," I said, and lightly touched his arm. "I really appreciate you getting us here in one piece, but I won't put anyone else in jeopardy."

Bailey agreed. "We can take this from here."

He blinked several times. "I think maybe *you're* the ones who should be called Loco. They *shot* Suka. You don't even have guns!"

"We have one," I said. "We'll be fine. How far is it from here?"

"Mile, mile and a half, straight that way, but—"

"Her mind is made up, Maniitok, really," Bailey said. "We'll be fine. Echo wouldn't risk putting us in danger if she could help it."

Maniitok shrugged helplessly. "I'll wait here then. Right here. If you're not back here at noon, I'll head back to Nome and bring a search party."

I shook his hand, but Bailey hugged him. "Thank you so much."

We trudged through the snow, partially melted by Cinder's heat. Taylor was right behind with me and Bailey pulling up the rear.

"He could have dropped us off," Bailey grumbled.

"He'd never have left. I won't put any naturals in danger if I can help it."

Bailey looked at me, an eyebrow raised in question.

"Taylor's different. All of Delta's team are different."

"How do you figure?"

"Haven't you noticed? They each have some skill or talent superior to just about any other natural. Connie and her computers, Taylor and her magianship, Sal and her electronics, Megan and her people-reading skills, and Delta..." My voice trailed off. "I don't know *what* she is. She's not one of us, but she's not wholly one of them, either."

"So, they don't count as naturals?"

"They don't. Besides, they thrive on the adrenaline of danger.

They seem to look for it and embrace it when it arrives. We avoid it. They seek it out."

Bailey said nothing, so I pressed on. "You love her?"

We walked twenty more steps, crunching snow as we went, without a word. When she did answer, I could barely hear her.

"I'm afraid to."

And there it was. The same fear we all had about not loving for fear of losing. "You've not told her?"

"Not all of it. She knows I am an animist. She knows I can make shit from nature. She doesn't know, nor does she seem to care, about the label that is…well…us."

"Afraid to tell her?"

She let out a sigh. "It's not for me to tell until you okay it."

I stopped. She stopped. "Where on earth did you get that idea?"

She shrugged. "Mel's orders were for all of us to wait on anything involving the group until you ascertained the appropriateness of the discovery. In other words, I can't until you clear it."

I thought my head might explode. Was there a mentor handbook out there somewhere that I'd missed reading? "I don't…I'm not sure—"

"Relax, E. I'm not ready. Right now, it's fun and new, and we really get along."

"But?"

"But I'm a creature. My heart of hearts believes I need to be with the same kind of spirit, someone who can truly understand my need to be alone in nature—someone who can understand that I can hear things she never will. That's a lot to ask of someone."

Nodding, I continued walking.

"What about you and Finn? How's that faring?"

My last thought about Finn made me wince. "Hard to say. I only recently told her I love her, but since meeting her, we haven't had a moment to really be together, to spend that kind of time couples need to connect."

"In other words—"

"We're in a wait-and-see holding pattern. I'm hoping we

have some real time to talk when this is over and we've settled in Marin."

"I sense some hesitation."

That was precisely how I felt. "I don't know. I can't protect her all the time. I worry that loving me is a dangerous proposition. I know you understand what I'm talking about."

"Like you said, though. These ladies love them some danger. Keep that in mind when you start wavering. I love that Taylor has basketball-size balls. That's what makes her so much fun."

Suddenly, we all stopped walking. About fifty yards away was the door I had seen in my dream, leading to ice I'd seen around Tip. It was smaller than a regular door and looked like something a Hobbit might live in. The mound around it was covered in snow and there were icicles hanging from the lintel.

"That it?" Taylor asked, pointing. She was so little, she wasn't much taller than Cinder, and looked like the Michelin Man in her white parka. Where she had managed to find form-fitting white leather pants was beyond me. I'd never seen her in anything but black leather jumpsuits like Cat Woman wore.

"That looks just like it." I looked to the left of the burial mound and saw the tree line. I had seen that tree line in my dream and it was almost exact. "Let's head over there. I'll get as close as I can and see what I can read down there before we go in."

I left the three of them at the tree line, safe behind some larger pines—safe from the prying eyes of any helicopter. When I reached the mouth of the burial mound, I closed my eyes and tried to feel the emotional energy inside before I took any unnecessary risks. To my surprise, I felt the energy of three people.

Three?

That didn't make sense. But, before I could make any sense of it, the familiar sound of chopper blades made its way toward us. I made a beeline to the trees where everyone was waiting, making it just as the black chopper crested over the top of them, kicking up snow from the pine branches.

Pulling the Glock out, I handed it, butt first, to Taylor, who took it from me without question. "I need you to distract the pilot long enough for us to follow them in, but be careful you don't hit the gas tank."

Her eyebrows flew up. "What do you mean, *follow them in?*"

Just then, the chopper hovered over the burial mound as three figures cloaked in uniforms of the Red Cross lowered themselves on zip lines.

"No time to explain. Go."

She regripped the gun and took off running.

"Echo?" Bailey asked, watching her lover zigzag across the snow-covered ground. "What are you doing?"

"Tip would never go someplace she'd be cornered. I don't know who's in there, but it's not her."

"And we're following them in *because?*"

"Because we need that chopper."

When the three figures landed, they ran to the burial mound, ripped the door open and then disappeared. Shortly after the last one vanished into the mound, bullets zinged off the hovering helicopter, which whirled around to see who was firing at it. When the helicopter made its move, so did we.

"I need their uniforms, Cinder, so no fire."

"No fire?"

"No fire. We really do need their outfits."

"Because?"

"Because we're commandeering that helicopter."

"Wolves, Bailey?" I asked.

"Way ahead of you, boss."

"We're hijacking their uniforms, taking that chopper, and heading back to Nome."

"Back to Nome?"

"I'll explain later. Let's just get those uniforms."

Following the three Genesys members into the mound, I realized the burial mound went down a little bit beneath the ground. The people we were following were not supers. They were Genesys collectors: well-armed, equipped with sedatives and other drugs to keep a super under that they were ready to collect, and I was ready to stop them. I shuddered at the thought of these people hunting supers like deer or bears. A slow-burning anger built up within me. Hunting my people. Corralling us like animals.

It was time to stop this madness, and I had a plan of attack that I was sure was going to surprise the hell out of Genesys.

I could see their lights as they made their way down a short tunnel, thinking they had either cornered Tip or the triplets. I wondered how they knew they were here...or almost here, because I had no doubt that the people they would soon discover were not who they expected to find.

"When I say now, Cinder, I need a blast of light. Bailey, cover your eyes. I need it blinding, Cinder. Make it as white and as bright as you can."

Nodding, she began warming up so much I could feel it through my layers.

As we crept closer, I yelled, "Now!"

Cinder lit up the cavernous tunnel so brightly, I could still see some light even with my gloves over my eyes.

"*Done.*"

Opening my eyes, I watched as all three Genesys workers reeled from the blinding light. Lowering my head, I concentrated on pushing out the same kind of energy I'd used in an SUV in Vegas. The energy was much like a percussion grenade, knocking them backward before knocking them out. They crumpled to the ground without getting off a single shot.

"Light."

Cinder gave us some light, though the dropped flashlights would have been sufficient.

"You two get their uniforms off and put them on. I'm going to see who the hell lured them down here."

Twenty feet further, I found my answer: Three Inuit natives sat in a small burial chamber calmly playing cards. For a second, I considered blasting them as well. Cooler heads prevailed.

"You must be Echo," the oldest one said, standing. He wasn't much taller than Cinder and had more wrinkles than a Shar-Pei.

"I am," I replied. "And you are?"

"Here to help. We brought Redhawk from Russia to here. She says people follow, so we wait for you to give message."

"And what message is that?"

"She is taking children to Nome. Could not wait here once helicopter arrived."

"Thank God. So they are together, Redhawk and the children?"

"They left together, yes, by boat. Our boat, but she will not stay with them."

"What do you mean?"

He turned and spoke his own language to the other two before turning back to me. "She is going to turn herself in to the group following her to buy you time to get children to safety."

"Turn...oh God...you don't mean—"

He nodded. "She said..." He looked up as he tried to remember her words. "*Throw a dog a bone so he doesn't eat the chickens.* It is an old Inuit saying."

A dark sense of dread washed over me. Tip had offered herself up in place of the triplets? It didn't make sense. Why would she do that? "Anything else? Did she leave any other message?"

He nodded solemnly. "She said you would know what to do, and she will see you soon."

"Thank you so much for taking care of her and giving her breathing room. It means more than you might realize." I ran back to the opening, where Bailey and Cinder waited with my uniform. As I put it over my own clothes, I explained what had happened.

"She handed herself over?"

It was so Tip. She was expecting me to know what she was thinking, where she was going with the plan. I was only now beginning to understand what she was up to, and was irritated with myself for taking so long to get it.

"Why in the hell—"

I held my hand up. "Because she's expecting us to find her and do what needs to be done."

"They'll kill her."

"No, they won't." I flipped the hood up and reached into the pocket and pulled out syringes meant for Tip and the children. "She's using herself as a bargaining chip, not just for the triplets, but—" I looked at Cinder. "Cinder as well. She is trying to protect as many of the children as she can."

"She would never give Cinder up."

"No, but they don't know that. They know a lot, but not that."

"What do you think they know?"

"I think they might know about Mel being sick."

"Oh shit."

"They expect Mel to be out of the game, and they don't realize we have the firepower we do without her."

The chopper turned back around and this time, landed, kicking up more snow. The pilot was expecting to pick up six. I hoped three for now would suffice until I could convince him to fly us to Nome. "We're going to commandeer that chopper and get the hell out of here." I could feel the three Genesys people coming to.

"What about them?"

I shrugged. "Who cares? Just keep them there. Come on."

Bailey nodded before taking off for the chopper with me and Cinder right behind her. When we reached the helicopter, I looked back to the entrance of the burial mound and watched as four huge gray wolves stood guard at the door. Those Genesys goons wouldn't go anywhere near that door.

Hopping into the chopper, and helping Cinder get in, I sat next to the pilot, who looked at me, turned to look at Bailey, before looking back at me. "What the fuck?" He started reaching for a weapon when I pinned him to his seat with nothing but a thought.

"You know how some people are afraid of burning alive?" I asked, leaning closer to him.

He made the huge mistake of spitting in my face and before I could stop her, Cinder sent a laser beam-size flame from her finger that sliced across his cheek and set his hair on fire.

"Shit! Shit! Shit!" he said, slapping at his head to douse the flames.

"Let's try this again," I said softly. "If you don't want to be tossed out into the snow as a burnt french fry, then you will do exactly as I tell you. Think you can manage that?"

He swallowed loudly and nodded.

"Here's how this is going to play out. You're going to call your boss in Nome, and tell him you have the triplets. You get your orders, you acknowledge with a ten-four and sign off. You do anything else, you're a dead man."

He looked over at me and laughed. "Besides your little flame thrower, you girls don't even have a gun."

"She doesn't, but this *girl* does," Taylor said, climbing into the helicopter. "And I have absolutely no compunction about splattering your brains all over the windshield. So, it's your call, tough guy." Taylor leveled the gun at his head. "You have three seconds to pick up that radio. One."

"I'm just the pilot!"

"Two."

"Okay, okay."

I handed him the radio. He tried, but we were still in a dead zone.

"When we get closer to Nome, you'll call them. In the meantime, get us out of here."

The pilot did as he was told and we lifted above the ground. "Stay low and along the coast, and you'll live to see your family again."

"Steve."

"Steve?"

"I'm really just the pilot."

"And I'm Little Red Riding Hood," Taylor said from behind his chair. She was looking at me as I shook my head.

He was lying.

"All I know is I am to deliver those kids at Bearclaw Pass, a couple miles outside of Nome, get my money, and that was it."

Taylor hit him in the head with the butt of her gun. "Try again, asshole."

"Shit! I'm telling you all I know!"

"I'm an empath," I said, seeing his eyes register that he knew the jig was up.

"Fine, yeah, I work for them, but I don't know anything other than what my orders are. Honest."

I nodded to everyone that this was true. "Then if you work

for them, you know we are every bit as dangerous without a gun, so if you step out of line, it will be the last thing you do."

He nodded. "I read you loud and clear. Where am I taking you?"

I saw the coastline and was relieved to see he wasn't going to do anything stupid. "Just keep heading toward Nome. We have a GPS system and will know the second you deviate from the course."

"Signal!" Bailey yelled from the back. "One and a half bars."

"Keep it here," I ordered Steve, pushing the mic into his hand. "Make that call…and be very careful with it."

Taylor placed the muzzle behind his right ear. "Keep your hands on the stick and do exactly what she tells you to or I *will* kill you."

"While we're in the air?"

Taylor got real close to him and said, "Don't assume we can't fly this. You're only needed to make the call, *Steve*. After that, you're expendable."

With the radio on, Steve confirmed a rendezvous at Bearclaw Pass in less than an hour. He did precisely what I had told him to do, then he signed off and looked over at me. "They'll kill you the moment they see you."

"Oh Steve, even after all you've seen, you have such little faith."

"What is it you want?"

"Well, I personally want to delete Kip Reynolds and his chain of command."

"Kip isn't even here."

"I know. He doesn't lower himself to collections. So, who is leading this little party?"

He shook his head. Taylor pushed the muzzle harder against his head. "Who. Is. He?"

"They just call him the Professor. That's all I know."

I nodded at Taylor to continue.

"What's his role in all of this?"

"He checks out the captured to make sure they have what he's looking for."

"Which is?"

"I don't know. It's all smoke and mirrors. They piecemeal information out in slivers at a time on a need-to-know basis."

Suddenly, Bailey was up in front with us. "Danica has us locked in, still no word from Mel, and Finn got the good to go from the doctor."

I nodded. "Good. Things are finally going our way."

"Dani says shoot this guy if he plays dumb. Playing dumb is Genesys 101."

Taylor slapped him upside the head with the tip of the Glock. "Tell us about the smoke and mirrors."

As she said this, I looked down and saw the familiar yellow and red snowmobiles below us. "Land her."

"Here?"

"Here, there, I don't give a crap. Set. Her. Down."

Steve did so, and when Bailey swung open the door, there were Pitt and Loco, wearing what can only be described as shit-eating grins.

"Okay, ladies, apparently we *did* underestimate you. My hat's off to you."

I looked over at Steve, who was finally figuring out how much trouble he was in.

"Either of you know how to fly a chopper?"

Both shook their heads.

"Gar does, though," Loco said. "Pretty damn good, too, from what I hear."

Pitt shook his head. "Bad idea. Last one he flew was a Blackhawk. It went down. You know how those pieces of shit are built."

Steve chuckled as if he were one of the boys. "Looks like you're stuck with me."

I shot him a look, followed up with a nice tap to the back of his head by the butt of Taylor's gun. He swore and tried to shake off the pain.

"Enough outta you."

I stepped closer to Pitt. "I need Gar to fly us to Nome."

Pitt shook his head again. "He's still detoxing. He has PTSD. Putting him behind the stick is a bad idea."

"Keeping Steve here is even worse. He's not really what I'd call trustworthy."

Pitt nodded. "Roger that. I'll see what the big guy thinks."

"Thank you. We'll meet you in the northwest corner of town. If Gar doesn't want to, then we're stuck with Steve and we'll have to make do."

Pitt and Loco were still arguing the point when we closed the door to the chopper.

"What will you do, kill me?"

"Nah. You'll just need to find your own way back to Nome. Got money?"

"You're kidding, right?"

Taylor yelled in his ear. "Does she *look* like she's kidding?"

In no time, we were back in Brevig Mission, landing the chopper once more.

"Think he'll do it?" Bailey asked as I hopped out of the chopper.

"I don't see why not. What else does he have to do out here?"

To my delight, Pitt roared in five minutes later with Gar on the back of the snowmobile with a heavy-looking backpack on.

"Need a lift?" he asked, grinning.

"Would you mind? We're in a bit of a pinch here."

Climbing into the helicopter, his enormous body filled half the bay. "Looks like your services are no longer needed, asshole."

The look on Steve's face was priceless.

"What...what about me?" he asked, exiting the chopper from the driver's door.

"Start hitching. Send out smoke signals. We couldn't give a rat's ass." This came from Bailey.

"Good luck finding a way home." Taylor followed him out, Glock aimed between his shoulder blades. "Pitt, would you mind patting him down and making sure he doesn't have any weapons or a way to phone home?"

Pitt roughly checked him over. "Tell you what. Why don't I sit tight with flyboy here for a couple of hours just to make sure?"

"That would be awesome. Where did Loco go?"

Pitt shrugged. "Didn't say. That boy marches to a different drummer. Who knows?" Pitt handed me a business card. "You ever need anything, call us. Friends of Sal are always welcome out here."

He saluted, I nodded, and five minutes later, we were airborne once more, only this time with Goliath at the wheel.

Gar spoke very little as he flew along the jagged coast. With every passing moment, he relaxed a little more until, when we were almost to Nome, he finally turned and said, "Where to?"

I loved his military manner and understanding of need to know. "Bearclaw Pass."

He laughed. "No clue."

Bailey handed me her vidbook with a GPS map of where we were and where we needed to be. I showed the vidbook to Gar.

"High-tech toys," he said. "Shoulda known. You gals aren't anything like you seem to be. Now, tell me what we're flying into. I prefer to be prepared if you don't mind."

I leveled with him as best I could and told him what had been happening. He listened intently as he flew, not once interrupting. His stock continued to climb in my eyes.

"So," he said at last, "when these Genesys folks show up for the drop, and you got nothin', what then? You can only bluff for so long."

"Then we make them take us where we want to go."

"Which is where?"

"To the top…or at least as high as we can go."

His face broke in half with a grin. "I like how you ladies think. Cut the head off the damn snake and watch its body twitch."

Finally, we were back in the live zone and all of our electronic gadgets sprung to life. Just seeing Nome in the distance made me feel like I was returning home from the Arctic. If I never saw snow again after we got out here, it would be too soon.

"Bailey, let Dani know we're going in. Tell her we're going after a guy who calls himself the Professor. See if she can come up with anything."

"Gotcha."

"Cinder? You're up."

"I'm ready."

"Okay!" I yelled above the whirling rotors so everyone could hear. "Until we know where Tip is, we can't just blast away randomly. We need to remain focused and on point. *Capisce*?"

Everyone nodded.

"We need someone to take us to where she is. We have to play it cool so they believe we have the triplets. They have to *believe* we're willing to deal."

"When will you let them know it's us?"

"At the last possible moment. Right now, I don't think they have a clue where we are and that we're still in play. It's harsh out there. They may think we're dead after the blizzard."

"Anything's possible," Bailey said. "Let's assume they still expect us. And let's not forget Sonja Satre. We don't need to face that demoness and her bag of fiery tricks."

Gar set the helicopter down in the powdery snow and shut off the engine. "Now what?"

"Now we wait. When they get here, we need the driver alive."

Gar turned from the stick. I read no judgment from him. "What do you want to do with the chopper?"

"How much further can it take us?"

He looked at the gauge. "Hundred miles, tops."

"We may need wings to get us out of here. Would you mind—"

"Hanging here while you ladies take on some corporate creepies? Not at all. So long as you let me in when and if you need it. I'm all for feminism and shit, but sometimes, a gal could use a guy my size."

"We appreciate that. Thank you, Gar. Really."

"No problem." He winked. "Detox was getting boring."

While we waited in the chopper, I tried contacting Tip again. We were no longer in a dead zone...I should have been able to reach her.

"Nothing?" Cinder asked.

"Nothing at all. It's just not like her."

"*Would you...you know—*"

"*Know if she were dead? Yes. She's not. She's just not open to me.*"

"*Maybe there's a reason.*"

I nodded. Maybe.

"Oh fuck," came Taylor's voice from the front of the chopper. "Company's here."

We all looked out the front window. Not one, but three black Hummers came barreling over the small incline.

Three.

"Damn it! They must have wanted the triplets separated."

"What now?" Taylor asked, checking the ammo in the Glock. "This just got a whole helluva lot dicier."

"Now, we improvise." Pulling everyone together, I made as good a plan as I could on the fly. When I was done, Gar turned to me and said, "You need all three drivers alive for this plan to work."

Nodding, I pulled the chopper door back open, tightened my hood around my face, and ran to the first Hummer as if I truly was one of them. My heart hammered beneath my chest as I ran straight into the arms of the enemy.

By the time I reached that Hummer, Bailey and Cinder reached theirs. I couldn't see what they were doing, as I had my hands full with the two in my car. The window was halfway down before he realized his mistake. I threw a percussion field out at them, knocking them backward in their seats and disorienting them long enough for me to rip the door open and pull the passenger out of the car.

When she landed in the snow, I hit her with another percussion shield before taking her cell phone and her gun from her. Then, hopping in the passenger side, I locked the doors. The driver was still disoriented from my blast and held his head in his hands.

As I glanced out the passenger door one last time, there sat a wolf next to my first victim, who also held her head. She wouldn't be going anywhere too soon. One down, one to go.

Putting my newly acquired gun up to the driver's head, I slapped him to bring him out of it with the other. Those percussion fields really ring your bell, and I was glad I taken the time to hone that particular ability.

"Can you hear me?" I said loudly.

He blinked, swallowed hard, and nodded, wincing.

"Good. Call your boss and tell him you have her. You do anything other than that, and I *will* kill you. You can get out of this alive by doing exactly what I tell you to do."

"What is it you want?"

"Two things. Tiponi Redhawk and your boss."

"Mr. Reynolds isn't in Alaska. I swear."

"I know. I'll go for him after I take down the Professor."

The blond man looked at me for the first time, his eyes registering slight fear. He was a natural. He was afraid, and he knew I would kill him.

And he was right.

So much had changed within me in such a short amount of time. Once I had accepted my new role as mentor, something clicked…something akin to maternal instinct. That instinct had made me believe that I could and *would* kill to protect my supernatural family.

I was feeling that instinct now.

"All you have to do is to get me to Tiponi or your boss and I'll let you go. It's that easy. Conversely, you make one slip up, and you can kiss your kids goodbye. You have kids, don't you?"

"No."

Lie.

"Yes, you do. And we will find them. We will find them and do to them what your people would do to my people. Are you hearing what I am saying?"

He nodded. "I don't know where either of them are. My job is to deliver the kid to the Grey Wolf Hotel."

"What room?"

"Two fifteen. All of the kids are being delivered to different hotels, room two fifteen in all of them. Please. Don't hurt my kids. This was the only real job I could get here and they are innocent. I'll do anything you ask me to do...just please leave my family out of this."

"Like I said: you cooperate with us and you will live to see your family. Will the Professor be at one of those hotels?"

So far, he'd been totally honest with me. Fear will do that to a person, and he was genuinely frightened for his family.

"I'm really just a driver. I've told you all I know."

That was true.

Flipping my vidbook open, I waited to see Cinder's face. Instead, there was Taylor.

"Yo. All's cool here. Cinder's got it under control. They're going to Hotel Chastaine, room two fifteen."

"Thank you, Taylor. Cinder will keep you both safe from here on out."

"Uh, Echo, you mind telling me how she's gonna keep us safe without a weapon of some sort?"

"Taylor, would you believe me if I told you she *is* a weapon?"

Taylor chuckled and shrugged. "Right about now, I'd believe you if you told me you were Santa Claus."

"Cinder is better than that Glock you're sporting. Trust me on that, and I promise I'll fill you in on who we really are when this is over."

She was still smiling when she said, "Oh, Echo, I'm not just beautiful, I'm pretty damn smart, too. I think I have a pretty good idea of what you all are. We'll talk later. For now, go get your girl."

Next, I checked in on Bailey. "You got it covered?"

"Me and my little friend, yeah."

"How little?"

She turned the vidbook toward an animal I'd never seen. "What in the hell is that?"

"Wolverine, baby. Beggars can't be choosers, you know? One of the meanest animals on the planet. I'll be fine."

"So where are they going?"

"Not *they*. I had to dispatch the passenger for calling me a bitch. You know how it is. We're off to Shiloah Hotel, room two fifteen."

"Okay. Tip has to be at one of those places. I can't imagine they'd let her out of their sight. She's their big prize."

"Roger that. Keep close."

"Bailey?"

"Yeah boss?"

"This is going to get ugly. You know that, don't you?"

She smiled softly, her eyes warm. "We've faced worse and kicked ass. Remember that."

"Thanks for reminding me. Okay, three honks and we're moving."

"Right behind you."

My final call was to Danica. When she and Roger answered, I gave them all the information we had: Hotel names and numbers, license plates, everything. With all of that information, if anything were to go wrong, they'd be able to zero in on our location much more quickly.

Danica took not one note. She didn't need to. All of our conversations were always recorded. "Give Roger ten minutes to pull up hotel registers. If they're online, we'll see who is waiting for you in those rooms. If there are any cameras in the lobby, we'll see if we can hack into them and come up with some photos for you. Roger?"

Roger's face came online. "Yo, Princess. Not only are we grabbing registers, Franklin and Carl are hacking into those new street cams the city puts up. We'll have you covered in as many places as possible. Once we have you in the frame, we'll be able to follow your route. You won't be alone out there in the hinterlands of the US of A."

"Thank you." I could hear them all typing away, my own personal research/security/intel team that gave me the confidence to do what needed to be done.

"Clark?" Danica scooted closer to the monitor, her voice softer.

"Yeah?"

Her face held an emotion I couldn't read. "We've been digging as deeply as we dare into this Professor. All we can find is a public statement from ten years ago when they were proud to present the new head of research and development: the Professor."

"That's what he's *called* in real life?"

"Yeah. Says here, Kip Reynolds searched long and hard for the right match for the head of his R and D department, and the Professor hails from Cybergine, a company based in Rio de Janeiro."

"Cybergine, huh."

Roger nodded. "Cybergine has spent the last twenty years trying to replicate certain genomes. The company literature says it's for curing some disease—"

I knew what was coming. "But that's just their cover."

They both nodded. "Cybergine is a cloning operation that had to move out of Korea because of their dubious experiments with animal and human genetics."

"Cybergine still exists? I thought I'd read somewhere that they'd abandoned ship due to some ethics committee and a whistle-blower."

"That was how they wanted it to go down, but they are still very much in the cloning game."

"Okay, so this professor worked there. Where did he work before? What country does he call home? What is his specialty?"

"I wish we could tell you more, Princess, but there's nothing on this guy. It was as if he surfaced from out of nowhere. It's hard to trace a pseudonym, but we're working hard to crack into Cybergine's database to find out."

"Good work, Roger."

Carl's face now filled the lower right-hand corner of the screen. "I went digging for who is paying for this Alaskan excursion. You know…follow the money? The rooms are registered to a man and a woman."

"In all three cases?"

"Ten-four. Mr. Jones and Mrs. Smith. Jesus, could they be any more obvious?"

I looked over at Cinder through the windows of our Hummer. "They brought women because they're not as scary or intimidating for the kids. It's brilliant, really, to give them the notion of a mother figure."

"Safe bet, Clark. We'll keep on the paper trail."

"Good. Okay, you got us on GPS now, right?"

Danica held her hand up. "Wait. I have all of you but Tip. Why is that? Is she still incommunicado?"

"I think it's safe to assume she doesn't have her vidbook anymore."

She nodded. "If we do get a bead on her, I'll call."

I studied Dani a moment. I'd known her long enough to recognize that expression anywhere. "Don't look so worried."

"That's easy for you to say. Come home."

"Will do. Good work, guys. We'll keep you posted." Closing the vidbook, I felt more at ease now, knowing she was watching every step we took in an area that wasn't a dead zone. Turning to my driver, I reached across and honked three times. "*Vamanos*, driver. It's time to finish this."

Hummer keys in one pocket, and gun in the other, I marched us up to the first hotel elevator and pressed the second-floor button.

"They'll kill you on sight," the driver muttered.

"Hardly. You people have no idea the giant you've awakened. You're lucky to still be alive."

"Since when did your kind kill humans?"

"We're *all* human…and to answer your question, since I took over. Your asshole boss wants a war? He'll get one. You *humans* are expendable to me…to us. We're done playing defense. Done."

"In that case—" He lunged at me and because of the confined space, my percussion field bounced off the elevator walls, completely scrambling his brain. He dropped like a rock, blood oozing from nose and ears. I was pretty sure I had just killed him.

"Shit."

When the elevator doors opened, I stepped out, left him there and pressed the top floor button. If someone was up there, they'd call the cops for sure. Cops were fine with me at this point.

At room two fifteen, I paused at the door and listened. I hoped my Red Cross jumpsuit was enough to gain me entrance.

Then I thought about something and got back to the elevator before the doors closed.

On my knees, I searched all of his pockets, and there it was: His key card. I grabbed the key card and exited the elevator once more. Inserting the key card, I flung open the door and charged into the room, powers at the ready.

"Who the fuck are you?" A woman asked, rising from the multicolored loveseat.

"Where's Tiponi Redhawk?"

Her eyes betrayed her even before I felt her fear. She knew who I was.

"Yep. That's right. I'm Echo Branson, and I've come for two things." I hesitated, waiting to feel any other emotions from anyone else. There were none. It was just me and her. "I want Tiponi Redhawk and that damned Professor."

Her eyes were darting all over, but there was no place to run.

"Sit down," I ordered. She hesitated, so I pushed her with a small field. "If you know who I am, then you also know I know truth from lies. Lie and you're toast."

"Please. Don't kill me. I'm just a courier. Nothing more. My job is transport, and that's all."

"Oh, sweetheart, everyone is *always* something more. I want Tiponi Redhawk and I'll kill you and everyone else in your fucked-up organization who tries to stop me from getting her back. So, let's start with the easy question first. Where is she?"

"He wouldn't tell anyone for fear you'd read our minds."

Truth.

"Does he have a name?"

"The Professor is all I know."

Truth.

"What supers does he have working for him?"

"None that I—"

"That's the only lie you get. Try again."

The woman began breathing hard as her fear started taking over. "Sonja Satre, but she was just the point of contact. She doesn't really work for the organization. There's also Rafe Webber, he's a—"

"High-level telepath, I know. Anyone else?"

"Yes, but not here and not that I know of. Mr. Reynolds only gives us information on a need-to-know basis."

"So Rafe is the only psi here?"

She nodded. "That I know of."

Truth. Now things started to make sense. Was Tip's silence a result of not wanting Rafe to know where we were? Were her shields so thick to prevent him, and the rest of us, entrance to her mind in order to protect me? That made more sense to me than anything else I'd come up with.

"What's going on with all these rooms in all these different hotels?"

She hesitated long enough for me to shake my head. "I gave you *one* lie. You used it up, so be very careful with the rest of your answers."

"The Professor wanted the triplets separated."

"Why?"

She stared at me. "You don't know?"

I knew, of course, but I wouldn't let her know I knew. "No."

She shook her head. "My job was limited to sedation and transportation."

I shuddered at the word sedation. "Transportation? How?"

"Boat. There's a boat off the coast. We were to take the kids to the dock, where the helicopter will take them to the boat."

"It's a big enough boat to land a chopper?"

She managed a faint grin. "Genesys has deep pockets. We don't do anything on a small scale."

"What next? How does Tiponi play into all of this?"

She stared at me, weighing whether or not I would do something rash or violent when she answered.

"I won't hurt you for the truth…but I *will* blow your brains out your ears if you tell another lie."

Resigned to her fate, she said softly, "He is planning on trading Tiponi for Cinder."

That was unexpected. "Where?"

"On the docks."

"Is that where she is?"

"I really don't know."

Truth.

"He was going to what? Contact me and tell me he wanted to make an exchange? Did he really think I would?" It was a rhetorical question and she heard it as such.

"How...how did you get the triplets?"

I didn't answer, and there wasn't anything else I needed to know. "Is this the sedative?" I asked, picking up a syringe laying on the kitchen counter. Anger poked its head through my calm veneer.

Her eyes grew wide. "Yes."

Tossing it to her, I said. "Use it."

"What?"

"Inject yourself."

She blinked, a swirl of emotions emitting from her. "I won't tell on you. I swear. I'll—"

"You'll do to yourself what you were willing to do to a child. Now."

I watched as she did so with trembling hands. "Before you go down, you need to know I'm going to rip this organization apart, so you might want to find a new job."

As her eyelids got lower and lower, slower and slower. I pulled out my vidbook and dialed everyone. Bailey's and Danica's faces came into the square on the top left.

"You okay?" Danica asked.

I nodded. "Getting closer." To Bailey I asked, "I take it all went well on your end?"

She nodded. "Where's Taylor?"

I shrugged. "Might just be taking her longer." Back to Danica. "Can you pull up the dock or marina for Nome?"

"Already got it. What do you need?"

"There's a ship off the coast—probably a very large one capable of taking a helicopter. Tell me anything you can."

I watched Danica work another monitor while Bailey leaned closer and whispered, "Fuckin' A, these people are jacked up."

"Everything okay on your end, Bailey?"

Bailey nodded and told me a story only slightly different from mine. It had been somewhat awkward getting the wolverine into the hotel, but the natives knew enough about the dangerous animal that no one really stopped to question her. "I got the bitch's gun, too. She actually considered shooting us with it. Needless to say, my little hairy friend's teeth convinced her that probably wasn't a good idea. We've got it all covered on our end. I just wish Taylor would chime in here. You need us to go to the docks?"

I shook my head. "I need you to go to Gar, then the docks. We're going to take that chopper to the boat. That's where the Professor is."

"What about Tip?"

"We're getting her first if we can, but I need you and Gar to be ready to hit it."

"How we going to find her?"

"Rafe the telepath is part of this little group."

"Oh, I *hate* that guy! Came to the bayou once and acted like his shit didn't stink. I'll be more than happy to sink some pearly whites into his arrogant flesh."

"You might get your chance. Rafe doesn't know it, but he is going to lead us to her."

"Awesome. Cinder?"

"No word yet. Too much distance for her telepathy to work."

"Don't be worried. She can do this, E. Have faith."

Just as she finished, Taylor's face appeared, so I went to conference mode. I felt a huge weight lift knowing all of us were okay. "Everything okay?"

Taylor nodded. "Ummm...you might have warned me a little about...well...why she's called Cinder." Shaking her head, Taylor looked off camera, presumably at my flaming charge. "She was simply amazing, though I think I shit my pants."

"What happened?"

"Nothing, at first. I started asking questions, and the woman refused to talk. Acted all superior and shit. I did everything I knew how to get her to open up, but she wasn't biting. Suddenly, her eyes got really big, and so I turned around and saw something I'm still not even sure I saw. Cinder was bouncing what can only be called a fireball in her hand. A flippin' fireball!"

"I should have told you, Taylor. I'm sorry, but there just wasn't any time."

Taylor replayed the same story Bailey had told me. "The bitch is sedated and tied up, and let me tell you, gagging her was a pleasure. Not nearly as cool as seeing Cinder juggling a damn ball of fire, but close. What now?"

"You two meet us at the dock. We're not taking another step without Tip."

"But the triplets—"

"Are secondary. I know that's harsh, but that's the way it's going to be. I'm sure Tip has them securely sequestered somewhere. She set this whole thing up and is expecting me to know where she is going with it. I have a good idea that Genesys is flailing right now. We have about thirty minutes before they realize this has gone south on them and send for reinforcements."

"Meet where?"

Danica pulled up her map of the pier with a blinking red dot. "This red dot is off-road from the north entrance to the pier. Meet there. I've got it programmed into your GPS. You're each a different colored dot: Echo blue, Bailey green, Firefly red, Taylor orange. Tip is brown, if she ever comes back on the grid. We'll have eyes on you the entire time, so if any dot starts moving away from the dock, we'll call in our guys."

"Perfect. Thank you, Dani."

"No problem." She typed something into the computer before turning back to the vidbook. "Roger is hacking into a satellite feed to find a photo of the ships in the bay. We'll get back to you as soon as I have a positive ID."

"Awesome. Okay, Bailey, Taylor, we'll meet there ASAP. We're on the clock now. They're going to be expecting the triplets, or at least word of them, pretty soon. Once they realize they don't have them, Tip's life is at risk and this thing is going to go right down to the damn wire, so shake a leg."

I made my way to the port, wishing I could contact Tip, wishing Danica were here with me, wishing for a lot of things I couldn't have. Maybe this was what being mentor was really all about—the aloneness of making and implementing hard decisions. The problem wasn't in making them nor in implementing them. My issue was the aloneness I felt that hadn't been there in fourteen years—the silence was deafening.

"Where *are* you, Tip?" I muttered, glancing occasionally at the vidbook perched on my lap. My mind was racing with all the possibilities of which way this could go. I knew I had to get Tip first. If she was here at the docks, then she had hostage takers we would have to deal with. If the triplets were to be delivered to the helicopter, and then to the boat, we were going to have to take a chance and land the chopper on the boat.

The boat.

Danica had to find the right boat.

The right boat. Ice. I kept thinking of my dream and Tip being in a room or ice cave. Had they literally put her on ice? If she wasn't on that boat, I didn't know how I would keep from panicking—how would I push forward if she wasn't alive? Just the thought made me want to vomit. It was as if not hearing from her made me off-centered. I felt a little out of balance. I needed to know she was okay. I *needed* her to be okay. Fine. Healthy. Good. I needed Tip, period.

Maybe I had just been fooling myself all along that I could make something work with Finn when Tip and I were inextricably bound…or *were* until this collection went south on us. Maybe I should just stop fighting the inevitable and just be with the woman I was clearly lost without.

I was beginning to hate maybes.

I pulled up to the meeting place and Bailey pulled in two minutes later.

"I'm sick of this shit," Bailey said. "Taking our people. Trading with us like we were a commodity. It's bullshit, E, and it's time we let these motherfuckers know who they're dealing with."

Before I could respond, I watched in awe as the wolverine clambered out of the Hummer. "I hear you. Is that the same wolverine?"

Bailey smiled. "She is one of the baddest ass animals on the planet, E. This guy could tear you apart in less time than a bear. Wicked sharp teeth and claws. You don't want to get into a fight with one of these."

I nodded and watched as it sat staring at Bailey like a dog might. "I completely agree with you, Bailey, but they didn't take Tip. She gave herself up to save those three kids."

"Then she's put a lot of faith in you. She's expecting you to pull out a Melika-sized miracle."

"We don't need a miracle this time. What we need is a good, solid plan—the kind that Tip makes…or in this case…made. She knows what she is doing. She's just praying to her gods that I do as well."

The third Hummer drove up quickly and slammed its brakes, spraying snowy gravel everywhere. Cinder was out before the car could stop.

"These people suck."

I nodded. "Yes, they do."

"I accidentally showed Taylor what I am. I'm sorry."

I laid my hand on her shoulder. "Don't be. There are times when we have to learn to trust our friends. This is one of those times."

Taylor joined us, a gun tucked in her waistband. "God damn, that woman was an asshole! I enjoyed knocking her out. What's with separating the triplets? What is it we don't know that we need to know, Echo?"

"They, uh…"

"Come on, Echo. I just watched Cinder pull a fiery rabbit out of her hat. I'm pretty certain none of you are what you appear to be. It's no skin off my nose if I don't know, but I'd prefer keeping the skin *on* my nose, if you know what I mean."

A part of me was thrilled to know that Delta and Connie had not shared our secret with her even though she had already risked her life once for us. While Bailey had shared her own secret, it was time for me to confide in someone who had put her life on the line more than once for us. It was time.

Nodding, I started toward the pier. "I do know what you mean, Taylor, and I'm sorry we haven't been straight up with you, but now isn't the time. You deserve the whole truth. Can you wait until we get back home?"

"I can put two and two together, Echo. You guys are super heroes, right? That's why Danica calls you Clark. Oh my God… are you Superman?"

I laughed for the first time in days. "Thank you for that, Taylor."

"You guys are good people, Echo. I don't really give a shit if you can shoot flaming farts." Taylor paused and looked at Cinder. "You can't, can you?"

I didn't wait for the answer.

The Nome port harbor was an interesting formation of two levee-like protuberances; one with a road and one which is an extended arm that created a bay of sorts. A larger opening led to a smaller entryway that was the door to a U-shaped inner bay. I did not see a boat beyond the levee, but that didn't mean anything. Given the shape of the bay, you would want your boat outside of the two entrances for faster escape. It reminded me a bit of Pearl Harbor: too easy to get trapped inside.

As we walked down Steadman Street, I lowered my shields. If Tip was near, I would feel her energy. Paranormals have a much different feel than naturals. There's more hot energy to us, like when you put your tongue on the prongs of a battery. I would sense her emotional energy a hundred yards away.

"E, this place is too big for us to locate Tip psionically." Bailey glanced over at Taylor, who smiled and muttered something about her girlfriend being a superhero.

I told them everything the woman at the hotel had shared with me and why I thought Tip was here. "She's here, Bailey, and I'm certain she's not alone."

Suddenly, I felt it. It was like that feeling you get when you get before playing a ballgame or going on stage. I should have felt both their energies, but Rafe obviously had his shields up to prevent that. She wasn't alone, that much I knew, but I couldn't tell what direction to go.

"What are you gonna do? Walk around until you feel it? We don't have that kind of time."

I nodded. "I know."

My vidbook vibrated. It was Danica and Roger.

"Glad you're still in the game, Clark. I have Franklin calling the hotels to have them notify the cops of strange goings-on in room two fifteen. That should keep them on ice for a spell."

Roger turned from the screen and gave Franklin more directions before turning his attention to the monitor. "We've located the vessel, Princess, the only one in the Bering Sea large enough to land a chopper."

"Excellent. Can you send those coordinates to Cinder's phone?"

Danica cut in. "Why isn't she with you?"

"She is. We left Gar a vidphone. He's waiting for directions in the chopper."

"Smart. We'll send them to everyone. From here on out, what one of you gets, the other gets. Any sign of the Big Indian yet?"

"Not yet. As soon as we do, we'll meet up with Gar and head to the ship."

"What else can we do?"

"Find out as much as you can about that boat."

"We've been working on that dummy corporation, but damn, it's hidden deep. We'll stay on it. Be careful."

I hung up and turned to my little group. "Okay. She's here somewhere. We need to split up and look for the containers."

"Containers?"

I thought back to my dream. "Yeah. Storage containers. Refrigerated ones, to be exact."

"Umm, E, if Tip is in a freezer—"

I nodded. "I know, but Tip's body temperature runs really high. If she's in a refrigerator unit, she'll be cold, but not frozen. Trust me. If she were dead, I would know it."

"I'll go to the front office and get a map," Bailey said. "You three get moving."

"And the wolverine?"

"Comes with me."

Everyone was relieved, not just because it had scary teeth, but because it stunk. "Everyone keep in touch. Stay fast on your feet. Expect Genesys around every corner, and no one takes them on alone. No one. We don't need another hostage situation. Any questions?"

We all looked at each other. It was Taylor who spoke first. "You sure we ought to split up?"

"We have to. I can't feel Tip's energy as easily if I'm near Bailey and Cinder. It's a supernatural thing."

"So, you're a what? A feeler?"

I grinned slightly. "Something like that."

"Cool. It suits you." She looked over at Cinder. "It's pretty clear the little one can take care of herself."

"Cinder *can* take care of herself," Bailey replied. "So if you want to come with me—"

Taylor shook her head. "I'm no pussy, Bailey. I can hold my own, with or without super powers."

With that, we went in four different directions in search of Tiponi. I rounded a corner and closed my eyes. I knew she was here, not just from any paranormal feeling, but something deeper, more mammalian in nature. I *knew* she was here. It all made perfect sense. Keeping her here meant they could make the exchange for Cinder on land and keep Tip on ice. Genesys' greatest mistake was that it had gotten greedy. Instead of just collecting the triplets from Tip, they had decided to go for broke.

Well, be careful what you wish for, because broke was how they were going to end up.

As I pressed on, I could feel her expectancy. What did she expect me to do? What would she have done? I stood there in relative silence, eyes still closed. Tip had been our leader when we were kids, our protector. She taught all of us how to negotiate our way around the real world. She taught us to protect ourselves with mental shields and how to go on the offensive. She had taught me enough that someday, I would be able to lead. Right now, I knew she would never walk into an ambush. This wasn't that. I doubted they were onto us yet, but time was running out. This operation was huge for Genesys. At least twenty people on the ground, who knew how many on the boat or with Tip? It was their greed that would get the best of them. They were not going to get Cinder nor were they going to harm my ex-lover. Not on my watch.

"Come on, Echo, think."

She wasn't expecting me to be her. She was expecting me to be me. She wanted me to lead in the manner most comfortable to me. She would expect that. So she knew I wouldn't be alone… that I'd bring backup.

Opening my eyes, I barely caught a glimpse of a sniper atop one of the cargo bins. Pressing myself flat against the building wall, I held my breath. A sniper? Now *that* was interesting. Given Genesys' penchant for sedating supers, I'd lay money on those rifles being tranquilizer guns, and tranq guns didn't have a very long range.

I smiled to myself. I was getting closer.

Pulling out the vidbook, I let everyone know we had snipers and to chime in if they saw one. Mine was on a blue cargo box.

Not two minutes later, Taylor came on with one on a yellow cargo holder. Hers, she said, was facing west. Mine was facing east. Now I had a better idea of where Tip was: she was somewhere in between them.

"Echo?" Taylor whispered softly. "You three get to Tip. I'll take out the two snipers so we can get away cleanly and without being seen."

"You sure?"

Taylor grinned into the camera. "If I don't pull my weight here, Delta won't let me play anymore. Sneaking around is what I do. I'll be fine. Just go."

I told Bailey and Cinder to meet me at the corner of West and Comen streets. The harbor was off West Street, and I was pretty sure they had a smaller boat in the harbor as well, though I wouldn't give them the opportunity to use it. I was fed up with these cat and mouse games, and once I got Tip back, we were going to cause some irreversible damage.

When we were at the corner, I could tell everyone felt the same. Energy was high. We were more than ready to release it, and were ready to go home.

"Their locations point to one of the streets between West E and West C Street. If Tip took a boat here, it's still in the harbor. It means they nabbed her from the harbor. She's too powerful a telepath to risk moving very far—"

"So she's down one of these streets," Bailey finished for me.

I nodded. "The problem with lowering my shields to find Tip, is it could alert Rafe I'm nearby."

"So...how are you planning on finding her?"

Looking down at the scary wolverine, I said, "Sorry, sweetie, wish I could use you, but I need a dog."

"There was a husky at the harbor center. No human."

"How good is their sense of smell?"

She stared at me. "They're *dogs*." Closing her eyes, she waited ten seconds, then opened them. "She's on her way."

It was Taylor's turn to stare. "How do you *do* that?"

Shrugging, she answered. "I pet her when I was looking for someone to help me with the map. We bonded. She's looking for me the same way she'd look for a pack member."

"With her nose."

"Bingo."

The brown-and-white husky reached us in less than a minute. She walked right over to us and sat down as if waiting for her orders. It never ceased to amaze me.

"You got something of Tip's?" Bailey asked.

I pulled my vidbook out and held it out to the dog. The hand-tooled leather cover was a Christmas gift from her last year. She'd made it while cleaning up a mess in Santa Fe, New Mexico. It had my name on it. It also was imbued with oil from her hands.

"Perfect, E." Taking it from me, Bailey knelt down and communed with the dog.

"She has the weirdest powers," Cinder said.

"Stranger than being a human matchstick?"

"Uh-huh. Way weirder. Look at them. They're like soldiers waiting for their orders. I can command fire molecules. She commands life! And what about that badger thing? How come it's not attacking the dog?"

"You're asking me*? I have no idea."*

"Well, a dog is a good idea. I don't know about that other thing. It scares me."

"Yes it is scary. Now, just so we are clear, we're not killing Rafe, Cinder. No matter what he's done, we are not going around killing supers who do things we don't like."

"Not unless he's hurt Tip. You can't ask me to hold back if he has hurt her."

I thought about that for a second. *"Right. If he's hurt her, turn him into ashes."*

She smiled. *"You know it. Look!"*

I followed her gaze and saw the husky make her move. When the dog took off running, I started after her, but Bailey stopped me.

"She'll come get us. It's safer that way."

Cinder and I exchanged glances. Maybe Cinder was right about Bailey's powers. Maybe she had the best of the bunch.

"What's the plan after we get Tip?"

"It depends on what condition she is in. If she's up to it, we're going to that boat and destroying it."

They both stood, jaws gaping.

"Just like that?" Bailey asked.

I nodded. "Genesys left us no choice. They can't collect my people. Not now. Not ever. I want Kip Reynolds to *know* what happens if he keeps threatening us. The time for words is over. We need to show what will happen if they continue down this dark path."

"E, there could be innocent people on board. We can't just blow it up."

"I never said we'd blow up the ship. We'll land, find this Professor, and take him out—but not before I squeeze every ounce of information from him."

"Fair enough. And the triplets? You're sure Tip knows where they are?"

"Absolutely. I'm sure they're safe somewhere. Wherever she's left them, they're in good hands."

The husky rounded the corner, barked twice, and waited.

"She found her."

My heart leapt in my chest. Thank god. "Excellent. Okay ladies, it's showtime."

Taylor must have secured the snipers, because I didn't see any as we made our way to the shipping container holding my ex-lover. By this time, I was getting used to following Bailey's menagerie. They were the best secret weapon we had. No one expects animals to think, to lead, to do what Bailey asked them to do, and right now, this big dog was waiting in front of a small fishery building. Just sitting.

"Fish?" Bailey uttered. "Ugh."

"This is where they gut and clean the fish brought in from all those Alaskan deep sea fishing trips. There's a freezer in there. I'm sure of it."

Bailey nodded. "That smell is disgusting."

I felt a brief chill in my bones as my dream kept coming back to me. Flash freeze. That's what they do with the halibut caught by guys who paid handsomely to go out on one of the coldest seas in the world and fish for the biggest fish on the planet. They flash freeze the fish after it's cut up. Flash. Freeze.

That was when I saw it…and her in my mind's eye.

Tip was in there.

"Isn't it weird there's no one around?" Bailey asked. "I mean this place feels like a ghost town."

Cinder nodded, and then pointed to a rooftop.

Looking up, I saw Taylor, a big shit-eating grin on her face. She bounded off the roof like a cat, landing in a crouch position like some movie. Maybe *she* was the superhero.

"Snipers out of commission, but they had walkie-talkies, which means someone will be expecting them to check in. We're really on the clock now, ladies. Time to shift into fifth gear." Reaching into a pocket on her thigh, she pulled out a ring of lock-picking devices. "If this is the building, let's get a move on. Ticktock, ticktock, and all that." Kneeling at the door, she waited for us.

I issued my orders. "Nobody dies until I can talk to them. We need information, and Rafe has it. Leave Rafe to me."

Taylor turned back to the door and in two seconds, popped the lock. "Ready?"

Cinder had her hands up, ready to fire. Bailey and her pair of fang-bangers were poised and ready to rush in.

I nodded. "Go for it."

Pulling her gun from her waistband, Taylor nodded and swung the door back before quietly entering, gun poised. "Drop it!" Taylor ordered, drawing down on a tall blond natural, who hesitated a little too long. A fireball from behind me landed at his feet. He jumped back, cussing.

"One more time, Bubba. Fucking drop it *now*!"

He did and raised his hands in surrender.

"Where's Rafe?" I asked, stepping closer. I could feel Cinder on my heels. "And I have the best bullshit detector around. One lie. One small lie, and Cinder here will turn you into a crispy critter."

Cinder tossed a ball of flame up and down in her right hand. I immediately felt blondie's fear.

"I'm not fucking around. Where is Rafe?"

"Back...back there."

"In the freezer?"

He started to nod, then his eyes caught the fireball and he shook his head. "Refrigerator."

"With Tiponi?"

He nodded.

"Turn around."

"P-Please. I...I did what you—"

Taylor gun-butted him and down he went. "Asshole."

"Leave the dog, Bailey...and that wolverine as well. It's sort of scaring us."

She nodded. The dog was inside with us, the wolverine was sitting outside the door. No one would be leaving any time soon, and not without teeth marks and blood.

There was an opening with those hard, clear plastic strips found in meat packing refrigerators hanging in the doorway. The distorted images on the other side were creeping me out, so I lowered all my primary shields to make sure we weren't blindsided. Even lowering those, I was still invisible to his mind-reading abilities.

"I'll go first, then Cinder. Taylor, you watch our backs."

She held up her gun. "Ten-four."

Creeping across a foul fish-smelling, gut-strewn floor, I saw another opening like the one we came through. Telling emotions washed over me. "There," I whispered. "He's there. Rafe. I feel him. He'll know Taylor is here, but with our shields up, he doesn't know the rest of us are here. I'm going in first. I want the rest of you to stay here."

"Echo—"

"No, Taylor. Please. Do as I ask and stay here." I knelt down and laid my hands on Cinder's shoulders. "I need you to show some self-restraint here, okay? Remember our discipline training. Be strong. Be patient. You understand?"

Cinder nodded. "*I do.*"

With that, I walked through the plastic sheets and stood eight feet from Rafe, who started for the gun in his waistband. That one action told me all I needed to know about him. He was a thinker only. No telekinesis. No fire. Nada.

"Don't do it, Rafe. I'm not alone, and killing you is an option I would love to explore. Just give me a reason."

He paused and tried to force his way into my head, but was met with a shield Melika and Tip showed me how to make years ago. Amateur.

"I mean it, Rafe. I'll bury you here and now if you make another move."

He studied me with deep brown eyes. He was a handsome man, graying at the temples, with a Roman nose and square chin. He stood well over six feet tall with lanky limbs that hung loosely at his side. "Don't be a fool, Echo. This place is surrounded by snipers, by—"

"Shut the fuck up," I ordered. "Slide your weapon across the floor and then open that unit." I nodded to the door with my chin. "Make one bad choice and it will be the last thing you do."

He shook his head. "I know all about you, Echo Branson. We've all studied up on you, your life, your strengths and weaknesses. And there's one thing very clear...you are not a killer." His blue eyes fairly sparkled as he said this. "You may hang with them, but you are not one of them."

"I don't know where you get your intel, Rafe, but it needs to be updated. Now, slide the gun over there before I prove you and your sources wrong."

He hesitated one split second too long, so I gave him a mental shove against the wall. "Don't piss me off, Rafe. I'm so not in the mood for your bullshit. I'm willing to let you live if you toss the gun. Now."

Rafe reached too quickly for the gun, so I slammed him

against the wall once more, the gun clattering uselessly onto the fetid floor.

Shaking his head he said, "Well *that* little gem certainly wasn't in your dossier. Appears you're a bit more than an empath."

I stepped up to him, unafraid and resolute. "Just open the goddamn door. The next blast won't be so gentle and you won't live to tell anyone about it."

Rafe shook his head. "It's not you I am worried about. *She* will kill me."

Cocking my head, I crossed my arms. "And you don't think I will?" I shook my head and tsked. "Either way, it looks like you're a dead man."

"Can you guarantee my safety from her?"

I laughed. "Of course not, but I can try. I can guarantee you this much: if you don't open the door, you'll be laying on the floor with the fish guts, so I suggest you just hop on down there and open the damn thing."

Rafe blinked a few times before opening the refrigerator door. There, handcuffed to a metal shelf, was Tip. My heart nearly leapt into my throat seeing her like that. Her head hung down, chin on chest. Sedated.

I should have known. No wonder I hadn't heard her.

Turning to Rafe, I growled. "Unlock her."

"I don't have the key."

He was telling the truth.

"Who does?"

"The Professor. He has the key. I swear."

"Did someone mention a key?" Taylor asked, sauntering through the door and holding up her lock pick set.

Rafe's emotions changed from feigned disinterest to immediate attraction. "Well, well, well," he said, brushing his hair back with one hand. "Who is this?"

"Are you kidding me with this?" I said. "Focus in here, Rico Suave."

Taylor glared at him with disdain. "Not on your best day, asshole. Step aside." Taylor flitted by me and stopped when she saw Tip. "Oh shit, man. You've gone and done it now." Kneeling down, Taylor pulled Tip's head back. "Fuck me, E, she's seriously drugged up."

I shoved Rafe back down on the metal table, surprised by my own strength. "Why?"

Rafe struggled a moment. "Oh come on! She's Tiponi Redhawk: one of the world's most dangerous telepaths alive. It was that or kill her. Why do you think she's—"

I was on him in two strides, connecting to his left jaw with my right fist and immediately regretting it. I'm pretty sure I hurt me more than him. "I know why she's sedated, you goddamned traitorous piece of shit."

"Fuck you."

I would have gone at him again, had Bailey not stepped in. "Save it, E. He's so not worth it."

Rafe wiped his lip where it split when I punched him. "Ah, the shaman speaks. Still all about passivity, Bailey? Letting your animals do all your dirty wo—"

A flaming ball of heat whipped by his head, the shock of it silencing him.

"Cat got your tongue, asshole?" Bailey said. "Nobody does my talking for me but me, so listen up when I tell you, Echo may not take your life from you, but I have no compunction about doing so. Passivity is overrated."

"Play nicely, Rafe, because I'm leaving. I'll leave you in the hot hands of the super your people would die to have."

I left Rafe under the watchful eyes of Bailey and Cinder.

"Kill him if he moves from that table, Cinder."

Taylor had Tip out of the handcuffs in no time. When I knelt next to Tip, I felt the enormity of the drugs coursing through her. Lifting her chin up, I stared into her glazed eyes. She was totally jacked up.

"Tip? Babe, it's Echo. It's me. You're going to be all right. Everything's going to be all right. Do you understand me?"

She blinked a few times and I could feel her trying to focus on my face. "Took you...long...enough." She wiped her mouth with the back of her hand.

Brushing the hair from her damp face, I saw a big bruise on her right cheek. The chill I felt in my bones wasn't from the cold of the refrigerator, which was pretty damned cold. It came from the iciest part of my heart as vengeance chilled me to the bone. "Oh, Tip. Sorry I'm late."

She smiled. She actually smiled. "No worries. Payback's... a bitch." Shaking her head, she closed her eyes. "I'm all fucked up."

She was wrong about payback. *I* was the bitch...or would be soon enough. This was one transgression people would pay for. "Can you stand?"

She tried, but her legs were rubbery and she slid back down the wall.

"Caneven shtand," Tip slurred, eyes still closed.

"We have to get out of here, Tip. We're on the clock. You *have* to get up." I put her arm around my neck.

"Trying."

Suddenly, Bailey was at my side. "Come on, E. You get one side, I'll get the other. Taylor—"

"I got Rafe. Come on, asshole. Your turn in the cold."

As Bailey and I helped Tip out of the refrigerator, Cinder stood glaring at Rafe. I knew she wanted to torch him, knew every bone in her body was itching to turn him into a pile of smoldering ashes, but I couldn't allow that. He was still one of us and hadn't yet shown that he was a danger to us. If he did, she would get her wish.

Stopping, with my right arm around Tip, I turned to Rafe. "You have one of two choices: The cold where you kept Tip, or the heat of one of Cinder's blasts. You have one second to decide. One."

He moved quickly into the refrigerator, where Taylor handcuffed him to the same metal shelf.

"Where are the sedatives?" I asked.

"All gone."

I turned. "Lie."

Taylor smacked him on the head with the butt of her gun. "Don't mess with us, cowboy. Where are they?"

"I'm telling you—"

Suddenly, Taylor's gun was jammed into his groin. "You're beginning to piss me off. One, two—"

"Inside jacket pocket."

Taylor pulled out a syringe and looked at it. "Is this the same shit you pushed into Tiponi Redhawk?"

He didn't answer.

"Guess we'll find out, huh, big guy?" Taylor took the plastic protector off and jammed it into his neck. "Nighty-night, asswipe."

Bailey, Tip, Cinder and I were almost at the door when Taylor joined us.

"You guys get her to the street. I'll go get one of the cars."

"Hurry, Taylor. Once they sound an alarm, that boat out there will take off."

She took off running before I even finished my sentence.

"The...kids...safe?" Tip mumbled.

"We have no idea Tip. Do you remember where you put them?"

Her head lolled over to her shoulder. "Don't...be...shilly. Of course I...know."

Bailey and I sat on the sidewalk and leaned Tip against a building. "Chew this," Bailey said, handing Tip what looked like a piece of beef jerky. "Chew it up really well, okay? Don't swallow until it's practically mush."

Tip took the jerky and struggled to bite a piece off. We all waited while she fought with whatever it was Bailey had given her.

Bailey then examined her cheek. "Just a bruise. I'll take care of that later. Right now, we need to neutralize the sedative they've given you, and that neutralizer in the meat should help with that."

Nodding, Tip kept chewing slowly, blinking as if to clear her eyes and her head. Her chewing was slow and methodical, and a couple of times, she stopped chewing altogether, as if she forgot to keep going.

"Keep chewing, Tip." Flipping open the vidbook, I told Danica we had Tip. I heard cheers in the room behind her. She said there was still no GPS for the triplets. The cheers died down.

"Not...till...midnight," Tip muttered. "They'll turn vidbook on...at midnight tonight."

"We'll be all over it then," Danica said. "You just get the hell out of Nome. Go someplace safe. Go—"

"We're going after that ship."

"Of course you are."

"I need to take care of Tip, then we're out of here. I'll keep you posted."

I knelt next to Tip and watched her chew like a cow chewing its cud. With every passing second, she got stronger and clearer. I could feel it in her energy.

"How you doing?"

She swallowed and breathed in through her nose. "Getting... better," she softly whispered with hazy eyes. "Done good."

Kissing her forehead, I let my lips linger there for a moment, relieved to finally have her back...relieved to know there was a reason why she hadn't been able to contact me. "God, am I glad to see you."

She nodded and reached out to touch my face. "Miss... you."

I turned her palm and kissed it. "I know. I miss you, too." And at that moment, I knew somewhere not so deep inside me that my life wasn't truly complete without Tiponi Redhawk in it. I knew she would always be more to me than mentor and ex-lover. She was just...more.

The Hummer Taylor was driving skidded around a corner, stopping in front of us. "Get in! Get in! Get in!"

Bailey and I nearly threw Tip into the vehicle before we jumped in after her. Taylor already had the car moving before the doors had closed.

"What's happened?"

"Genesys cars on their way. Two I could see from the road. I think they're going to the harbor."

"You sure it was them?"

"Trust me. It was them. I could see rifle necks leaning against the windows." Taylor left rubber as she hauled ass out of the Nome docks and hit the road to the airport. I called Gar and told him to get her started, that we'd be there in less than ten minutes.

As Taylor drove like a woman possessed, I called Danica for

the ship's coordinates and had her send them to Gar. Then, I ran over my plan with everyone.

"We're going to land right on that ship, and Cinder and I are going out first, followed by Bailey."

Tip shook her head. "No..." came a groggy voice.

"I'm sorry, love, but yeah, that's how it's going to go. I want the Professor to know we got you, the triplets, and anyone else he's thought of going after. And then I am going to kill him." I looked right at Tip. "It's time you put as much faith in me as you did in Melika. I know what I'm doing. As long as the triplets are safe—"

"They are."

"Then you need to put some faith in me."

She opened her mouth to respond, but just nodded instead. "You got…it."

"Good. Now, here's where it gets tricky."

Gar had the chopper off the frozen tundra less than thirty seconds after we all got in it. It was an amazingly smooth liftoff considering how quickly we all jumped in.

"The ship radioed me five minutes ago wanting to know if there was a problem."

"Oh shit."

"No problem. I answered we were en route. I seriously doubt anyone would remember a pilot's voice. I thought it was better than sounding an alarm that I hadn't answered."

"Good thinking."

As we neared the ship, I realized why it was this far out. It was huge. Too big to come into the harbor. Too big to hide, but large enough to handle the weight of the helicopter.

"Jesus Christ, that's not a ship. That's a luxury liner!"

"What do you need from me?" Gar asked as we approached the ship. "I gotta feeling this thing might slide sideways on us."

"Just be ready to fly us the hell out of here."

He looked over at me. "Is that all?"

"That's good for now. We need an exit strategy and you're it."

"Roger that."

Sitting next to the slow-chewing Tip, I laid my palm on her face. It was clammy. "How are you doing, love?"

She nodded, still pretty out of it. "Stuff...shit like taste."

"Look at me."

She did. Our faces were inches apart. "Listen to me. Are you listening?"

She nodded. "Too loud."

"I know, but listen, okay?" I could tell by her pupils as well as her emotions that listening and understanding were worlds apart. "I need you to stay here and protect Gar, okay?"

"Who's Gar?"

Oh God. She really was jacked up, but I needed her to stay with the chopper, to get her head together in case she had to protect the helicopter and Gar. I couldn't risk her being out there half in the bag.

I pulled her face closer. "Protect the pilot and the chopper, okay? We need this ride."

"Gotcha." She struggled to keep her eyes open. "Echo?"

"Yes?"

"You don't love me anymore."

Oh God. Now? She wanted to have this conversation right now? I tried not to look at the uncomfortable faces around me. "Don't be silly. Of course I do. I'll always love you, Tip. You know that." I felt every awkward emotion from everyone in the chopper even through my shields.

"Uh-uh. Not true..." Her eyelids fell slowly. "That's why—"

Her voice faded and I waited for her to finish. "Why what?"

"Why you can't hear me anymore? I called and called...and yelled and yelled...*nada*."

I stared at her. "What are you talking about? What do you mean you called?"

Tip shook her head. "Mel shoulda told you...long time ago... our connection...is based on love. Real love. Deep love. Love love. If you still loved me like *that*...you could hear me...and I could hear *you*."

I was speechless.

"You, Echo. It has…always been you. I can't believe you don't know that." She shook her head. "Now, it's too late."

This was just the drug talking.

"Tip—"

She kept going. "Not being able to hear you…it's the worst…feeling. Like I am lost in a maze. It's the—"

"E, we're coming up on it."

Leaning over, I kissed Tip's forehead again and whispered, "Oh, Tip, I really will love you forever. You were my first and best. We'll talk later, okay?"

Turning, I prepared to leap from the helicopter the moment it landed. "Any word from the ship?"

Gar nodded. "We are all clear to land."

I immediately felt Cinder and Bailey behind me.

"Right behind you, Boss."

I looked at Bailey and then to Cinder. "Take out anyone who could hurt us. Anyone." Pulling up our hoods, we prepared to jump when the feet touched down.

They nodded, and away we went.

The first three people who came to greet us were women. Like those women in the hotels, they were there to put the triplets at ease after the handoff. I knocked all three back against the ship's railings and Bailey dispatched them quickly by tying them to those same railings. A quick pat down revealed five more syringes, candy and a Taser gun. We used the syringes on them.

"Those assholes were just going to keep those kids sedated, sedated, sedated?" Bailey chuffed. "Fuckers."

"Sure looks that way," I said, starting to the belly of the boat.

The first person we ran into, I blasted back into the room he came from. He crashed into boxes that fell on top of him, knocking him down and out.

One down.

Then I came to the energy of someone who could lead us where we wanted to go—someone in power here on the ship. I pushed him against the wall with another shield. He was unprepared for my aggression and stuttered and stammered when I demanded he take us to the Professor.

"If you don't take us there right now, *she* will turn you into a pile of ashes."

Cinder held out a ball of flame. It crackled with a preternatural sound that gave even me goosebumps.

"Truth or death. It's your call."

He agreed that living was preferential to being burned alive and practically ran to the lower deck of the ship, where we stood facing cage-like containers of all kinds. There were cages with steel bars, Plexiglass cages, and even two cages that looked frighteningly like the jail cell of Hannibal Lector. I was rooted where I stood. I knew exactly what this was: this was Genesys' portable laboratory.

"What the fuck?" Bailey muttered. "Is there...there's a fucking kid in that last one!"

Cinder ran over to the cell.

"Cinder, stop!"

Too late. She ran to see who was in the final cage, and I had a flashback of the first time I peered into a cell and saw a drooling empath rocking back and forth...a victim of her own powers.

"*Echo, come here! Hurry! It's a little boy. And he looks really scared.*" She gripped the bars and stared in the cell.

"Cinder, step away from the bars, please. You don't know what he's capable of."

She did as I asked, and I stepped behind her and looked in.

"*Who is he?*"

The young man hesitated, staring at Cinder. "My name is ...Tack. I'm a...they call me a techopath."

"*We have to let him out, Echo. He doesn't belong in here.*"

"*I realize that, Cinder, but we can't have a loose cannon running about.*" Looking in, I knelt down. He could have been ten or he could have been fifteen, it was too hard to tell. I knew he was one of a rare breed of supers capable of commanding technology and electricity, but other than that, he was closed off to me because of the drugs. "We're gonna get you out of here, okay?"

When he looked at me, I saw the same glazed look Tip had had on her face and felt the same drugged emotions. "Sedated," I growled, rising and glaring at our hostage. I think I was most amazed by how many naturals they had working for them.

"Where is the Professor? And don't yank my chain, buddy, because I just became one pissed off empath!"

"He's…in the lab. Beyond those doors."

I glared hard at him, my suspicions confirmed. "Lab? This *is* a floating lab, isn't it? Of course it is. That way you don't have to stand and fight. You can flee in the dead of night like the cowards you are."

He shrugged, keeping one eye on Cinder. "He'll be in there… I swear…prepping for the triplets. He's been very excited about their…capabilities. Please don't kill me."

I opened a cage. "Get in."

"What?"

"You heard her, asshole. Get. In!" Bailey shoved him in and I closed the door. "Make one sound and I'll come back here and kill you myself."

He nodded and stepped away from the bars. "He's crazy, you know?"

I walked back. "Who?"

"The Professor. He's insane. He has cloning ideas that are off the charts nutso. Pushes kids too far, over medicates." He shook his head. "Nutbag."

I turned and approached the lab door, stopping dead, my emotional bells clanging loudly.

"What is it?" Bailey whispered.

"I don't feel him."

"You don't mean—"

I nodded. "He's one of us. That creep is one of us." I tried to keep it together, to remain calm and somewhat detached, but I couldn't. Sedating Tip was one thing, but caging and sedating children…well…oh hell no.

"E?"

I shook it off. "I'm ready. Cinder, keep your hands ready, but be careful. Labs can have all sorts of flammable liquids. You'll need to have pinpoint accuracy. Remember when we were working on that?"

She nodded. "*I am ready, Echo, really.*"

I took a deep breath and busted through the door, coming face-to-face with the Professor. For a nanosecond, he seemed slightly shocked to see me, but he quickly recovered and took several steps away from us.

"I take it this means the triplets aren't coming?" He said it almost cavalierly.

"Good guess, asshole," Bailey said, stepping behind him. "Fingers laced behind your head. Move them, and Cinder here will brand you forever. Understand?"

He did as she asked. "Really, Echo, there's no need for such—"

"Shut up." I walked up to him. He was vaguely familiar. "Lower your shields or I'll have her do just that. This is no bluff."

The look on his face told me he hadn't expected that. "Lower my shields?"

Cinder raised her hands.

"Fine. Fine."

When he lowered them, a foreign emotion skittered across the room just out of reach.

"What *are* you?" I asked, sensing a variety of emotions I hadn't experienced before. They were pinballing all over the place.

"I'm an empath, like you, Echo, though Genesys has heightened that awareness to include a little telepathy as well. Heightening abilities is something we are very capable of doing if you're ever interested."

He was telling the truth, and that only made me hate him more.

He cocked his head at me, and something like a slow realization crept across his face. "Oh my." He looked over at Bailey before looking back at me. "I get it now. You really don't know who I am." It was a statement.

"Don't know and don't care. If you give me Kip Reynolds, you can live to find new employment. If you don't, then you are of no use to me."

He was staring hard at me. "Look at me. Look very carefully at me."

"Just answer her question, asshole," Bailey said.

He ignored her and locked eyes with me, saying something

to me only three seconds after I figured it out myself. "Charlie, I'm your father."

The word punched me in the gut, and I stepped back a few paces, the room spinning slightly. I lost my breath.

True. It was the truth and I was so not prepared for it.

"You didn't know." He shook his head. "Of course you didn't know. How could you?"

With everyone staring at me, I struggled to pull it all together. "I…I thought you were dead. I *hoped* you were dead. You *should* be dead."

"You sound like your sister."

I stepped back up to him, my emotions changing quickly from shock to intense anger. "Do not ever talk about my sister, you scumbag. Don't you *ever* say her name," I growled, feeling venom in every word. "You lost that privilege when you handed her over to Genesys all those years ago. Do you understand me? If you say her name in my presence, I will kill you. I can, too, you know. I am no mere empath with enhanced telepathic powers. I am more than any of your goddamn reports can convey. Are we clear?"

He nodded. "Handed her over? Is that how she spins it? It's not what you think, at all, Charlie. Genesys—"

"And don't call me that. I swear to God, if that name ever comes from your lips again, I will have Cinder turn you into a lump of coal."

The Professor did not turn his face toward Cinder. "Hello, Cinder. It is good to meet you at long last. I have heard so much about you."

"This is not a goddamned social visit," Bailey snarled. "We want to know where Kip Reynolds is. This little reunion needs to be put on the back burner. So save us all the headache and give us the info we want."

Professor Hayward never took his eyes off me. I was five when he had dumped me at an orphanage in order to protect me from Genesys, the company he and my mother worked for. He dumped me there, burned our home down, and left the country with my sister, Kristy. My mother admitted herself into a sanitarium for nine long years in an effort to escape Genesys and to keep an eye on me from afar. Genesys had done more than destroy my family…they set me and my sister apart for many years and changed the fate of our existence. To know that my father now worked for them after all the three of us had been through after the fire was almost more than I could bear.

Almost.

"You *erased* my memory," I said more evenly than I felt.

This was not a scene I had ever played out in my mind. He was a stranger to me; a man who had used my sister as a bargaining chip: a dangerous doctor who sedated children so he could probe them like lab rats and change their DNA.

"I had to. It was the kindest thing to do under the circumstances."

"Kind? *Kind*? I was a scared five-year-old girl left alone. *Alone*, Mr. Hayward! Don't tell me it was *kind*, you piece of shit. Was it *kind* to leave my sister with this group of demented scientists? *Kind* to let her experience unspeakable pain? Was it *kind* to change her into something she could barely handle being? I ought to kill you with my bare hands, you sonofabitch. You make me sick."

He pushed his glasses back up the bridge of his long nose. This man looked nothing like either Kristy or me. "You've only heard one side of the story."

I stepped back up to him. He was a good eight inches taller than me. "Oh no I haven't. I've spoken with my mother and Jig as well." I could see that amazed him, and I felt his surprise. "You left her in that sanitarium for nine years. Nine years! What kind of man does that? What is *wrong* with you?"

He stepped back a step. "It was more complicated than that. We were trying to do right by you. We were trying to protect our family. Surely you can understand that much."

"So you protected us one minute only to turn around to join the enemy the next? What are you, schizo?"

"It's not like that—"

I shook my head. "You know, I don't really give a shit why you work for Genesys. You are nothing to me. Less than nothing. You and Kip Reynolds deserve each other." Stepping away from him, I turned to Bailey.

"Can you get Tack out and bring him with us?"

"You got it, boss. Want me to keep my eyes on him?"

"Please."

"You're not taking my—"

"Not yours!" I yelled, pointing my finger in his face. "Not yours. Never yours! You will never again cage another super. He's going with me. Are there any others in here?"

"No."

Truth.

"Then you came up here specifically to get the triplets."

"No. We had them. Took us months to get them to a place where we would be able to enter Russia and get them. Then your Tiponi Redhawk managed to abscond with them, ruining thousands of hours of work and hundreds of thousands of dollars." He was actually sneering as he said this. "We came after her to get—"

I held my hand up in his face. "Don't say it. People aren't owned. Children are not yours, and supers are off-limits for collecting purposes. Do you understand what I am saying? It is over for you. *Over.*"

He didn't even blink. "Oh, daughter, you have no idea about the tiger whose tail you've grabbed. This is far from over."

"No, daddy dearest, it's *you* who doesn't understand that the tiger you're looking at is two steps away from clawing your eyes out and two more from pulling the plug on this whole sick operation. It should have been done years ago."

I hated him not only for how he'd treated me and Kristy, but for the role he played in other children's lives.

"And why do you suppose it wasn't? Have you asked your precious Melika that? Why has she and her aging band of geriatrics not come after us or tried to stop up? Because they were smart enough to see it for the losing proposition it is. You can't win this game, Ch—"

I blasted him hard against the wall, knocking the wind from him. The look on his face was priceless. He hadn't been expecting that. Then I locked eyes with him and stepped so close, he backed up into the wall. "People's lives aren't games, Mr. Hayward, and *your* people have no idea the shit storm that's coming their way."

He leaned away from me and sucked in some air. "My *people* have more resources than you can imagine, daughter. Kip has very deep pockets in very high places. *You*, my dearest, have no idea of the shit storm *you'll* rain down on *your* people if you mess with him or his backers. What do you think this is? Some game for bored billionaires? Do your homework, Charlie. This is—"

And before he could finish, Cinder sent a laser-like flash that sliced his shoulder wide open.

"Jesus Christ," he said, grabbing his shoulder, blood slowly seeping between his fingers.

"She told you not to call her that," Bailey offered. "So open your fucking ears, asshole, or next time, that'll be your neck."

Holding his bleeding shoulder, Hayward slowly shook his head. "You have no idea how quickly and easily they will dispatch you. All of you. You are all expendable." Then he looked at Cinder. "Well, almost all of you."

"That's a chance I'm willing to take. *We* are willing to take. You'll never get Cinder. She will never be a weapon for this country or anyone else's. If you come after her again, I will spend the rest of my life coming after every last one of you."

"I didn't take you for a fool, Echo."

"We're done here." Stepping away from him, I nodded to Bailey, who pushed him to a desk. "Get your people in those lifeboats. You have five minutes to load everyone in. After that, people will die. I don't have time for any of your bullshit."

"And then what?"

"What else? I'm going to blow this floating torture chamber sky-high." I watched his reaction as I said this. "And me and my people will seek any others like this and destroy those as well. It's a new game, Hayward, and my team plays to win."

"Oh, Charlie, that wouldn't be—" Before he could finish, Cinder send a thin line of flame at him again, burning his other arm.

"She told you not to call her that, asshole," Bailey said. "You a slow learner or what? There is no Charlie here. Just a bunch of pissed off supers who are tired of your shenanigans. Consider this your pink slip."

Hayward cursed under his breath as both shoulders bled, but didn't say anything else.

"Five minutes. You take any more time than that, and we'll blow this thing up whether they're off it or not." Grabbing the mic, I handed it to him. "Don't be stupid. You can save people or you can sign their death warrant. It's your call."

Taking it from me, he put it to his mouth, then paused. "This is an expensive mistake you're about to make. He'll just build another...and another."

"Then we'll just blow up another and another. What don't you get about this? The party is over. You're through experimenting and torturing young supers. Make the goddamn call."

Hayward put the mic to his mouth, hesitated, and lowered it again. "Look, maybe we can work something out."

"Make. The. Call."

Bailey punched one of the wounds, causing Hayward to grimace and swear. "You're beginning to really piss me off. Do what she says right now, or I'll have Cinder blind you with her next shot. Understand me?"

"Echo, listen to me. Please. Kip Reynolds is not the kind of guy you want to go up against. Why do you think your people have never gone after him? He is that dangerous."

"You know what? I don't really care why. I'm stopping Genesys, with or without help."

"You've really gone rogue? You're really willing to take on the United States government? Maybe you're more like your sister than you realize." Putting the mic to his mouth, he ordered his crew to evacuate. Gave them five minutes, then he set it down, shaking his head once more. "Big mistake."

"Won't be my last. Come on."

"Where we going?"

"You're going to take me to Kip Reynolds. If you do that, I'll let you live. If you refuse, then you are no use to me. You, Hayward, are expendable."

"You're going to kill him? Since when did your kind start killing people?"

"Since I took over. Welcome to the twenty-first century, *Daddy.*"

Bailey shoved him toward the door.

"There's no need for brutish behavior, but you should know, Kip is not an easy man to track down. He moves every week to an undisclosed location. Very few people know of his whereabouts."

I wondered who he was most afraid of. "Scared of S.T.O.P? Of us? Who?"

"Not scared. Prudent. He is a valuable asset to Genesys."

"Who are you kidding? He *is* Genesys, and it's time the walls came tumbling down."

As we made our way through the bowels of the ship, I felt an anger and rage I'd never experienced before. I wanted to kill him. I wanted to put him in one of those cages and make him suffer for what he did to my sister, to Cooper's girlfriend, Eve, to so many others whose names will never be known. As a man, he was despicable. As a father, he had chosen to ruin the lives of both daughters in order to save his own.

I had never hated anyone more than I despised that man, and it took every ounce of maturity I possessed not to tell Cinder to turn him into a burned french fry.

When we reached the deck, Taylor jumped from the chopper and helped Bailey tie Hayward's hands and feet. His people had made it off the ship in three lifeboats, but the captain, in a show of unneeded heroism, chose to stand fast and aim a rifle at the helicopter.

"Anyone move, and I'll blow that chopper to bits."

As he took aim at us, the husky jumped from the chopper and sat there staring and snarling at him. The captain lowered his rifle to shoot him, not seeing the wolverine coming from behind. When he realized what was happening, he was too late to swing his rifle around at it, and the damned thing nearly tore his arm off. He was a bloody mess by the time Bailey called him off. The rifle clattered to the deck, and Bailey scooped it up and jammed it against her shoulder like she had known how to fire one her whole life.

"Get in a fucking boat," she ordered. "Before you become his lunch."

The captain held on to his shredded arm and propelled himself away from the wolverine and over the side of the ship. I didn't see where he landed and didn't care. I had to hand it to Bailey—her powers were far scarier than even Cinder's. Burning alive is one thing: being eaten alive is something from a horror flick.

"Keep your eyes peeled," I said, opening my vidbook and waiting for Danica.

"Glad to see you in one piece, Clark. Everything okay so far?"

I nodded, seeing Roger's and Carl's faces pop up in the picture-in-picture mode. "I need to know where to shoot fireballs in order to blow up a ship the size of this one."

Cinder tugged at my arm. *Echo, I am strong enough to do it on my own.*

Looking down at her, I nodded. "Let us get far enough away—"

She shook her head. *I need to start it in the engine room, otherwise, they might be able to save the ship before it sinks. I want it to sink.* She cast her eyes over at Tack, who hadn't left Bailey's side.

"Can you get out in time?" I hesitated to put Cinder in that position, but she wasn't a little girl asking to play on the freeway; she was a valuable member of my team asking to do her job.

Yes. Just be ready to take off. Tack can go with me. He knows this ship better than we do.

I nodded, though every fiber of my being told me to let it go...to take Hayward and be gone. I knew I shouldn't risk her safety or anyone else's, but I had to do it. I wanted to send Kip a message—a loud, fiery message—one he couldn't ignore.

"Go for it."

As Cinder took off, Tack was right beside her, yelling something to her and pointing to the ladder.

As Bailey corralled the wolverine and Taylor stayed with Hayward, I looked down at the vidbook. "I want a video of the next five minutes here on the ship Then I want it sent to Genesys with these words: *You're next.* Address it to Kip Reynolds."

Danica nodded once. "Hit the camera icon and shoot the footage. When it ends, I'll retrieve it from your book and send it to Genesys. Anyone else?"

"No."

"Clark, are you okay? You're...scaring me a little."

I looked into the camera and nodded. I was scaring me a little, too, but I had figured out along the way, that this was the mantle of a leader. You either made the tough calls or you let someone else do it. It was time I was willing to do it myself. "I'm fine. Everyone is fine. Including my father."

Danica's mouth moved but nothing came out.

"*He's* the Professor?" Her hand went to her mouth. "No fucking way."

"Way. And I'm using him to find Kip Reynolds."

"Whoa. Whoa. Wait. You're not ready. *We're* not ready. Where's Tip? Goddamn it, Echo, not now. Not like this. We need time."

"We don't have time. We've given Genesys all the time they are going to get. Gotta go, Dani."

I climbed into the passenger seat and waited a few moments before turning the camera on and pointing it at the ship.

"You ladies mean business," Gar said. "I like that."

"When you see those two kids come out that door, get this bird ready to fly."

"To?"

"Brevig Mission. We need to regroup before we move on out. They won't expect us to stay in Alaska, and we need to do the unexpected."

"Who's that dickweed?" Gar motioned to Hayward with his chin.

"My father."

He looked over at me. "No shit?"

"Yeah. Piece of shit."

We didn't have to wait long, because suddenly Cinder and Tack came running toward us. "Go! Go! Go!" Tack yelled, helping Cinder into the chopper before diving in after her.

Gar lifted the bird off the deck and away from the ship moments before the first of many explosions rattled our windows. The smoke rose almost as quickly as we did, and the whole ship began exploding, sending flaming parts of itself in all directions.

I taped the whole explosion, with Gar keeping the chopper steady. Orange and yellow balls of flame shot from the ship. When the boat began sinking in earnest, I ended the videotaping and nodded to Gar, who peeled away from the charred, sinking wreckage toward Brevig Mission.

"Remind me never to piss you off," Gar said, shaking his head. "What the hell did you use? TNT?"

"Something like that."

"And...uh...I've been waiting long enough, but can one of you explain the wolverine?"

"Maybe later. Right now, just please get us out of here."

As the chopper made its way toward the wilderness, I got out of my seat and knelt next to Tip, whose eyes were closed, but I knew she wasn't asleep. "Hey."

Opening one then the other, she studied my face. "You're doin' good." Her forehead was sweaty but some of her color had returned and her eyes were not as glassy. "Proud of you."

I brushed her hair over her shoulders. It felt so good being close to her again. "I had a good teacher."

"He's really your dad? The asshole who left you for dead and erased you?"

"That would be him."

She struggled to get up, but I placed a hand on her shoulder. "Now is not the time for personal vendettas, Tip. Later."

Her brown eyes drank in my face. "Later."

We rode in silence the rest of the way, even during a refueling stop along the coast. Helicopters are abnormally loud, so it left each of us with our own thoughts as the rotors angrily beat the air.

And I had many thoughts.

Twenty-three years ago, that man on the boat had erased five-year-old Charlotte, a.k.a. Charlie Hayward's memory. One minute, she was a happy little girl and the next, she was homeless, alone and anonymous, with no memory or her parents or sister. For thirteen years, I went by Jane. Jane Doe. As foster family after foster family rejected me, I grew further and further away from myself, often blaming that five-year-old for having done something so heinous, she wasn't worth keeping.

Not long ago, I'd accidentally discovered I had a sister; Kristy, also known as Scion. Technically speaking, a scion is a detached living portion of a plant that is joined to a stock using a grafting method. Genesys had employed this particular technique on Kristy, changing her chemical makeup into something far more powerful and dangerous than a regular supernatural. She was like a turbo-charged, overly caffeinated, eminently powerful version of herself. They destroyed the girl to create the hybrid woman: an angry woman who finally escaped from Genesys only to join a group of other angry and vengeful supernaturals known collectively as S.T.O.P. Their goal was the utter destruction of Genesys. At the time, I refused to join her merry band of killers, thinking that I was somehow better than them. The problem was I hadn't supported their methods or the *way* S.T.O.P went about attacking Genesys. I hadn't fully understood.

Past tense.

Now, I got it. I understood Kristy's anger. I understood why offense was our best weapon. I understood the anger that drove my sister to hunt them down. I finally understood.

Kristy had asked me to join her, and I couldn't. I still wouldn't. My job was to mentor young supers like the three, make that four, I would be returning with. I understood my role only too well but, unlike Melika, I would not sit idly by while some government subsidized company picked us off one-by-one. While I wasn't interested in joining Kristy's group, I was *very* interested in protecting my new charges and all those other struggling young paranormals.

I had expected a fight. I had even anticipated my own anger. What I wasn't prepared for was to discover my father was one of the top dogs in this flea-ridden kennel. How had Kristy not known this? Or did she? I wasn't sure. We weren't really on speaking terms. She viewed my passivity as weak and I saw her aggression as misdirected. Needless to say, we didn't really hit it off very well.

Glaring over at him, I wanted to punch him in the face.

He had destroyed our family only to join ranks with the very organization he'd ruined us for. It was enough to make a girl dizzy.

But I wasn't dizzy.

I was pissed.

Nine years my mother had waited for him. Nine years he let her linger in a sanitarium. Nine years I was passed around from one family to the next, never feeling wanted, never having anything of my own, never being loved. Nine years is a long time.

I hated him.

But I didn't think I could actually kill him.

Of course, there was a first for everything.

When we landed in Brevig Mission, Pitt and Loco met us at the chopper and helped us all out.

"She needs to lay low for a bit," I said to Pitt as I passed a limp, semi-awake Tip to him. She was more lucid, but I could feel the effects of the sedative still lingering in her.

As Pitt walked away with Tip's arm over his shoulder, I saw Loco frozen. He had spotted the wolverine as it sat there licking its paws.

"He won't bother you," Bailey said, helping Tack out. "Trust me on that. I am sending him home now."

"You're…" he shook his head. "Never mind. Thank you," he said softly. "I saw one of those take down two pit bulls once. They are far fiercer than even their reputation."

I agreed.

Once Taylor and Cinder were out, I had Loco gag and secure Hayward with duct tape to a chair in the small dining room and told him not to let Hayward out of his sight.

When the propellers finally wound to a stop, I waited for Gar to get out. It took some doing, since he was so huge. He stretched and yawned.

"Thank you so much for this," I said. "We couldn't have done it without you."

He chuckled. "Pardon my saying so, but what, exactly was 'it' that we did? We blew up a ship, kidnapped a man who you say is your father, grabbed a kid, and have even managed to keep a wolverine under your control. So what was that all about, Echo?"

I wasn't going to lie to him anymore or withhold any truth he was ready to hear. "See that boy?" I nodded toward Tack who was playing in the snow. "You just helped us save his life."

"So that's what we've been doing out here in the wilderness? Saving kids' lives?"

I nodded. "Among other things."

"Cool. Works for me. I'm starving. You?"

I hadn't thought about food, but now that he mentioned it... "Got dinner up your sleeve?"

"Gimme thirty minutes and I'll whip up something for the troops." Gar lumbered away, leaving me with Cinder and Tack.

"Cinder, can you give us a moment?"

Nodding, she went into the house.

I put my arm around Tack's shoulders and walked him toward the house.

"I'm sure you have a lot of questions for me, but why don't you get out of those lab rat clothes and grab some dinner? We can sit down after and talk."

He stopped walking and looked up at me, tears in his eyes. "Thanks for coming to get me. I thought for sure I was going to die like the others."

"No need to thank me, Tack. We take care of each other." I had to reconstruct my shields to keep from feeling the depth of his sadness. "The others...didn't live?"

He shook his head sadly. "Nope. The experiments were too harsh or the DNA got screwed up or some stupid story. Guess it doesn't matter why. Dead is dead, huh?"

"But it does matter, Tack. It matters very much. What Genesys is doing..." I shook my head. He didn't need this lecture from me. "You've been very brave, but you're safe now."

"Cinder says you might teach me. She says you have a safe place for us to live."

"Would you like that?"

He nodded eagerly. "I really would. I can do stuff, but I am not always sure how it works."

"We'll see what we can do once this whole thing is finished."

He looked up at me, tears in his eyes. "I hate them."

"I know you do. So do I. They'll never get to you again, Tack." I brushed his brown hair across his forehead. "What's your real name?"

"Mike Cross, from Alabama."

"How old are you, Mike?"

"Thirteen, ma'am, but you can call me Tack. I'm used to it now. I prefer it actually."

"Tack it is. What's that name about anyway?"

We reached the front door and he grinned. "It's actually Tech, but the way Mr. Reynolds always said it, it came out Tack." He shook his head. "Whatta jerk."

"You go on and ask Gar for some clothes. Grab a shower and dinner will be ready in about thirty minutes."

When Tack walked into the house, I blew out a deep breath. I was exhausted. I needed to talk to Hayward, but I was simply too tired to put up with his crap. I needed to be fresh before dealing with him. I needed time to catch my breath, to feel my own feelings for a change.

That my father was alive and playing for the bad guys, I wasn't at all prepared for, but if I could use it to my advantage, I would.

Feeling the cold now, I went inside, checked on everyone, and lay down next to Tip. It had been a while since we lay together. The last time was right after she'd been shot in New Orleans.

Turning her head, I felt her lips on my forehead as she pulled me deeper into her embrace. It was a hug more familiar to me than my own face, and one I hadn't realized I had been missing.

"Rest, Echo. I gotcha, love. I gotcha."

And she did. She always had and I suspected she always would. Studying the side of her face, I felt a tear escape my eye and run down my temple. "I really do love you, you know."

She let that hang in the air awhile before replying, "Not like that. Not anymore. Shhh. Rest now. Now is not the time or the place."

Another tear fell as I scooted closer. "You've been in my head over half my life, Tiponi. I feel...like something is missing."

She held me closer to her. "I'll always be here, Echo, but you made your choice. You're an empath. Your mind is open only to the one you love. That, sadly, is not me. As much as I wish it were, it isn't. I will just have to find a way to get used to that. Now, close your eyes and take a break."

"Dinner is ready in thirty."

"Thirty then. Just let it all go, love. We're all safe now, and Mel would be really proud of how well you handled it back there. You rocked it, for sure."

"I wanted…to kill him, really I did…" My eyelids were so heavy, I fell asleep in mid-sentence, but I could have sworn I heard her say something about killing my dad. I floated away on a cloud of exhaustion, safe in her arms, my head on a tear-stained pillow.

When I pried my eyes open, Tip was still lying next to me on her side, holding me, her eyes open and caressing my face. It looked like whatever she had been chewing had worked. Her eyes were back to normal and I could feel only a little wooziness from the sedatives.

"What time is it?" I looked out the window. It was dark.

"A little after four."

I started to sit up. "What? I told you thirty minutes!"

She pulled me back. "Everyone is resting after eating Gar's spaghetti and meatballs. Loco, what a guy, is just sitting there staring at Hayward." She chuckled. "Dude deserves his name. Batshit crazy loco he is, but with a heart of gold. If Hayward so much as twitches, he gives him the stink eye."

My stomach growled loudly enough for her to hear it.

"Come on. Maybe Gar will heat you up something to eat, and you can tell me how you came to know this cast of characters."

We walked out to the great room, the fire blazing away. Cinder and Tack were playing checkers, Taylor and Bailey were nowhere in sight. Loco was, as Tip had said, just sitting there staring at Hayward. No sign of Pitt or Gar.

"I can get my dinner," I said.

"Sit. I need to get my muscles moving. I don't think I have ever been so stiff."

I hesitated.

"Please."

I sat on the stool and watched as Tip heated up the spaghetti and was reminded of all the wonderful times on the river when we all hung out together while Melika cooked. Tip would stand there, her eyes never leaving my face. It used to disconcert me—this tall, broad-shouldered Indian woman staring at me. I got used to it about a second before I left the bayou to attend college.

Ever since I was fourteen, Tip had been inside my head. Distance didn't matter, time apart wasn't an issue—she could always peek in to make sure I was all right. While her invasion often irritated me, I'd found comfort in knowing I was never truly alone. All I needed to do was call her name, and she'd be right there. We were tied together in such a way as to never really be far apart.

I'd cut that rope, and now the void she'd left, the yawning, gaping chasm sat heavily on my chest. I missed it. I missed her. I just hadn't realized how much.

Sliding off the stool, I said, "Be right back."

"Where you going? It's zero degrees out there."

I grabbed my parka off the hook. "I'll just be a second. I need to clear my head."

She looked at me, probably trying to get in. Force of habit. "Don't be gone long."

I lowered my eyes and went outside, into the biting cold that froze my cheeks and nose almost instantly. Pulling up the hood, I jammed my hands in my pockets and walked out a few yards to look at the purple sky.

Only a couple of months ago, if I needed either Melika or Tip, all I needed to do was call their name in my head. Now, with Melika dying of a brain tumor, and me being in love with Finn, I was truly on my own.

And I felt it deep in the crevasses of my soul.

I *was* in love with Finn, wasn't I?

"Jacob, can you hear me?" Two tears rolled down my cheeks. Jacob's death in the bayou and everything after it had happened so quickly I never really had had time to mourn. I had faced Malecon, the Katrina aftermath, my girlfriend being hurt, and the news that my real mother was alive and my true mother was dying.

I had never felt more alone in my life here on this hard, cold earth.

"I miss you, Jacob. I miss you and Zack more than you could know. Isn't this a cosmic joke? To find my father is still alive and playing for the other team? All I want to do is tear him apart for what he did. But I can't. Not yet. I have this enormous responsibility to teach those kids the way Melika taught us and it weighs heavily on my heart. I...I just don't know if I have what it takes."

Bowing my head, I let the tears fall. They had been a long time coming. The pressure of caring for everyone. The fear of losing Tip. The sadness from knowing that in the near future, I would be without Melika for the rest of my life. It all had caught up with me, and I was feeling every single emotion.

"Sure you do. You're a natural-born leader."

I wheeled around, but didn't see anyone. Ever so slowly, Gar emerged from the shadows.

"Gar. What are you doing out here?"

"Keepin' watch. Folks like that guy in there never just walk away from a fight, Echo. Trust me. He's in there scheming and plotting and planning his way out. If it were up to me, I'd slit his throat and leave him for the wolves. Maybe your spirit folks will give you better advice."

I nodded, feeling a blush crossing my cheeks. "I...uh..."

"No need to explain. I talk to my dead buddies all the time out here. Can't help feeling closer to God in this godforsaken wilderness." He chuckled. "Can I say something?"

"Can I stop you?"

He chuckled. "Probably not. It's pretty clear you gals aren't what you appear to be, but I've learned no one truly is. I have no issue with that. I've seen a lot of military leaders in my time, Echo. Good men, bad leaders. Bad men who were good leaders.

You're that rare quality of good woman, good leader. Those people in there? They know it as well. They'll follow you to the depths of hell, even that new kid, Tack. You have a natural ability to lead. Don't let your feminine insecurities dampen that."

I stepped closer to him. He was enormous. "Feminine insecurities?"

He nodded. "It's a woman's way to always wonder if she is good enough. A great woman still questions her greatness. Men think they are, even when they aren't." He stepped from the shadows, looming like a statue. "And you are. Now is not the time for self-doubt, Echo. Now is the time to believe in everything you know you are."

I looked up at him and nodded. "You're right. My mentor would not have doubted herself."

"Your mentor would be proud, Echo. You sank that ship, returned with all your people, saved a hostage—or whatever Tack was—and nabbed their leader. A good day's work if you were in the military."

"Thank you, Gar. I really needed to hear everything you just said."

"We all need to be reminded of who we are, Echo. Some of us more than others."

Reaching for the door, I turned back to him. "Thank you for standing watch over my people. It means more to me than you know."

He stepped back into the shadows of the porch. "No worries. It meant a great deal that you trusted me, Echo. For a while there, I wasn't worthy of anyone's trust."

"You're a good man, Gar." I paused, then asked, "Just what is Gar short for?"

I heard his rumbling chuckle. "It's short for Gargoyle, my nickname in the marines."

Smiling to myself, I nodded. "It's fitting."

"Yes it is."

When I came back in, I watched as Cinder beat Tack in checkers. Bailey and Taylor sat yakking it up with Tip and filling her in about everything she'd missed, and Loco was still staring at a now sleeping Professor Hayward.

These *were* my people. I *was* their leader, and with or without Tip and Melika in my head, I would take them all home.

"So, what happens at midnight?" I asked Tip as we all gathered around the fireplace. "You mentioned midnight earlier."

"At midnight, the triplets will turn my vidbook on for one minute, allowing Danica and the boys to gather their coordinates. It was the best I could do under the circumstances. I had to disconnect from them because I was too great a liability. I figured I'd divide and conquer."

I'd set my open vidbook on the coffee table so Danica and the boys could be in on the discussion.

"Sent the video everywhere we could. Needless to say the press was on it, too. They heard that explosion everywhere in Nome. Very impressive, Clark. You sure know how to crash a party."

"One minute is all the phone will be on," I reminded her.

"We don't even need a minute," Danica said. "Once we get that position, we'll give you the coordinates and the best way to get there. Roger has the best topo map ever made of Alaska's wilderness."

Bailey leaned toward Tip. "How is it *you* don't know where they are?"

"I knew I had to give myself up in order to buy them time. So I got on a fishing boat and came to Nome while they headed in the opposite direction. As long as *I* didn't know where they were going, Rafe could not pull it from my mind. They could sedate me all they wanted and it would get them nothing as long as I knew nothing. And I don't."

"They set out on foot?"

She shook her head. "Sled. I was sure they thought the kids were with me. When they nabbed me and sedated me thinking Rafe could read my mind once the sedatives kicked in, they waited until he located the three images in my mind. I burned those images deep in there. He's good, but not as good as I am."

"The Inuit," Bailey said, referring to the indigenous people of Alaska who sat in the berm pretending to be the triplets." "Good one."

Tip nodded. "As long as I didn't know where the kids were, they were safe. It was important I not know where they were. I was buying you guys some time and buying the kids some distance."

"Buy...*us* time?"

She caressed my cheek. "Of course. I knew you'd come looking for me when you hadn't heard from me. I can always count on you, Echo Branson, to pull my ass from the fire."

I nodded. "You can't seem to stay out of trouble, can you?"

Bailey cleared her throat. "Lover's quarrel later, please. Continue."

"Anyway," Tip continued, "I was able to pay the three of them to hang out in the burial mound, giving me some time to set up the next part of my plan."

"Good plan," Taylor whispered. "Separating from children in the wilderness and leaving them alone would never be an expected move. I mean, who leaves three kids alone in the Alaskan outback?"

Tip turned to her. "Alone? You think I sent those kids out on their own? That would be insane."

All of us looked at each other.

"Tip?"

Looking at me, she shook her head. "Echo, the reason you can't hear me anymore is because *you* love someone else. The reason *I* can't hear *you* is because *I* love someone else."

The room would have been silent but for the crackling logs...or was that sound my heart breaking some more? It was hard to tell.

Tack broke the silence by mumbling, "Awk-ward."

"Oh." Was all I could think to say.

"The kids are with Ivonne. Ivonne Darkwater. We met in Russia. She helped us out of there and got us safe passage to Alaska. She's...well...for lack of a better word...my girlfriend."

I didn't know whether to applaud or cry. Tip had a...a girlfriend? I so wasn't prepared for this.

"You met in Russia?" Bailey asked, leaning forward, but keeping one eye out on me. "How?"

"She belongs...*belonged* to the European Chapter of S.T.O.P."

"You've got to be shitting me," Bailey said, leaning back. "They have chapters?"

"They're all over," I said, recovering my voice. "They've managed to spread to several other continents. They've made it their mission to seek out Genesys collectors and destroy them." I was babbling. Tip had a girlfriend? How did I not know this?

"Destroy...as in kill?"

"As in," I said.

Tip nodded. "Ivonne came to Russia to collect the triplets for S.T.O.P, but I had already snaked them from a sleeping Genesys. Ivonne got the four of us out and helped secure passage across the Bering Sea. You all pretty much know the rest. Genesys found the Inuits, giving me enough time to throw them off the scent and Ivonne enough time to get the kids to safety."

"But you knew they'd make a deal for Cinder. How?" Bailey asked.

"They'd do anything for a Cinder. *Any*thing. Mel forewarned me this would happen when she realized the extent of her powers. And my guess is, they won't stop until they have her."

"Don't they have the bitch who warned us at the hotel? Sonja What's-her-name?"

Tip shook her head. "No. Sonja is a free agent who goes to the highest bidder. If she came to you with a warning, that's probably what she was paid to do. Besides, she's too old and doesn't posses the genetic makeup they need to complete the experiments they have in mind. They want Cinder's unique DNA. She has the genetic code to actually live through the experiments. Genesys wants Cinder like a starving man wants food. I knew they'd agree to an exchange. I just never thought—" She looked over at me and shook her head. "You sank his ship." She laughed. "I'm impressed. Mel will be, too."

"I had a lot of help."

Tip looked around at all of us. "Yes, you did. And now, we're going to call on your help once more. At midnight, when the GPS goes on, we make a beeline to wherever they are and grab them up."

"'Copter can't hold that many," Gar said. "You'll need to decide who goes. If we are picking up four, I can take four of you, tops."

Tip nodded. "When I am one hundred percent—"

"No." I said it with cold steel, decisive, sharp. "You aren't at peak condition, and I need everyone at one hundred percent. You're not at your best, and this is not up for discussion. I'm taking Cinder, Bailey and Taylor with me."

Tip opened her mouth to argue, but Bailey laid her hand on Tip's shoulder to silence her. "Tip...this is...well, it's Echo's lead." She looked over to me for permission. I nodded. "We'll go after the kids as per your directions, but this is Echo's game. We're following her. End of story."

Tip looked from Bailey to me and back again. "What do you mean? Didn't Mel send you? Give me your cell, Echo. I'll tell her what's going down."

This so wasn't how I wanted to tell her, and for the first time, I was glad she wasn't able to get into my head, but she knew me well enough to know there was something amiss.

I shot Bailey a look she instantly picked up and she slid her hand down Tip's shoulder to take Tip's right hand. I held her left. It was going to be a bumpy ride.

Tip's eyes grew larger with alarm. "What? What's going on?"

My heart ached at what I was about to tell her. I knew this wouldn't be easy, but I would have given anything to have been able to tell her on the river, and not here in this frozen wasteland. "Mel didn't send me because...she's sick, Tip. Really sick."

She visibly shuddered, her skin paling immediately. "What do you mean sick? How sick?" Her voice held a panic I had never heard before.

I swallowed back my own tears. "Brain tumor."

Tip was on her feet instantly, letting go of both our hands. "No, no, no. That can't be. I would know. After all these years, I would—"

"She hid it from us for a long time," I said softly. I never imagined telling her this news in a room full of people. "She's had it for quite some time."

"What do the doctors say? We'll get her to the best specialists in the world. What are you doing to get her the help she needs? Wait." She looked around the room at each of us. "If you're all here, who's with her now? Zack? Tell me you didn't leave her with just Zack. Unless we can find Malecon's body, we have to assume he might still be alive."

Now came the second bomb to drop. This one even bigger than the last, and I dreaded it. "There's no easy way to say this, Tip. She's with Malecon."

"*What?*" Her voice heated, her anger palpable as it seared through my shields. "Are you fucking kidding me? Tell me you're not serious." She turned to Bailey. "Tell me this is—"

I pointed back to the couch. "Please. Sit down. It isn't what you think. *He* isn't what you think."

"He's a murderer. He's a psychopath who should have stayed dead. He's—"

"He's trying to save his sister, Tip. I know it's hard to digest. I had a hard time with it, too, but he knew something was wrong with her and he offered to do what he can to help."

"And, just like that, you *let* him?" She turned to Bailey again, her eyes boring into her. "What the hell were *you* thinking? You know better than this! Have you all lost your minds? Malecon? Fucking Malecon?"

"Easy, chief. Desperate measures," Bailey said quietly. "And we are at that point of desperation. Melika wants her brother with her. That's her call, Tip, not ours. Not ours and not yours."

Tip stared at me, waiting.

"Apparently, he's changed. When he heard she was sick, he came immediately. And like Bailey said, it's not our call. Mel wanted him with her, and now he's spending his time with Melika on the bayou."

Tip sat there shaking her head. Finally, she muttered, "I don't like it. I don't like it at all." She looked to me and whispered, "Is this why I can't hear her?"

I nodded. "The tumor is why she hasn't been able to communicate with *any* of us."

She blinked rapidly, but the tears came anyway. "I need some air." Grabbing Gar's parka, she ran out the front door before even putting it on.

Bailey came to her feet, but I stopped her.

"I'll go after her. Everyone else just get ready." Grabbing a parka and gloves, I followed Tip out the front door. I found her on one knee in the snow, sobbing the kind of sob that wrenches your soul from your body. It was the kind of pained weeping that burns your insides and makes your heart ache. My arms were around her in a heartbeat and she clutched onto me for dear life, burying her face in my neck and sobbing.

I knew the depth of her despair—that sickening feeling of being left alone by someone you can't imagine living without. I'd been battling it myself for days. "Shhh. I got you, Tip. I'm here."

She hugged me so hard I could barely breathe.

"No, no, no, no." She cried. "Not Mel. Not her. Not now."

I rocked her in the snow, oblivious to the cold. "Shhh. She's not in any pain and she's happy to have Malecon with her. They are exhausting all options to see if there is anything they can do to shrink it." I held her as she cried out, slowly releasing the pain of the truth with every tear.

Wiping her face, she pulled back and looked into my eyes. "Promise me she's not in any pain. Swear to me."

Brushing her hair away from her face, I nodded. "I promise. She's not in any pain. She's lost some of her abilities, but it doesn't hurt her. She's not afraid, either, and she's not alone. She has the one person with her she truly wants." I kissed her forehead and wiped her cheeks. "I'm so sorry you had to hear it like this." I had never seen her like this...so distraught, so afraid. It rattled me to the core to see her this way, but I understood why. I'd been there, only I didn't have Tip's arms to crawl into.

"I couldn't figure out why I stopped hearing her."

"We all have. The tumor has shut down that particular component of her powers, and who knows what others? She's conserving her energy to battle the tumor."

Tip wiped her face with the sleeve of Gar's big jacket. "I want to call her."

I shook my head. "I've tried. She hasn't answered in a couple of days, but don't worry, Malecon said he would—"

Holding her hand up, she shook her head. "I'm sorry, but

it's too weird hearing you talk about Malecon without some expletives. I can't believe he's still alive. You really don't think he's a danger?"

"So far, he has been the best thing for her. He dotes on her, has consulted all sorts of specialists all over the world, and is taking really good care of her. He has the money and the means to make sure no stone is unturned."

"You really trust him? Just like that?"

I looked out into the darkness, feeling the strange tingling of a few wild animals in the mist. "I do. To be honest, he's been a lifesaver. He's totally devoted to her. But if it'll make you feel better, you can call her and leave a video message."

"I'd like that." Tip rose and pulled me up with her. "Thank you, Echo."

"It's what we do, Tip. It's just the way we are with each other."

She stared down into my eyes, but I couldn't make out anything in the dark. "Losing the two women I love most in the world will wreck me, you know? I…I don't know what I'll do or how I'll manage all of this without you."

"You won't have to. I promise. We will get through this together."

She nodded, fresh tears coming. "Promise."

I pulled her to me and held her until it was just too cold. "Can we go in? I think I am freezing to death."

We went back into the house—she peeled off to the bedroom to get herself together, and I grabbed my vidbook.

"She okay?" Bailey asked.

I shrugged. "She needed to know. It was bound to happen sooner or later. It wasn't quite how I envisioned it, but improvisation is just how we roll."

Taking Tip the vidphone, I handed it to her. "Be upbeat, Tip. Be happy, and keep smiling. She needs positive energy."

Closing her eyes, Tip centered herself in the same way she had taught us all those years ago. "Will do." Opening the vidbook, she grinned. "Hi Dani."

"Hey there, Tip. Good seeing you. You bring my girls home soon, will you?"

"I'm trying, but I think they are the ones who will be bringing me home."

"As long as you all get home safely, I don't care who leads. Just come home soon."

"We're trying."

"I'll call as soon as we get their coordinates."

I left Tip alone and returned to the great room where the others were waiting. "She's leaving Mel a message."

Bailey joined me by the fire. "Are *you* okay? That couldn't have been easy."

"No it wasn't. I've never seen her cry like that before. It was tough seeing her like that, but she'll step up. She always does."

"And my other question, E? How are *you*?" she lowered her voice. "I saw the look on your face when she sprung that girlfriend news on us. You all right?"

I turned away from the kids and whispered, "It was a shock to hear she has a girlfriend, but so do I, and..." I paused. How could I really call Finn my girlfriend when I'd barely kept in contact with her since I'd been here? What kind of girlfriend was I when, the moment I had Tip back, I hadn't given Finn a second thought?

"Echo?"

I looked at Taylor, who had obviously asked a question. "I'm sorry."

"I asked if you have anything else you need us to do besides wait, and are you sure you want me to go instead of Tip?"

"I do. Tip is still recovering from the massive amounts of sedatives they shot into her, and after hearing about Mel, her head won't be fully in the game. No, she needs to stay here and I need you with us."

Bailey whispered, "You sure?"

"I am. This should be a simple collection...well, not simple, but, we want to get in, out, and go home."

"You're the boss."

"Thanks." Glancing at my watch, I realized we had less than an hour before the GPS would lead us to the triplets. Loco had finally fallen asleep, and Gar was doing his rounds. The kids were sitting at a chessboard playing chess, and I could feel Tip's energy depleting. She was physically exhausted before, but now, she was emotionally drained as well.

"You need to talk to Tack. He says he can help."

Cinder had taken an immediate liking to the boy. I couldn't blame her. Ever since she came into my life, she'd had no friends her age.

"How? We don't know anything about his powers. Too unpredictable."

"Try him."

I looked at her. "You sure?"

She nodded. *"You have to learn to trust more, Echo. What good is your power if you don't follow what it tells you."*

"When did you get so smart?"

She smiled but didn't say anything.

Kneeling down, I made Tack face me. "Tack, would you mind telling us a little about your powers?"

He bowed his head, slightly embarrassed by all the attention. "Like I told you, Mr. Reynolds calls me Tack because I'm a technopath. That means I can figure out how to work almost anything electronic or technological. My mind fires like a computer when I'm figuring out how something works. With some electronics, I can even change how they work. I can shut some powers off, I can reroute others."

I was impressed. He was very young to have such control already. "No control on that last one, huh?"

He nodded.

"Telepathy?"

"No, ma'am."

"TK?"

"No ma'am. Wait. I can't move things, but I can move energy like in wires and stuff." He looked up at me. "Can I go with you?"

"I'd love to take you, Tack, but I can't risk it right now. I need to know more about how your powers operate first."

"But you'll let me come to your school?"

Messing up his hair, I nodded. "Absolutely, but we'll have to check with your parents first. Are they alive?"

"Yes, ma'am."

"Well, we'll see what we can do about that, okay?"

"Okay."

Just then, Tip came out.

"You okay?"

Nodding, she handed the vidbook back to me. She had cleaned up and looked better. "I need a few minutes alone, if you don't mind," and out the front door she went.

"She'll be fine," I said. "Just give her some time."

Opening the vidbook, I called Finn from the bedroom, and was so glad she answered. From her position, it looked like she was in her kitchen.

"Echo! Damn, I've been worried sick! I'm so glad to see you!"

Setting the vidbook on the dresser, I let out a loud sigh. God, I was missing her more than I thought. "You look great." And she did. Her eyes had their flirty luster back and her color had returned as well.

"Getting stronger every day. Shoulder hurts like hell, but at least I'm not in the hospital. That food was taking years off my life. How are you, love? You look tired."

"I'm hoping to wrap this thing up tonight and be on the plane in the morning."

"Awesome. Feels like forever since I've kissed you. I'd give anything just to put my arms around you."

As good as that sounded, I needed more than mere words right about now. I needed some sort of direction only Finn could give. "Finn?"

She stopped talking.

"When I get home, I want to sit down and talk about where we are going with all of this."

"Going?"

"Yeah. What *are* we? A couple? Fuck buddies? Friends with benefits? Just pals? What in hell are we doing here? I want that conversation. No, I *need* that conversation. So many things are unsure in my life right now. I need something consistent. I need to know if we are on the same page."

She ran her hand over her face. "Consistent? Whoa. Echo, maybe I haven't made it very clear, but I'm in love with you. I'd love nothing more than for us to be exclusive...to be a couple, and now is probably not the best time to have this discussion, but if you're asking what you mean to me...well, I'm not interested in seeing anyone else. I'm just waiting for you to come to your senses and be mine."

My eyes washed over her face. "Officer Finn, I'm more yours than you realize."

Leaning closer to the camera, she whispered. "Let me ask you one thing. Is Tip with you?"

The question caught me off guard. "Yes she is, but—"

Finn held her hand up. "That's all I need to know. We'll talk about her, about us, about your relationship when you get home. I won't have this conversation with her around."

"Finn—"

"I'm sorry, Echo," her voice was as cold as the ground around us. "But I really don't want to have this discussion on the phone. I deserve better than that. Just know I really do love you, and I'm glad you called. I've been missing you." The warmth from her eyes was gone now, replaced by what could only be suspicion and distrust.

"I miss you, too."

There was an awkward silence we seldom experienced together.

"I'd better go."

She nodded. I could tell this conversation had saddened her. We hung up without any mushy sentiments or hugs and kisses. I should never have called her when I was still feeling raw about Tip's news. It had been a huge mistake.

As an empath, I may be capable of sensing other emotions, but I seldom recognized my own. It was one of my greatest weaknesses, and Finn knew it. She knew I still had feelings for Tip, that I probably always would. Hell, she probably even guessed why I had called.

Before I realized it, before I was even aware that I had, I called Dani. "I have one question. Am I a crappy girlfriend?"

She squinted into the camera. "Shit. That's a tough one. I guess it depends on which girlfriend you're talking about."

"Great." I felt foolish for even bringing it up. "I seriously suck, huh?"

"You don't look so good. What happened?"

I told her about Tip seeing someone else. "I guess I wasn't ready for what that means or how to feel about it."

"Uh-uh. No you don't, girlfriend. This is a *good* thing. It's a *healthy* thing. You two need to push past whatever feelings linger between you. It is time to move on, Clark. Actually, it is way past time."

"It's not just that. Finn so often…feels like an afterthought, and I'm pretty sure she feels that way, too."

"Well, that's not good, but Jesus, Clark, look at your life. You haven't even had time to enjoy the luxuries at the chateau. You're globetrotting all over the place putting out one fire after the next. Until you tell her the truth, she'll always be on the periphery. She'll always be on the outside looking in. Besides, now is not the time for you to even be worrying about this. Focus in! Do your job and then come home and clean up your emotional bed."

"That's just it, Dani, now is *never* the time, and Finn is never a priority. Am I just doomed to not have a relationship?"

"Once you get settled into the chateau, you'll have plenty of time to see Officer Yummy and get your bearings. That's all you need, you know. Just finish this and come home. We'll take care of the rest. I promise."

I looked out at the darkness. It was darker than dark out. "Dani, I have a bad feeling about this. I don't know what it is, but I can't shake it. Maybe it's because Hayward is so calm even under these conditions."

"What are you planning on doing with your…with the Professor?"

"Make him get me as close as he can to Kip Reynolds, and cough up information we can use against Genesys."

"You're not going to…kill him?"

"I want to, I really do, but I don't have it in me right now. Not because he was my father, but because I don't think Melika would kill him. We don't kill naturals just because we hate them or disagree with what they're doing. If I don't follow her code, then what good am I as a mentor?"

"Your creepy-ass sister would disagree. She'd already have finished him off."

She was right on that account. If Kristy had her way, everyone in Genesys would die a horrible death.

"I'm not Kristy, and I don't believe in their ways. I'll think of something."

"You know, with you sinking his battleship, he'll go to ground. He will be even harder to find."

"Let him. There's no place he can hide, no place they can go where we won't find him. And I *will* find him, but first, I have to train my kids...build an army, as it were. I won't go in unprepared. Mel wouldn't. Tip wouldn't. I won't. We're done letting them hunt us. Done."

"That's a one-eighty from Mel's point of view. If you want the backing of the Others, you probably won't get it with that attitude."

"I realize that, but Dani, they're a bunch of retired psions living in the quiet comfort of the San Juan Islands. They are not part of this world anymore. They sit up there like gods on Mount Olympus, dictating what we, who *do* live here in the real world, ought not to do. Well, I won't have it. I won't sit around letting a group of octogenarians tell me how to live my life."

"They saved your life once."

"I'm grateful for what Rose and Lily did, but saving my life has only led me to want to save others. This is something I have to do, Dani. If I don't, they'll never stop coming after Cinder."

Danica's eyes narrowed. "They want her that badly?"

I nodded. "Yes."

"Then let's fuck them up but good."

I tried not to smile. "That's the plan."

"And when will you do this? You've sent them a warning, thrown down the gauntlet, so to speak."

"Right. They'll be scrambling for sure, but we're a long way off from going after Kip Reynolds. We have homework to do, and intel to gather."

"And armies to train."

I grinned. "And armies to train. Look, I'm not planning on teaching these kids how to kill. I just want them all to be aware of those out there who would do them harm if they could. I understand Mel tried to give all of us the good life, a normal life, but we're not normal. I just want the kids to know both sides of the coin...good and bad."

"Fair enough. Well, the chateau is ready for you and your charges. Sal finished up the last of the security measures. Connie has the whole thing wired like something from a James Bond flick, and the boys have added their own touches to make this the most technologically advanced house in northern California. All permits are signed, sealed and delivered. Everything is a go."

"I'll take everyone out to dinner when I get back."

"What have you decided to do about your job?"

"When I asked Wes if I could take a year to just do contract work, he gave me the green light. He doesn't want to lose me and he knows I can write my own ticket just about anywhere else."

"That's a good idea. You need some balance, Clark. I won't let you be like Mel was—chained to the bayou. He may not want to lose you, but *you* don't want to lose you, either. The paranormal world can eat you alive. You need more than just that. Keeping your hand in the news game is a great idea."

"I've already been writing an article in my head about dog sledding and the guys who run them."

"Perfect. You just need balance, Clark. Once you get that, you can make the hard decisions. Don't do anything about Finn until you find center."

My watch urged me to finish the conversation, and so we said our goodbyes and I rejoined everyone in the great room—everyone including Tip.

"Leaving me here is a good idea, Echo. When I get back to one hundred percent, I'm going to crush Hayward's shields and clean him out...see what he knows, what he won't tell us about Genesys. I'll pull every goddamn piece of intel from his messed up head. Once I have that, do you want me to fry his brain?"

She was serious.

"No. We're not Kristy's group, and we won't start acting like them. I want him alive long enough to explain a few things later. You get what you can, but no frying his mind." Touching her arm, I kept her from walking away. "You okay?"

Her eyes welled up again, and I was amazed at all her

emotions. Tiponi Redhawk embodied the word "stoic," so it was strange seeing her so emotional.

"I'm mad at her for not telling me, I'm mad that it happened, pissed off that I'm here in the fucking cold dealing with these assholes instead of in Louisiana helping Mel. I'm irritated that Malecon, who doesn't deserve her, gets to be with her while she goes through this. I'm just angry all over, which is better for me right now than feeling this chasm of sadness threatening to swallow me whole."

"We'll get through this, Tip. I swear we will."

Cocking her head, she pushed her tears away. "That's just it, Echo. There is no *we* anymore. Jacob Marley is dead. Zack is busy living a normal life. Mel is dying, and you...you have your hands full with..." She waved her arms around. "All of this."

All of this. This was a lot. Tip would need time to process what Mel's death would mean to her. She would need time to prepare. Now that she had someone else, I didn't doubt Tip would hightail it back to the bayou...to her home. She would not be joining me in the mentoring process. That ship had sailed. I would need another number two.

"You'll be heading home after this, then?"

She nodded. "I'm taking Ivonne back with me. She's really looking forward to seeing New Orleans. How soon can we get the hell out of here once this is done?"

"Private jet waiting for us in Nome. We can leave at first light."

"Private jet? Don't tell me Danica finally bought herself a Lear."

"It's rented, although, Malecon did offer his."

She cursed under her breath.

"Let it go, Tip. If Mel trusts him, we can do no less. If you can't trust her judgment, trust mine."

"It doesn't bother you she's not answering her phone? It doesn't seem odd that—"

I held up my hand. "I can't worry about that right now. He came when she needed him most, no strings attached other than the chance to make amends with Melika. He has. Let it go and try to focus on what we're doing now."

She turned away angrily. "You may forgive and forget, Echo, but not me. I'll hate that asshole forever."

"You do that, but not around Mel. If you go home, you're going to have to suck it up around him. I'll not have you bringing discord to her in her final days."

Tip whirled around. "You'll not *have* me? Who the hell do you think you are?" She towered over me, eyes blazing. "Look, I know you're her replacement, but don't think for one second—"

"Tip, hold on—"

"No, Echo, *you* hold on! Don't you think for one minute you have stepped into her shoes and can start telling me what I can and cannot do. You're a fucking rookie. A newbie. Don't you ever presume—"

"Tip—" I felt my ire heat up my neck and cheeks.

She threw her hands up. "Talk about getting too big for your britches. I mean, really. Who the fuck do you—"

Before she could finish, Bailey was in between us shoving Tip backward with both hands so hard, she lost all the air in her lungs when she crashed into the wall. "*She's* Melika's replacement, asshole, so fucking back off!" Bailey stood in the fighting position, ready to do something for me I'd never seen her do: actually fight.

Tip's eyes flared and she made a move like she was going to retaliate, so Bailey bridged the gap and stepped right up on Tip. "I said, back off! The way you protected Melika is the exact same way I am going to protect Echo, so if you don't want to be spitting your teeth out, you'll take it down a few notches."

"Bailey," I said. Tip could drop her to her knees on a good day. Today was not one of those.

"You move, Tiponi Redhawk, and I'll take you out." Bailey pushed her face closer to Tip's. They were almost the same height. "And if you doubt that I can, try me."

Tiponi looked from me, to Bailey and back to me. "You really think you can replace Melika? Just like that? Step in and start commanding everyone around you? You have no idea what you're doing. You drag a child to Alaska when you should have—"

"That's enough," I said coolly. I nodded and gently pulled Bailey off her. Tip's energy was waning. "Melika handed the reins over to me, Tiponi. Me. As hard as it may be for you to accept, I am now a mentor and I am calling the shots. So you can accept that and help or you can get the hell out of my way. It's your call."

"When did all of this happen?"

"It's been on the burner for a while, but you knew that. None of this is a surprise to you so why are you acting like such a horse's ass?"

She sat down, holding her head in her hands. "I guess you're right. I guess there's a whole helluva a lot changing and I am just having a hard time accepting it all."

Bailey backed out of the room taking everyone else with her and leaving us alone again.

Sitting next to her, I did not touch her. "You need to accept it. I need you to accept it. Hell, I'd love it if you supported it, but I'll settle for acceptance."

She shook her head slowly before looking up at me. "I do accept it, but you're asking me to accept more than that, aren't you?"

I knew it for the rhetorical question it was. "It's what Mel wants."

"Will you move to the bayou?"

The question surprised me for a split second until I remembered she hadn't been privy to my thoughts for quite some time. "No. Danica bought a winery in Marin and has—"

"California? You're going to try to teach supernaturals in San Francisco?" She shook her head. "It'll never happen." Standing, she pushed by me, her anger palpable. "And you're a fool to think that it will. The bayou is the only place safe enough from prying eyes." She shook her head again. "Your first major decision is for shit."

"Thanks for the vote of confidence. You don't even know what—"

She whirled around. "I don't *need* to know! I know what's worked in the past! I know what Mel did was safe and sane, but apparently you're too good for that. Apparently, you're too good for the bayou."

"It's not that, Tip, it's just—"

"Save it, Echo. You go after those triplets for your own little mentoring program, but I'm going back to Louisiana where I belong."

With that, she walked out of the house.

"Tip!" I started after her, but Bailey stopped me.

"Let her go, E. We don't have time for this bullshit."

I shrugged, feeling winded. "She's just hurting over the news about Mel. That's…that's all."

"Well, let her take it out on someone else. What she said was mean and vicious whether or not she's hurting."

"Cut her some slack, Bailey, please."

"*You* cut her slack. We've got work to do." Bailey pointed to the clock on the wall. Two minutes to midnight.

As I watched the clock, my heart slowly broke into tiny pieces. I had just lost Tip, felt like I was losing Finn, and was scared to death I'd lose the triplets as well. Was this what I had to look forward to as a mentor? Was this why Melika had always been alone? The weight of my supernatural world settled heavily on my chest, but I really didn't have time to feel it or deal with it. Bailey was right: we had work to do. My personal issues would just have to wait.

With thirty seconds to go, Tip came back in. She moved toward me but Bailey slid in front of her.

"You need to back off, Tiponi. *You* may not recognize her as your leader, but the rest of us do, and I'll protect her from anyone. Anyone including you."

Tip narrowed her eyes at Bailey. "You know, I could drop you like that." Tip snapped her fingers. "Even at half my speed."

Bailey pulled herself up so she was eye-to-eye with Tip. "Bring it."

"That's enough." I started toward them when the vidbook buzzed. It was time.

"Okay, Clark. Great news! Your triplets sent us a GPS signal for barely a blip on the clock, but we got it."

"Excellent. How far?"

"In between Brevig Mission and Wales. Not too far, really. Based on the topo, you have one of two choices: Try to make your way in the dark or wait till dawn and take the chopper. One's sneakier, one's faster. Your call."

Yes it was. "We'll wait till dawn, then take the helicopter. It'll be faster and safer."

"Those kids are with Ivonne, and they've been out there far too long," Tip growled, "and *she* is worth the risk of going *now*."

I silenced Bailey with a look. "I didn't say we *weren't* going. I said—"

"I *heard* you." Tip walked to the door. "We're leaving at dawn? That's how you're going to play this?"

"Not playing, Tip. It's the smartest decision under the circumstances."

"Under the circumstances, if *I* were leading this and *you* were out in the fucking freezing weather, I wouldn't still be standing here arguing. But that's just me." With that, she was gone.

"Damn, harsh, Redhawk," Taylor muttered when Tip blew by her. We all joined the kids and I pulled everyone together.

"Cinder, go get some sleep. You, too, Tack. I'll wake you at five so you can have breakfast before we go."

They were so tired they didn't even put up a fight.

Once they were gone, I sat in front of the fire, refueling my own waning energy. Hayward was asleep, his chin on his chest, but not Loco. His ability to sit still was almost as good as Gar's, and any time Hayward even breathed too loudly, Loco slapped him in the head.

"I'm sorry Tip's being such an ass, E."

"It's okay."

"No, it's not. She was totally out of line and she better start reeling it in or we're going to dance."

"Bailey, *we've* had time to digest the news that Melika is dying. Tip has never known another mother and this came out of nowhere at a time when she's off balance. She's hurting. Please cut her some slack."

Bailey shrugged. "I'll try, but she'd best remember who she's talking to or we're gonna have it out for good. I guaran-damn-tee it."

Taylor stood next to Bailey, held her hand and nodded. "She's right, Echo. Just because she's hurt doesn't give her carte blanche to crap on you. It's best you leave her here. She's too unbalanced by her grief."

"Point taken, but let me handle her, okay? I know her. I know how to handle this. You two get some rest."

"What about you? You need some sleep."

I remembered when I first arrived on the bayou. I slept for twenty-two hours straight. Whenever I woke up, either Mel or Tip or Jacob was in the room watching over me. That was what a mentor and a family leader did; they watched over you. They protected you. They made sure everyone was safe.

That was exactly what I was going to do with or without Tiponi Redhawk's support.

When the first ray of light poked through the cotton-white clouds, the chopper lifted off with me, Bailey, Taylor and Cinder in it. I don't know if Gar slept or not. I was pretty sure he could sleep standing up…and probably did.

We were all quiet as the helicopter made the short jaunt to the little red dot on the vidbook map. We were maybe thirty minutes away by air, and before I knew it, we were landing next to a tiny cabin with a plume of gray smoke curling out of the chimney. It was nearly hidden within a cluster of snow-laden trees that were bending like it hurt.

"Okay. Cinder and I will go in. If anything goes south, Gar, I want you to get them out of here. No questions asked."

"Roger. But by them do you mean—"

"My people come first. If this gets dicey at all, and you have to make a decision, leave the kids."

Bailey and Taylor both said, "Whoa. Wait a second."

I shook my head. "It's not up for discussion. If there's any problem, you guys are out of here. We are not risking anyone else. Period. Are we clear?"

They hesitated before both of them nodded.

"Thank you."

Cinder and I ducked as we ran to the front door of the small cabin. I knocked three times and waited. Cinder had her hands up and ready for fire.

"Ivonne, it's Echo. Echo Branson. Tip sent us."

The door opened and standing in front of me was one of the most beautiful women I'd ever seen. Long black hair, and clear sharp blue eyes that dug into me, questioning. She was Native American mixed with something else. It was hard to tell. I guess I expected her to be Russian. Hell, maybe she was.

"Prove it."

I pulled out my vidbook and showed it to her. "Only our team has these. It's how you let us know where you were. Tip told you to turn it on for one minute at midnight and you did just that. We followed the GPS signal here."

She looked around me at Cinder and then motioned us in. "Helicopter? Nice ride."

"We need to make haste, Ivonne." Cinder and I stood just inside the door as she corralled the sleepy triplets, three adorable towheads, two boys and a girl.

"No need to be rude, Ms. Branson. Some introductions are in order." She set her hand on the first boy. "This is Alexei, he's a TP. This is Boris, a TK, and this little sweetheart is Nika. We aren't sure what she is. So far, she's shown no supernatural powers, but she's a wonderful kid."

Kneeling down, I started to say something when Cinder moved by me. I watched in silence as she tilted her head and then pointed to me. She was talking to Alexei, who could probably communicate with his siblings. I didn't know for sure, but I would when we got back.

Taking Boris's and Nika's hands, Alexei walked up to me and nodded. "We go now."

And so we did, again, in silence. The three children did not huddle together afraid. They sat ramrod straight in the helicopter, looking about, blue eyes curious about their surroundings. I liked them right away. Their lack of fear, their poise, their curiosity, were all traits I wanted in my students.

My students.

I liked the sound of that.

"Hit it, Gar!"

He did, and when we landed, everyone was out waiting for us. I was thrilled we'd made it without any interference or obstacles. I had expected some issues and was grateful there were none.

Everyone piled out, the triplets stopping to stare at Gar as he stood stone-cold still. He must have been close to seven feet tall, but probably looked twenty-seven feet tall to the triplets.

"I need to gas her up, Echo, then the first group can go." Gar looked down at the three blond-headed kids and grinned. "What? You never saw a giant?"

All three shook their heads.

So they understood English, but couldn't quite speak it very well yet. Good to know.

"I give rides."

Before I could stop him, Gar scooped the two boys up in one arm and Nika in the other and swung them all around. "This is what a helicopter really feels like." They all giggled.

"They're sweet," Cinder said.

"Yes, they are."

"They don't speak much English, though."

"They will."

When everyone was out of the helicopter, Ivonne ran to Tip and hugged her for a long time. Their intimacy was evident. I suppose I should have felt something akin to jealousy, but I didn't. Tip deserved happiness, and if Ivonne gave that to her, so be it. I had bigger fish to fry.

"Everyone in by the fire to warm up while Gar gases up the helicopter. I'll go over our exit strategy while we wait."

Nika wriggled out of Gar's grasp and ran back to me. "Choclate?"

"We don't really have—"

"She means hot chocolate, Echo."

"Oh. Hot chocolate? Bailey?"

"Coming up!"

When everyone huddled around the fireplace with a mug of hot chocolate in their hands, I stood with my back to the fire and asked everyone to listen quietly while they enjoyed their drinks. Standing there looking at all of them, something happened to me…in me. I *was* ready for this. I had whatever it was Melika had seen in me to hand the mantle of mentorship to me. This was my family now, and I would make sure they were safe.

"It's going to take two trips to get us all to the airport. We need to act as if Genesys is still out there waiting, which they are. So Tip, Ivonne, Tack, Taylor and Pitt will go in the first group. You can do a little recon and see what you can see. Scout around, get a lay of the land and make sure all is clear. If anything looks hinky, you have time to notify us. That leaves me, Cinder, Bailey, the triplets, Loco and Hayward in the second group. I'm obviously keeping more firepower with us because of Hayward and the triplets. Are there any questions?"

"What plane are we flying out of here again?" Tip asked.

"The only Lear jet on the tarmac. The pilot will be there. He was told to wait and Danica is monitoring the plane. Anything else?"

"What do you want us to do if Genesys does engage us?" Taylor asked.

I didn't hesitate. "Blow them to smithereens. Do not hesitate, do not doubt, do not give them room to escape. Tear them apart."

Pitt, Loco and Tip all nodded as if that was the right answer.

"Look. We all came here to protect these kids and that task doesn't stop until we land in California. Let nothing and nobody stand in our way."

"What about *him*?" Pitt asked, hooking his thumb in Hayward's direction.

"He'll go with us to the airport. Tip's already gotten into his head, so we don't need him any longer."

"What did she find out?" Bailey asked.

"Kip Reynolds does move around a lot, but the main facilities are now in New Mexico and New York. There are, of course, labs in Europe and Asia, but the main lab is in New Mexico. Reynolds is making a big play for all supers under the age of thirteen for experimentation. He is also employing supers over eighteen who are in need of someplace to belong. He's using them as a bait of sorts to attract the younger kids. He offers room, board and big bonuses for those who want to come collect other supers."

"What is their main goal with all this experimentation?" Bailey asked.

Everyone looked at Pitt and Loco.

"Dudes," Loco said. "Like we haven't figured out you all ain't normal." He shrugged. "Don't matter none to us. The Big Guy's never looked better, so it's all good. You can talk in code if you want, but we kinda figured you guys got something over on the rest of us."

I looked to Pitt, who nodded. "We get it, Echo. We don't need to know the specs on this end, so Loco and me will go wait for Gar."

"Thank you."

When they were gone, I returned the floor to Tip.

"Cell mutation," she said softly. "Cell replication. They've received the attention of one Senator Stephen Maxwell, who is all up in the Department of Defense's grill about creating superior ground weaponry. The wars in the Middle East have shown how weak we are on the ground, in Afghanistan, especially. Senator Maxwell has pushed some of his own friends to donate to Genesys through a maze of corporations impossible to locate."

"With what goal in mind?" Taylor asked.

"Creating a super armed force of what Genesys calls TASS, or temporary armed super soldiers."

"You've got to be kidding."

Tip shook her head. "Maxwell wouldn't go for the permanent creation of supernaturals. He feels we're too uncontrollable and unpredictable. What he wants Genesys to do is find a way to *temporarily* enable soldiers to carry just a part of the construct of our cells."

"Like transplanting DNA?"

Tip nodded. "Pretty damn close. These cells could have a short shelf life, thereby preventing soldiers from becoming addicted to their powers, which is always the fear with our powers and naturals."

"Too weird," Bailey said. "Who *wouldn't* want to talk to animals?" She turned to Taylor and softly said, "Now you're *really* in. If you tell anyone, I'll be forced to kill you."

Taylor started to laugh until she realized Bailey wasn't kidding. "I'd never betray that trust, Bales, you know that. It's not in my character. I have lots of secrets locked up in here." Taylor tapped on her temple. "And not even torture could tear it from me."

Bailey nodded. "I know. That's why you're here. I just need to make sure you understand how important it is that our secret be kept. It would change everything if it got out."

Tip cleared her throat. "I think she gets it. Moving on. Genesys believes they can re-create our genetic makeup and temporarily create soldiers, or a Cinder who could walk into a camp full of soldiers and blast them to ashes in a single moment and more effectively than a drone missile and without civilian casualties. They have practically guaranteed it to the senator."

"Shit..." Taylor muttered, then covered her mouth as she glanced at the triplets. "Sorry."

"We all know our powers are all pretty amazing, especially since no metal detector or detector of any kind can sniff us out. We are invisible, and would make the perfect soldiers for even more undercover operations such as political assassination."

"So they want to create more Cinders?"

Tip nodded. She still looked tired, but she had rebuilt all of her walls and I could barely read her. "Hell yes, but there's one set of powers the military has been trying for years to tap into and that's remote viewing."

"Astral projection in the military?" Taylor said, shaking her head. "You've got to be kidding me. That's the stuff science fiction is made from."

I smiled softly. "*We* are the stuff science fiction is made from."

"I wish I were kidding, but I'm not. In nineteen seventy, a research program called SCANATE was funded by the CIA at Stanford Research Institute. In nineteen seventy-nine, hundreds of remote viewing experiments began using dozens of individuals who possessed a certain level of psionic capabilities. In nineteen eighty-three, the Department of Defense trained four US Army officers and a female civilian in remote viewing. In nineteen ninety-one, a United Nations team approved the US military section PSI TECH for help in locating bioweapons facilities. By that time, everyone was questioning PSI TECH's usefulness, so Senator Maxwell approached Kip Reynolds at Genesys. PSI TECH moved to Seattle in two thousand, which prompted the Others to relocate as well to the San Juan Islands, so they could more closely monitor their actions. In two thousand and one, PSI TECH built a research facility in rural Hawaii. If you go to their website, you'll see them admit to being involved in technical remote viewing, or TRV. They've now become all about making money from their "students."

"Okay, okay," Bailey said, holding up her hands. "What does this have to do with Genesys and these three adorable kids?"

Tip ran her hand over Boris's head. "Remember Rose and Lily, a.k.a Nitro and Glycerin?"

Who could forget two octogenarian supers who, when touching each other, created an explosion like a miniature atom bomb? They had saved our bacon once. I would never forget it.

"When they touch, their power is quadrupled. We saw it in New Orleans. Well, these two boys, when they touch, have the remote viewing capability." Tip paused here while we all processed this.

"They're remote viewers?"

"Only when touching, and only when both are concentrating on a specific locale, but yes. They are remote viewers, and our Senator Maxwell wants them badly."

Taylor raised her hand. "Umm, excuse the ignorance of a mere mortal, but by remote viewing, what exactly are you talking about?"

"Remote viewing, in the simplest sense, is the ability to acquire information about things, even events, far away physically, as well chronologically. It's a data collection skill. A very valuable data collection skill that would allow our military intelligence to extract information without putting bodies at risk."

I nodded, wondering how in the hell I would be able to teach these kids something I knew so little about.

"That's why Genesys is moving mountains to get to them. Senator Maxwell and the Department of Defense would pay enormously for any sign of proof that remote viewing exists. The CIA would finally be able to *validate* their expenses on all sorts of psionic experiments. This would open up all sorts of doors for the CIA, the DOD, the FBI and the NSA."

"Wait," Taylor said. "So the government *knows* you all exist and are coming after you all the time?" She slowly nodded.

"Hence the layers of security at the chateau. It's all beginning to make so much more sense now."

We all nodded.

"They know, but can't prove it, and, quite frankly, don't want to. They want to keep a lid on any potential human weapons. They would keep our secret even tighter than we do because it would be strategically advantageous to do so. They would set up experimental facilities so far underground, you'd need a ten mile long drill to get to it. We would become human guinea pigs and then, human weapons of mass destruction."

Bailey looked at me. "That's why you're all fired up to go after them, huh, E? If we don't start protecting ourselves, we'll never be free from not only Genesys, but our own government and every other one seeking a way to replicate what we can do."

I nodded. "Yes. With or without the Others' support, I intend on putting an end to these secret, privately funded science projects. I am done hiding. Done running. I want to go on the attack and send a really loud message." My eyes locked onto Tip's. We stayed that way for a protracted moment before I looked away.

She opened her mouth to say something, but just then, Pitt walked in from outside. "Everybody ready?" he asked, letting the cold air sweep into the room.

As the first wave of us filed out of the cabin, Tip walked over to me, leaned over and whispered, "You and your personal vendetta are on your own after this. Ivonne and I will be returning to the bayou as soon as we can. Respect my wishes and don't come back."

I blinked and tried to catch my breath. "What? Tip—"

"No, Echo. I mean it. *Don't* come back. Don't call. Just... don't. We're done here." With that, she turned on a dime and walked out.

Bailey passed her, and glanced over at me. "You okay?"

I wasn't, but I had no choice but to be. "Yeah. Time for a change."

"E, she's being an asshole. Hell, she's always an asshole. Stay focused here. We just need to get out of this godforsaken ice cube and then we can get started on those changes."

Following Tip out to the helicopter, I made sure all vidbooks were accounted for, and that everyone understood what to do when they got there. Once everyone was fastened in, I signaled to Gar to take off, and stepped back into the doorway to watch the chopper lift off.

I felt Bailey behind me, her chin resting on my shoulder. "So close to the finish line. I gotta say, I don't know if I will ever come back here. This place is desolate. It is cold, devoid of color, and did I mention it's cold?"

"But the shaman—"

"I know. I'd love to come learn from her, but I can't stand this cold. I need me some good old California sunshine."

I turned and studied her. "You really do love Taylor, don't you?"

She answered, her eyes glued to the helicopter as it got smaller and smaller, "I'm pretty sure I do. She makes me laugh. She's sensitive and caring. She's smoking hot, and to top it all off, she's taken all of this quite well, don't you think?"

"Under the circumstances, yeah. I'm pretty sure she's never been with anyone who talks more to creatures than to humans." Closing the cabin door, we both went back to the fireplace and fed it one last log. "She does seem to care about you, and she has that edge to her that makes her like living dangerously."

"Which is kinda how our lives have been recently, huh?"

I shook my head. "I so want some peace and quiet. I could use a break from all this."

"I'm sorry about Tip."

I shrugged, not at all feeling committed to the action of nonchalance. "It was bound to happen. We've been orbiting around *can't live with her and can't live without her* land for far too long. Maybe it's better this way."

"She didn't have to be such an ass about it."

"She just needs time, and I am an easy target right now."

"Don't shoot the messenger, you know? I don't know...I guess I just expected her to come be your right-hand man, like always. I sure as hell didn't think she'd be all up in your grill."

Shrugging, tears welling up once more, I said, "I guess we all thought so. Tip is a complex woman. If she doesn't want me in the bayou, then I'll respect her wishes. She has obviously decided it was time to move on, and she was right. It is."

"Give her some time," Bailey said. "She'll be back."

Wiping my eyes, I shook my head. "No, Bailey, I don't think she will. Not for a long time. If ever. The bayou is all she knows. It's her home. I was foolish to think she would leave there and come to San Francisco with me." I caught Cinder's eye and suddenly realized I had no time to feel sorry for myself or sad that Tip was so angry with me—or with life—or with whatever she was feeling. I had these kids who were counting on me to be strong, to be clear-headed, and that was precisely how I was going to be.

"Okay, everyone, I want you all to double-check every room. Make sure we close this place up tight. When Tip calls, I want everyone to be ready for that helicopter. Go."

As everyone scattered, I went over to Mr. Hayward and kicked his shoe to wake him up. "Wake up." I ripped the tape off his mouth and it made a satisfying *that must have hurt like hell* sound. "Okay, dickweed, here's how this is going to go down. We got what we needed from you, so we're going to kick your ass to the curb halfway between here and Nome. You survive the cold, good for you. You don't…" I shrugged. "One less asshole on the planet."

"You…you can't be serious. I'll freeze out there."

"Not my problem. You, sir, are not ever going to be my problem again. If you live, you tell Kip Reynolds I'm coming for him. You tell him there is no place he can hide that I won't find him. Tell him I'll come after his children, his grandchildren, and his motherfucking dog if he pushes me. You make sure he knows this is never going to end well for him. If, of course, you die, Reynolds will still get the message. Either way, I couldn't give a shit what happens to you. You've been dead to me for so long, you're like talking to a ghost."

"You *should* care, Charlie. If I make it back to Nome, *I* will come gunning for you and everyone you care about. I'm not someone to be trifled with, Echo."

"Shut the fuck up, Hayward. You're right. I'm not a killer, and as much as I would love to kill you, I have to set an example for those kids *you* would torture. So I'm going to let nature choose your fate." I leaned down in his face. "But, FYI. You *ever* come back into my world, I'll make sure the death you experience is filled with a kind of pain you read about. So don't sit here threatening me, you arrogant bastard." I retaped his mouth before he said something I'd regret doing something about. "Because in the end, you're a dead man."

Back at the fire, Cinder came up to me and put her arms around my neck. *"We can do this, Echo. Dani can be your right-hand man. I'll be your left foot."*

Smiling, I brushed her hair off her shoulder. "Dani's a natural, Cinder."

"And?"

Boris walked over to Hayward and tilted his head from side-to-side as he studied him.

"What can I do for you, Boris?"

Before I could stop him, Boris landed a telekinetic punch that sent Hayward reeling against the wall and bouncing from it like a pinball, the chair still firmly attached to him.

"Boris!"

"Bad man."

"Yes, he is, but there's no need to hurt him. That's not how we do things here."

Boris shook his head and walked away, muttering. "Bad, bad man."

"He's right. I can take care of him. Just say the word."

"No, Cinder. We aren't going to become those kind of people."

"You aren't, but I am already one of those kinds of people." With that, she walked back to the bedroom, leaving me a bag of guilt I'd been struggling with since she first killed for me.

Not long after Cinder went into the bedroom, I got a call from Tip that they had arrived without incident. They had decided it was safer to land outside the airstrip so as to not tip off Genesys.

It was a smart maneuver on Tip's part. She would have made the perfect counterbalance to the way I lead, but that was a pipe dream. When we landed in California, Tiponi Redhawk would leave me once more, this time for good.

"Bringing her down here!" Gar yelled, pointing to a patch of snow.

I nodded and moved next to Hayward. "Your stop."

We landed and I shoved Hayward out on the snow and pushed him away from the propellers so I wouldn't have to yell when I spoke.

"Okay, you disgusting piece of shit...if you make it back, and are foolish enough to bother me or mine again, I *will* let Cinder turn you into a pile of ashes. So listen up here, Mr. Hayward. You ever make another run at Cinder, I will kill you. If you so much as look at my people again, I will feed your eyes to a honey badger. If you so much as even think about me or my sister, I will have you skewered like a boar and roasted over an open flame. Are we clear?"

He stared at me.

"Are. We. Clear?" Tearing the tape off his mouth, I glared at him, the depth of my anger and hatred tangible as I locked eyes with him.

Holding his hands out, he didn't take his eyes off mine. "Crystal clear. You're not going to leave these on me, are you?"

I heard a branch crack behind a tree and shook my head. I knew what that sound was from. "No, I'm not." Pulling out my keychain, I opened the small scissors attached and started to cut it. Reading him, I stopped and watched as a gray wolf wandered out from the woods and sat about ten feet away.

"Unless you really think you can kill me before that wolf rips out your throat, I suggest you table whatever plan of attack you have going through that sick head of yours and just walk away. Do what you did twenty-three years ago and just walk away."

Following my gaze, he turned white and took in a sharp breath. The wolf growled.

"I don't think it likes you. Can't say I blame it."

Standing so he could face me and see the wolf, Hayward tried to regain his composure. "You have no idea the people you are dealing with Charlie."

"Charlie is dead. You killed her. You erased her, so she no longer exists. You killed Kristy as well. You almost killed our mother, but she's a lot stronger than you gave her credit for. Destruction is all you're good for, so let's be really clear here. The next time I see you will be the last breath you take. Now, move along."

"My hands—"

"Will remain bound. To think you believed you could actually attack me with a helicopter full of my people? Hubris, Daddy dearest, and that arrogance must get awfully heavy." Starting back to the chopper, I stopped and said my parting words, "You want to know the best part of you having me erased? I have no memory of you." With that, I joined my friends in the helicopter and headed toward Nome.

When we landed just outside the airport, everyone was waiting in what looked like a bus stop. It wasn't, but could have passed as one.

"You let Hayward go?" Tip asked.

"I did. We're not going to run around killing people, Tip. We'd be no better than them."

She shook her head in disgust so loud I didn't have to read her to feel it.

"Okay, the fact that they haven't blown up our ride tells me they're probably waiting for us." I looked up at Tip. "Now would be the time for all of us who have...weapons, to use them."

Pitt and Loco had rifles slung around their shoulders. "We'll cover you from the shed over there," Pitt said.

I shook my head. "I appreciate the backup, but I can't risk you guys going to jail for murder."

Pitt grinned. "Murder?" Who says anything about murder? You think they're the only ones running around with tranqs?" He grinned broadly. "My mama didn't raise a fool, Echo."

I stared at his rifle. Indeed, it was a tranquilizer gun.

"We've had to use these on some vets who go buggy during detox and take off running into the woods."

I put my arm around his shoulders. "Thank you for all your help. Will you let me know how Suka's doing?"

"Roger. You guys just get on that plane and get the hell out of here. We'll take care of anyone trying to stop you."

Motioning for everyone to gather around, I laid out my plan.

"We pretty much know they're waiting for us to get on that plane. Tip will stay back here with the rest of you while Cinder and I go check the plane out."

"Cinder?" Tip said. "Shouldn't she—"

"She's coming with me, Tip." I interrupted. "You are staying here." I stood as upright as I could in the confined space. She would never have second-guessed Melika in front of everyone. Perhaps her leaving was for the best after all.

"Echo—"

"No Tip. It is not debatable. This is the way we're playing it out. Ready, Cinder?"

She was right at my side.

"E?"

"Yes, Bailey?"

"Be careful. They're gonna be really pissed off and probably wanting to send you the same message you want to send them."

"I know. I'm not afraid. Matter of fact, I'm pretty pissed off myself, so it ought to be a good fight. Just remember…what they want are Cinder and the trips. They won't do anything to harm them."

Cinder and I walked briskly across the tarmac, and I heard the thoom of a tranq rifle shot. Not a bullet sound, but a sedative sound. That was why I took Cinder. Genesys wouldn't risk shooting her by trying to kill me. They would resort to their *modus operandi* and use sedatives. What they didn't know was that I had a field up that protected me just enough from the heat shield Cinder was casting: a shield hot enough to melt a tranquilizer dart before it could reach us.

Cinder heard it, too, because she immediately supernova'd herself, melting anything that came near her. Her heat penetrated my shield, and I barely distanced myself in time to keep from being burned by her heat.

A second thoom rang out, followed by a loud thud. Turning to look, I saw one of theirs on the ground, rifle by his side.

One point for our side.

As Cinder started up the metal stairs, I heard Hummer engines start. Five Hummers were quickly converging on us from all directions like black spiders zeroing in on a fly caught in their web.

Just as Cinder reached the door, I saw *her*, and it was too late for me to shout out a warning to Cinder.

"No! Cinder, look—"

It was too late. Sonja Satre appeared from behind the airplane door just as Cinder reached the top of the metal stairs. With one throw, Sonja knocked Cinder down the steps with a ball of fire I never even saw coming. She moved with lightning quick speed and I was barely able to break Cinder's fall and put out the fire burning her left sleeve.

"That's what happens when you send a child to do a woman's job." Sonja had two fireballs burning in both hands. "And your child is no match for me." She grinned. "Pun intended."

I was afraid to look at Cinder's chest, for fear the ball of flame had burned her badly.

"Cinder? Say something. Are you okay?"

"*Ouch.*" Cinder slowly righted herself. "*Bitch.*" Slowly turning, Cinder raised fireballs of her own.

"Oh look, the child wants more. Well, matchstick, bring it on, because it'll be the last thing you do."

I hadn't expected this. Kill Cinder? That completely went against Genesys' goals.

I held up my hand as Cinder stood protectively between me and Sonja. This was going to end poorly for one of us, and it wasn't going to be us.

"Don't do this, Sonja. We're not alone and don't want to hurt you, but we will if you fire one more fireball."

She laughed. "Of course you aren't alone. You are never alone, Echo. You surround yourself with people stronger than yourself because you know you are impotent as a leader. And your rag-tag group of naturals? Well…they have their hands full as we speak. There is no backup for you this time. You are completely isolated from your people."

Wheeling around, I could make out a flurry of activity beyond the airport proper. Genesys had engaged my people and there was thick animosity pounding at my temples. Five Hummers were heading toward my cadre of soldiers.

"Oh shit." Suddenly, I could feel Cinder's heat as she lowered all her shields.

"*Cinder—*"

"*I got this, Echo. Hit me with a fireball? Oh hell no. Only one time. One time.*"

"Here's the deal, Cinder," Sonja said, dropping the fireballs and turning to me. They sizzled as they hit the snow. "You get in one of those Hummers coming toward us, and I'll let Echo live." Sonja's hands were at her sides, all fingers glowing with whatever power she was going to send my way.

"*No, Cinder. Don't. She'll kill me anyway.*"

"*I know. That's why I have to kill her first...and I* will *kill her, Echo. I'm not afraid of her.*"

"Come on now, little Cinder. You are barely a novice. You cannot possibly believe you have what it takes to beat me. You'll be a pile of burnt bones before you blink."

Cinder stepped up one stair, her hands glowing as well. I wasn't at all sure what to expect from her and I was afraid of dividing her focus, so I said nothing.

Sonja cocked her head in surprise. "You have got to be kidding. You're a minor leaguer, Cinder. I mean it. Echo, call off your precocious peach before she gets hurt. Or worse."

I stepped up behind Cinder. "*I need to get close enough to her to knock her off balance When I do, blast her with everything you have.*"

"*I'm ready.*"

The raucous sounds coming from behind us were getting louder, but I could not take my eyes off Sonja for a second. We stood there, glaring at each other, no one willing to look away. Then, something strange happened. All five Hummer engines died, and they rolled to a stop fifty or sixty yards from the plane, engines completely shut down.

Cinder took advantage of Sonja's slight distraction over this and sent two fireballs at her, knocking her against the far wall of the jet.

"Can't start a fire near our ride, Cin. Be careful."

Cinder got up two more steps before Sonja recovered and fired a flame ball that roared past us.

Looking at the now stopped Hummers, I realized what had happened.

Tack.

He must have shut the engines off and locked our adversary inside. They were all beating on the windows. Good move.

"Echo?"

"Yes?"

"Go under the plane. You're too hard to protect out here."

She was right. I was no match for a full-fledged pyro. The question was, was she?

Before I could get under the jet, I watched in horror as Sonja threw two walls of flame at Cinder, the likes of which I had never seen. They rolled at her like a giant orange tidal wave and hit her with such force it lifted Cinder off the step and threw her to the ground, where she landed on her back, the air forced from her, her jacket on fire.

I started to make my move, but Cinder stopped me.

"Stay there. She'll kill you. Get under the plane."

Sonja came out to the top step and stared triumphantly down at Cinder, who rose slowly. "Stay down, little Cinder. If you know what's good for you, you'll realize this is the major leagues and you are but a minor league rookie. Genesys might want you alive, but I couldn't care less one way or the other. I've already been paid for this gig." Sonja moved to the second step as I prepared a field to knock her off the stairs.

As Sonja came down the third step, Cinder slowly got up, her eyes flaring with so much anger, I could have sworn her pupils looked like flames. "Is that the best you got, old lady?" Cinder said out loud.

Out loud.

I was more stunned by that than anything that had happened thus far in Alaska.

"Don't be a fool," Sonja said, shaking her head. "That was just a warning shot, little girl. Next time, I'll burn you to a crisp."

The sound of breaking glass made us all turn. The guys in

the Hummers were breaking the windows out with the butts of their guns.

Before Sonja could turn her full attention back to Cinder, I reached through the steps and grabbed her ankles while pushing energy at her back, sending Sonja toppling down the stairs in a bone-shattering avalanche of arms and legs. She landed with a loud crunch at the bottom the of steps.

Cinder didn't miss a beat as she threw a fireball at the first Hummer full of people. They quickly scrambled back inside even as the other Hummer windows came crashing out as well. We were woefully undermanned and I couldn't see or feel the rest of us anywhere around.

Stepping out from under the jet, I couldn't get to Cinder or Sonja in time to do anything other than get in the way. So, as Sonja rose to her knees, bloodied forehead and torn sweater, I feared for the worst and prepared to send her every ounce of energy I possessed.

"Cinder!"

Everything slowed down at that moment, as Cinder threw her hands up to defend herself from the flames shooting from Sonja's fingertips like red and orange lightning. It was the greatest show of fiery power I'd seen from a pyro, and had I not been scared out of my wits, I would have been impressed.

As it was, I was scared to death for Cinder, and that fear was all it took for me to ramp up the volume of my own energy resources.

"No!" As I pushed an energy field out at Sonja, she blocked it with energy of her own, knocking me against the hull of the aircraft. Then she returned her attention to Cinder with a wall of flames so hot, I felt it from twenty feet behind her.

I couldn't reach her in time. I knew that like I knew my own name. I was powerless against the heat and flames of Sonja's power, and Sonja was going to fry Cinder while I could only stand by and watch helplessly. It was the worst feeling in the world.

"Run, Cinder!"

Retreat truly was the better part of valor, and in this instance, all I wanted Cinder to do was to live to see tomorrow.

I knew she wouldn't run. Cowardice wasn't in her.

And then, just as the second wall of flames reached Cinder, something happened I would never have believed had I not seen it with my own eyes. Stretching her arms out in front of her, Cinder stopped the flamewall in its tracks and pushed it back. Slowly at first, she held her hands out in front of her and just started walking toward Sonja, who stepped back, bracing herself as her own wall of inferno heat came back to her. Cinder kept walking. Sonja, surprised by this sudden offensive maneuver, pushed back, and Cinder braced herself. The wall stopped between them with neither gaining advantage. There, in between them, swirled flames waiting to reach a target. They didn't care which.

I was going to give Cinder the advantage she needed when the second and third Hummers unleashed their people through broken windows. Some had tranq guns, others had real guns, and Cinder and I were in real trouble.

Whirling toward the first Hummer with three men, I prepared my best shield to protect her, but I knew it wouldn't be enough. My secondary skill of creating and using energy forces wasn't very strong. I might be able to change the direction of a dart, but I wasn't capable of stopping one. I needed far more firepower than I currently possessed.

We were screwed if I didn't think of something.

I resorted to the only power I had left: A human one. If my powers weren't enough, that didn't mean my brain wasn't as well. I had one talent left…one thing I could offer up for Cinder at this moment: My life. Gritting my teeth, I ran toward the Hummers, drawing attention from all three men.

Three rifles swung in my direction. There was nothing I could do but keep coming at them…give Cinder time to…to what? Stay alive against a veteran pyro twice her age? Give her time to make a run for it?

It was the only card I had left and I was going to play it for everything I had.

Or so I thought.

The three tranquilizer darts, which should have hit me, didn't, and the Hummer they'd exited from started up and barreled toward all three shooters who dove out of the way.

Tack. Again.

He was proving to be quite the asset already.

The other Hummers went in reverse just as everyone was trying to get out, spilling people everywhere.

Whirling around, I realized Cinder was losing her battle against Sonja.

Being human worked for me once, so I ran toward her. Sonja didn't bat an eye, and with one huge, final effort, slammed her wall into Cinder so hard she flew back fifteen feet, landing on her back as the flame dispersed and vanished.

Cinder didn't move. She lay there with her arms out like she was doing a snow angel. Sonja strode over to her and I willed Cinder to get up. I screamed at her in my head to get up. Get up, get up, get up.

She didn't.

"Sonja!" I yelled. "You can have the triplets!" The words escaped my lips before I even knew I'd thought them.

Sonja laughed with a sound I'll never forget. Like nails on a chalkboard. Standing over Cinder, Sonja said something as she pulled her right hand back, fireball ready to hurl into Cinder's face. She didn't want the triplets and she couldn't have cared less if Genesys retrieved Cinder or not. All she wanted was to snuff out the competition.

"No!" I could not stop her from where I was. I was helpless to save Cinder from Sonja's attack and a part of me died at the thought.

Then it happened.

I'd felt this once before in my life, over fifteen years ago when I first came into my power. Like a switch was turned on and the marrow of my bones ignited with mercury. It was the sensation of amazing power rippling from my brain to the ends of my fingers and toes.

"Stop!" I yelled, my body throwing off the same energy I'd experienced the day by the creek when Danica was in danger—it was a power I hadn't ever consciously tapped into—a power that, when unleashed, frightened even me. As I felt it course through my veins, my secondary power rose its head and fired an energy field so strong, it blasted Sonja ten feet away from Cinder, ripped into two Genesys shooters, and busted the windshield out of the nearest Hummer. My secondary power, as uncontrollable as it was, knocked down a cyclone fence, a stop sign and several traffic cones.

I couldn't control it. I couldn't stop it. It just pulsed out of my being like a beam from a lighthouse. I was pretty sure I was glowing.

When it stopped, I was breathless, down on one knee, and disoriented. Whatever *that* was, it brought me to my knees and made me slightly nauseous. When I tried to get up, I saw Sonja rise shakily to her feet and face me, holding the ball of flame still in her hand. She was quick, all right, and I was so disoriented, I never saw her throw it, but that ball was coming right at me, and I could barely lift my hands up to protect my face. This was going to hurt, and I had nothing left to stop it. Not one damn thing. The only thing I could think about was that I was glad I wouldn't die alone.

But I wasn't alone.

Just as the ball was within a yardstick of my face, something knocked it out of its path, sending it hurling harmlessly into space.

I knew another was on its way, and tried to stand, but I was spent. Sonja knew it, too, and readied one more fireball.

"Like Little Bit here, you're out of your league, Echo. Expendable. Finished." Raising both hands up, she prepared to blast me one last time when Cinder slowly got to her feet.

"You better have more than that in you."

Sonja blinked and wheeled around, chucking two balls that streaked toward Cinder, who was finally on her feet, but it was too late for her to get out of the way.

To my surprise, she didn't even try.

Instead, she stood up straighter and held up one hand. Both flame balls moved to her as if magnetically drawn, and hit right in the center of Cinder's hand and then... disappeared.

Poof. Gone.

I probably had the same look on my face that Sonja had on hers: awe and disbelief. Cinder had managed to absorb all of Sonja's power.

All of it.

"Im...impossible," Sonja stuttered.

"Was *that* your best, Sonja?" Cinder asked, stepping forward. Her hands were orange and red and it looked like a plume of smoke curled off each finger. "'Cause if that's the major leagues, then I think I'll pass."

I couldn't believe Cinder was talking. She sounded so much older than she did in my head.

Sonja found her own voice. "Cinder, I don't know how you did that, but taking me on would be fooli—"

Cinder hit her so hard with a bolt of something it lifted Sonja off the ground, over the hood of a Hummer and onto the tarmac, where she crumpled like a doll flung from a car on the freeway. Then Cinder fired some kind of fiery bolt of something toward one of the men coming toward her.

It was Rafe and he stopped dead in his tracks when she turned.

"Whoa. Unarmed," Rafe said, holding his hands up in surrender. The fire thing zipped by his head, but I could smell the stench of burning hair.

Before any of us could move, a sixth Hummer crashed through the fence and screeched to a halt in between us. Cinder did not move her gaze from Rafe nor did she lower her hands.

My team piled out, led by Tip, who strode over to Rafe in four giant steps and punched him in the mouth. He was nearly out cold when his head hit the ground. Bailey and Taylor tried to get to Sonja before her guys pulled her into their Hummer, but they managed to drag her in and speed off as my people surrounded us protectively.

Pulling Rafe to his feet, Tip shoved him at us. His nose and upper lip were bloody.

"You deserved that," I said to Rafe. "You're lucky that was all you got. Everyone please get into the jet."

Rafe laughed. "And go where? Do what? You don't even have a pilot."

We all looked at the cockpit window. He was right. Nobody home.

"What the fuck?"

"Everyone has a price, Echo."

"You paid him off?"

Rafe sneered. "What's your price, Echo? I'm sure I can get Genesys to deal."

Bailey and Cinder didn't leave my side, and it was at this odd moment, I realized I already had my right-hand women. I truly could let Tiponi go back to the bayou and still be okay.

"You don't have enough money, Rafe."

"Name it, Echo. You can walk away with a lot of money in your pocket if you just hand over those triplets. Think about it. Think about all the kids you could help if you just walked away."

Pushing past him, I shook my head. "Get away from me, Rafe. We'll be leaving shortly and I'd hate to see you run over by one of those fat wheels."

"Not in that, you won't. Face it Echo, these aren't your rules out here."

Stepping up to him, I growled, "Here is where I prove you wrong."

When everyone was on the plane, I stood at the doorway looking at them. Pitt and Loco stood like two sentries at the bottom of the steps rifles at the ready.

Pitt said over his shoulder, "We need to get you guys out of here. Pronto. They'll be back with more if we don't."

"A pilot would be good."

He nodded. "Gar's already heading back. It'll take us a few to find a pilot. You need to get your people—"

The sound of a chopper interrupted him.

I looked up, expecting to see our helicopter and Gar.

It wasn't him.

Flying over us and then away from us was S.T.O.P; my sister's collection organization.

I'd seen their black helicopter once before. Sleek. State of the art, it looked like a 'copter of the future.

"What the hell?" Pitt yelled, watching it fly overhead. "I've never seen anything like that."

I looked back at my group and made an abrupt decision I hoped wouldn't cost any lives.

"Tack, Cinder, Bailey, Boris. Come with me."

Tip started to get up, and I shook my head. "No. You need to search for a pilot. Pay him whatever he wants. If you find one before we get back—"

"We're not leaving without you."

"Yes you are."

We were locked in a stalemate. To my utter surprise, it was Ivonne who broke it.

"Echo's right, Tiponi. We must save those we can."

Tiponi ignored her. "No fucking way. I am not leaving without her…or the kids. It's not going down like that."

I turned to reply, but again, Ivonne stepped in. "She gave the order, Tiponi. Respect it." To me she said, "We will do that, Echo, if we must, but we'd all rather leave this place together."

"Thank you, Ivonne." I shot a glare over to Tip, happy for the first time in a long time that she was unable to get into my head because I was cursing her out big time.

The five of us ran to the nearest Hummer they'd just got out of, hopped in, and I put the pedal down as we crashed back through the fence after the helicopter.

"Where are we going?" Bailey asked, holding onto the dashboard.

"S.T.O.P didn't see us get on that plane. My guess is they saw Gar on his way back to the airport and think we're in that chopper."

"You think they're coming to help us?"

I shook my head. "They're vultures on this tour…scavenging the collections we've made. Trust me…they are not here to help."

"Crap, Echo. Are we ever going to get off this iceberg?"

I nodded, gripping the wheel tightly. "Today. Soon." As my Hummer four-wheeled over everything in its path, I could see Kristy's chopper just hovering there. They could see Gar's helicopter coming back toward us and then over us.

Coming to a stop, I asked, "Tack, can you bring that chopper down gently?"

He frowned as he thought. "Yeah. I think I can." Closing his eyes, he extended one hand and concentrated on the hovering helicopter. You could hear the engines slowing down.

"Bailey?"

She was halfway out the door before answering. "All over it, though, this close to the city, I'm not sure what I can come up with."

I looked to Cinder. "Well, Chatty Cathy, you got enough left in the tank to do some major damage?"

She smirked and nodded, mute once more. *No killing, right? I mean your sister could be in there.*

I stared at her. "What am I? Chopped liver?"

She grinned and shrugged. *Comes and goes, I guess.*

Rubbing her shoulders, I nodded. "For both of us. No killing. I have a sickening feeling my sister might be in that chopper."

Cinder climbed out of the Hummer, leaving me with Boris.

"When the chopper lands, I need you to keep an eye out on—"

The chopper fell heavily to the ground, damaging both feet in a horrid sound of crunching metal.

"Sorry," Tack said. "All that talking broke my concentration."

When I looked up, I saw my sister trying to get her door open. Thrusting my vidbook to Tack, I said, "Call Gar. Tell him to get the jet out of here. Remind him I know what I'm doing and I want my people safe."

Tack looked up at me, wide-eyed. "Leave? Without us?"

"I don't have time to explain. Just do it. Boris, you relieve anyone of their weapons. I don't want to see one handgun or rifle come out of the chopper, do you understand?"

The little towhead nodded.

I narrowed my eyes at Tack. "And that will be the *last* time you question my decisions."

Kristy's door finally popped open, and we both exited our vehicles at the same time.

Blond hair flowing like a mane, black leather jumpsuit like Taylor preferred, Kristy's blue eyes were on fire as she strode purposefully toward me.

She was angry—that much I didn't need powers to discern. This was not the first time I had gotten in her way, and I doubted it would be the last.

As a scion, she was far more powerful than I, but that didn't matter. I was not afraid of her or anyone else at this point. They wanted the triplets as well and I wasn't about to give them up.

"God damn you, Charlie! Why couldn't you stay the fuck away?"

I stopped walking and stood with Bailey on my left and Cinder on my right—a formidable triad if ever there was one. "You're entering the game at the two-minute warning, Kristy? You think you can just swoop in after all we've been through to save those kids and then just take them from us? You're a day late and a dollar short, and you'll leave here with bloody stumps if you get in our way."

She looked down at Cinder, unafraid. "Shows how little you know. Do your goddamned homework next time." She waved toward the helicopter, and out stepped Sonja Satre, shaken and pissed off, but none the worse for wear. "Ever hear of a mole?"

I blinked, trying to recover from the shock. "She...Sonja works *for you*?"

Cinder's hands glowed now and I lay my hand on her shoulder. *"Only if Sonja makes a move and then take her out for good."*

"And your sister?"

"Leave her to me."

"Sonja's a money whore, Charlie. She'll go to the highest bidder, and that's us. We have more money than you could spend in a thousand lifetimes. If you would have left well enough alone, you and your people wouldn't be in this mess."

"No can do, Kristy. You can't keep scooping up young supers for your army. They need training. They need a chance at a real life."

She laughed. "A *real* life? Gee. Like the one you had living out in bumfuck Egypt with the alligators? You call that living? Get off your fucking high horse little sister. There's a war going on and you can join it or get the fuck out of the way."

I shook my head. "You can't have them, Kristy, and if you press me, you will most certainly regret it."

She made a derisive noise and took a step toward me. Both Bailey and Cinder also took a step forward so Kristy stopped.

"Charlie, you've remained safe here in Alaska because *we*

allowed you to put a dent in Genesys' plans. Don't you get it? We've been using you all along. When we realized you and your people not only grabbed the triplets for us but bumbled into this snowball of a place, we let you do everything you've done along the way. Now, we're here for the payoff. We're taking the triplets."

I stared at her. I wanted to laugh, but pushing the buttons of a super as powerful as my sister wasn't a very wise idea.

As Gar's helicopter sounds faded in the distance, I was happy at least two of the triplets would be safe from harm. At this point, I could only hope I had chosen my aides wisely.

"Oh, Charlie, you are but pawns in a chess game you are ill-prepared to play." Kristy took another step and that's when I realized she was playing for keeps.

"*Echo?*"

"*Hold, Cinder.*"

"They're children, Kristy. *Children*. Not pawns, not soldiers, not something to be bartered with. Genesys can't have them and neither can you. I am going to give them everything Melika gave me."

"And what, exactly, was that, Charlie? A closeted lifestyle? It must be hard deciding which closet to live in every day. You're a gay supernatural trying to blend, trying to fit in. And for what? So you can be *normal*? Something you're not and never will be? I think those kids deserve *more* than normal because they are *better* than normal. So are you. So are your pals, here." She shook her head. "I just wish you realized we are on the same side." When Kristy raised her hands, they froze in midair as every sled dog within a mile radius converged upon us, sitting in a circle surrounding the five of us—two dozen dogs sitting in a circle, waiting. It was quite a frightening sight.

Kristy took a half a step back. "Your dogs will all die a needless death, Bailey. I *will* kill every last one of them if they make a move."

"You can't take them *and* Cinder out, Scion, and she's already bested your pathetic pyro."

Sonja nearly growled in contempt. She looked battered and burned, and I doubted she had much firepower left. I did not perceive her as a threat in the slightest. I had the upper hand and Kristy knew it, so I had one more card left to play. "You seem to keep underestimating me and my people, Kristy. There's one piece of this game you don't even see in play."

Folding her arms, Kristy waited.

"Here's what I'm offering you: A simple trade."

She shook her head. "There's nothing you have that I want except those three kids...and Cinder, of course, but she's made her choices."

I grinned almost malevolently. "Not true." Stepping close, I looked into the eyes that reminded me of our mother. "There's one person on this earth I *can* deliver that you'd move heaven and earth for. One person you would trade just about anything for."

She shook her head. "I seriously doubt that. Who would that be?"

I let a few seconds pass. "Our father."

Kristy looked like I had slapped her, her face blushing, her hands clenching. Her shields dropped and I read her disbelief and astonishment wrapped into one. "What the fuck are you talking about?"

"Who do you think the Professor is?"

She tried regrouping, but this news was too much even for her. "No way. That...that can't be. I would have known." Her breath quickened. "He's...he's *here*? That bastard has been running this shit all this time?" She started pacing back and forth. "How did I not know this?"

"Looks like it was you who needed to do your homework. He is here. And I can tell you where he is on the condition you leave me and mine alone. You can't have the triplets. You can't have Cinder. You can't. Period. You can fight me right now, where people will get hurt and possibly die. If you win, which you won't, you'll only have one triplet, and even then, you'll have to make sure Cinder is dead before you can take Boris. That's a lose-lose scenario that doesn't have to happen. If I win, your people will be hurt or dead, and you'll never find Hayward again. Another lose-lose. It's your call."

Licking her lips, she weighed her options, but we both knew

her decision was already made. She hated our father more than she hated Genesys.

"He...after all this...he *works* for them? That motherfucker."

I nodded, feeling a betrayal I hadn't expected her to feel. "Irony is a bitter pill, Kristy. He doesn't just work for them, he's one of the top dogs, and right now, he is wandering alone in the wilderness trying to make his way back to Nome."

She was dumbfounded. "Wait. You had him and you *let him go?*"

I nodded. "That's the difference between us, Kristy, and why these kids need to be with me. I'm no killer. As much as I thought I wanted to kill him, that cross was simply too heavy a burden to bear."

She shook her head slowly. "You're weak, Charlie, that's what you are. What that bastard did to us...to *both* of us...and you let him go? You're even weaker than your mentor."

All the dogs began snarling as Bailey strode up to Kristy. She would have popped her one if I hadn't have gotten a hand on her wrist. "Bailey—"

"You don't say her name, bitch. You don't even think about our mentor, or I swear to god—"

"Bailey, that's enough." I pulled her away as Kristy's anger mounted. "Please." Turning to Kristy, I continued. "His death might bring you a great deal of satisfaction, Kristy, because *you* remember him. *You* spent years with him that I didn't. He's a stranger to me. A nobody. Intellectually, I know he ruined my childhood and gave me away, but there's no emotional attachment to those thoughts. He's just a member of an organization I intend on putting a stop to."

She laughed. "A stop? Charlie, you couldn't even take down that asshole...one man. You can't stop Genesys with words and flowers. You don't have what it takes to go to war against those people. You've just proven that. You are soft." She shook her head again. "I can't believe you just let that fucker go."

"Maybe I'm not as hardcore as you, but I *will* stop Genesys one way or the other."

She stared at me a moment. "He's really here?"

"Yep. He is, and if you just get in your chopper and head

toward Nome, then maybe you can have the vengeance you so desire. But me? I'm going home." Just as I spoke, the sound of a jet leaving the runway filled my ears and lightened my heart some. Tip had done what I had asked her to do. "Your call."

Kristy looked over her shoulder at Sonja and her people before stepping closer to me. "If you're fucking with me—"

"I'm not. Trust me. I was as stunned to discover he was here as you are."

"That bastard. How could he? After everything he put us both through?"

I suddenly saw a glimmer of the little girl who had once been my sister. The feelings of betrayal and anger melted into pain and anguish. "The man has no soul, Kristy. He feels not one ounce of remorse. He's even learned how to build shields, but his are weak. The man is a snake, I'll grant you that, but I am not after him. I want the asshole at the top."

Pinching the bridge of her nose, she leaned toward me. "If I find him, I *will* kill him, Charlie. Slowly, from the inside out. I want him to suffer like I suffered. I want him to see what it feels like to be someone's lab rat."

"Do what you have to do. I really couldn't care less."

She nodded pensively and erected her shields once more. "Look, Charlie, it saddens me we are on opposite sides, but you truly are out of your element with Genesys. If you're going to play with the big dogs, you'd better do more than bark."

I shrugged. "Like I said: Hayward's just another puppet. I want Kip Reynolds. And after him, I'll go after the money."

"What will you do then? Slap his wrists? Spank him? Send him on a world tour? You're right about one thing: you are no killer and this is a death match where everyone is playing for keeps."

"When I find him, I will destroy him and everything he's ever created. I will crush every lab, every warehouse, and everything connected to Genesys. Mark my words, Kristy. I am not the pacifist Mel was."

"Was?"

"Is. I was her student, but now I am my own person, and I'll take out anyone who threatens us."

She chuffed. "Take out? See? You can't even say it, Charlie. Kill. You need to *kill* him."

"Destruction comes in many forms, but do yourself a favor, Kristy, and don't underestimate me. A lot has changed in my life since I last saw you. I'm not the same person, and I am not nearly as soft as you think I am."

She peered deep into my eyes. "I was sorry to hear about your loss. Jacob Marley wasn't it?"

I cocked my head.

She grinned slightly and shrugged. "What? You think we don't keep a close eye out on you? Like it or not, you're our competitor, and I always keep my eyes on my opponent. I know you've moved to California, though why on earth you chose Marin, I'll never know. It's not remote enough."

This was a revelation I hadn't expected and I suddenly realized I was not paying enough attention to all of the supernatural activities going on in the world. I would need to change that. It seemed I would be needing to change a lot of things.

"I have my reasons, Kristy. As for being competitors, that's where you're wrong. We're not even playing the same game. I want to teach them how to get the most out of life *even though* they are different, and you would use them as part of some super army to destroy Genesys and anyone else getting in your way."

"Tomato, tomahto. We both want young supers. Doesn't matter why. We both want to dismantle Genesys. Doesn't matter how. We just have different ideas about how to go about that. You can rationalize that away, Charlie, but the truth is, we're more alike than you'd ever admit. If you want Kip Reynolds, you're going to need soldiers as well. You can't do it alone."

"I'm not alone."

Her eyes suddenly looked very sad. "Maybe not literally, but I know you feel it deep down. I know there's an empty place that hasn't yet been filled."

Then she did something that shocked the hell out of me. She reached out and smoothed the hair from my forehead and I had a flashback of my real mother doing the same thing when I was just a little girl. It was the first real memory I had ever had.

"I'll forever be your sister, Charlie, and will always regret not being able to grow up with you...but my family is S.T.O.P now, and we have a duty I've promised to uphold."

"I understand that, Kristy. I really do." Turning to the Hummer, I motioned for Tack to come. I held my hand out for the vidbook. "I can show you where we dumped him." I showed Kristy the GPS map of the area where we'd dropped Hayward. "There's nothing between there and Nome except miles of snow."

She studied the screen a second before looking up at me. "I'll be damned. You really did leave him in the frigid wilderness." She chuckled and it sounded odd coming from her. "Maybe you *do* have it in you after all."

Shrugging, I shooed Tack back to the car before she became interested in him as well. "Life does that to you, I guess."

"And death," she said softly, knowingly, as she turned to get in the chopper.

I studied her wishing things could be different between us. "And death."

Motioning for her people to join her, Kristy turned back to me. "Charlie, when I kill him, when I am seconds away from snuffing out his pathetic life, is there anything you want me to say to him?"

I thought for a moment, a tear coming to my eyes. "Yeah. Tell him this one is for Mom."

We were halfway back to the airport when Danica called to inform me that the jet had returned and landed back in Nome. They were awaiting our arrival.

"They came back, eh?" Bailey asked as we headed for the cyclone fence we'd knocked down earlier. "Shoulda known Tiponi would never leave you behind nor would she follow your directive."

I let it go. What could I say? That she was right? "We need to pay for this," I said, stopping the car and getting out just as we reached the fence. "In fact, I'll bet there's a lot we need to pay for."

Bailey stopped walking and knelt down next to Tack. "We

need you to go into the airport and hand them this card." She pulled a card from her wallet and handed it to Tack. "Tell them to contact her for the repairs of the fence. If they give you any flack, describe Sonja and tell them she gave you the card. Then hightail it back to the tarmac."

Tack glanced up at me, so I nodded. "Hurry back."

He took off like a rocket, card in hand.

"Solved that issue. Anything else we need to do by way of cleanup?"

I nodded and stepped closer to her. "Thank you, Bailey, for everything. You've really come through for me here and I appreciate all that you've done."

She smiled bashfully. "You're the boss, E. That makes me… well…not the boss. My job is to support you any way I can."

"Thank you." Placing my hand on Cinder's shoulders, I stared into her eyes. She had grown up so quickly. "And you. You amaze me every single day. You took on a trained pyro and—"

"Kicked her ass!" Bailey finished for me, giving Cinder a high five.

"Yes, that, too. You showed incredible discipline and restraint—a true sign of maturity."

Cinder beamed.

"But," I watched her smile disappear. "Now that I know talking is possible, I expect to hear your voice at times other than when you are threatening someone. Is that clear?"

She nodded.

"Good. Come on. Let's get the hell out of here."

We were walking around the downed fence when my vidbook rang. It was Tip, her face registering unabashed concern. "We've landed, Echo. You okay?"

"We're good. Almost to you. Why did you come back? I thought I told you—"

"Not my call." She interrupted. "I wouldn't have, but Dani said she'd kick my ass so hard, I'd be a hunchback if we didn't turn around to come get you." She shrugged. "So here we are. Gar had no—"

"We'll see you in there." I hung up by snapping the book closed.

Bailey raised an eyebrow. "Um, you hung up on her."

"Because she's being an ass. She just said she wasn't going to come back for us, Bailey, and you know she wasn't kidding. She was going to follow my orders regardless of the danger, regardless of the outcome, regardless of whether or not we needed her." I shook my head.

"Wow. You two have never been like this, have you?"

"No, and if she wanted to take my place, she needed to bring that up with Melika, but I can't have her second-guessing every move I make. She needs to go home and see Mel. Until she does that, her emotions are going to be all over the place, and I have enough to worry about. Let her...new girlfriend rub her sore spots. I can't worry about her any more."

"Ouch, but yeah, she doesn't have to be such an ass."

As we neared the jet, Tack came running back. "They've called the cops, but there was something going on in town, so it might take a while."

"We won't need a while. We're getting the hell off this popsicle."

The stairs slowly lowered, and there stood Taylor at the top. The moment the stairs locked, she flew down them and into Bailey's arms, where they hugged for a few moments before Bailey pulled herself off. "Hey, we're okay. It's all good."

"I didn't want to leave, but that..." She shook her head in disgust. "Tip insisted."

"It's all good," Bailey repeated. "She just did what E told her to."

Taylor wasn't having it. "The day Delta leaves Megan or Connie on the frozen tundra to fend for themselves is the day I am cashing in my chips. It's not how we do things. It was bullshit."

"Come on, ladies," I interjected. "We can rehash all that later. Right now, let's get out of here." I was the last to enter the plane, and took one last look at Alaska before poking my head into the cockpit.

"We're good to go, Gar."

He nodded. "Soon as we get clearance."

Peering out the window, I saw Pitt and Loco waving madly at us from the tree line.

"Make a note, Bailey, to send those two whatever the veterans need at the retreat. If the list is a hundred pages long, I want everything on it. We owe them big."

"All over it."

I checked on all of the kids. Tack was sitting next to Cinder. It warmed my heart that she finally had someone her age to hang out with.

The triplets' heads were bobbing. All of this had taken its toll on them. The two boys who were very overly-protective of little Nika, resisted sleep even as Nika was sound asleep.

Bailey and Taylor had their heads together. It looked like love was really blooming for the two of them and I have to admit, I was slightly envious.

When I finally made eye contact with Tip, she looked away. She didn't act like a woman in love, and Ivonne didn't seem overly loving with her. Of course, Tip had never been the cuddling kind, so I understood that much, but her demeanor…it was… unlike how she had been with me.

Once we were in the air, I called Dani to let her know we were on our way home.

Home.

That used to be Louisiana, in the heat of the verdant bayou filled with crazy animals and colorful people, but now, I would be returning to San Francisco to start a new life…a life without Melika, a life without the river, and a life without Tiponi Redhawk.

When we arrived, Danica and a stretch limo were waiting. She hugged Cinder first and for a very long time. Her Firefly was home safe and you could feel the relief in the air.

"I need to say goodbye to Tip," I whispered. "Would you mind hanging with the kids for a few?"

Danica shot a look over at Tip and Ivonne. "Jesus, Clark, that woman is runway gorgeous."

I shrugged. "Say what you want about her, Tip has game."

"As long as you're not playing," she said, getting into the limo, "I couldn't give a shit what game the Big Indian is playing."

Tip extricated herself from Ivonne long enough to come say goodbye.

"Going home," she grunted. "Ivonne's never seen the bayou."

"Will you be staying?"

"It's my home."

The anger didn't ooze out her pores—it shot out like red laser beams. I'd never seen her like this. The best thing I could do would be to let her go.

"Take care, Tip."

"I will." With that, she took Ivonne's hand and walked toward the terminal, her pain evident by the way she carried herself.

Flipping open my vidbook, I called Melika and left her a message. "Mel, it's me. Tip is on her way home, and I sure hope you're there because she's really hurting about your health. I didn't want to tell her, but I had to. My hand was forced. She... I've never seen her like this. Please let me know that you get this. She really needs you. I miss you. Call me."

Closing the vidbook, I walked over to Danica who seemed to be trying to make sense of all of this. "I have one more thing to take care of."

"I'll meet you in the limo," she said, rubbing her arms. "It's too damn cold out here."

I laughed. "You don't know cold until you've been in Alaska."

"And that is never happening."

Climbing the stairs back into the jet, I sat in the small cockpit opposite Gar.

"Just shutting her down. This baby was like flying a dream." He grinned for a rare moment.

"I'm glad. So, what are your plans? Back to Alaska?"

"Actually, I was thinking about just heading south. Go home to SoCal. Try to put my past behind me. I think this little caper of yours was just what I needed to show me I could handle life and people on the outside."

"We owe you big, Gar. Without you—" I shook my head. "This whole thing would have gone south."

"Can I be honest with you, Echo?"

"Absolutely."

"As you know, I came to Alaska to get clean. I've been nursing my wounds for so long, I've almost forgotten what they were. But then you gals walked through my doors, and I haven't had that much fun in a long time. So, thank *you*. Not many people would trust their loved ones with an ex-oxy addict veteran, and I appreciate the faith."

"I'm not like many people."

"No. No, you're not. I don't quite know *what* you are, but you people are not like *anyone*. Period. But I'll tell you this much. I've had some good leaders and some crappy ones, and I'd follow you to the depths of hell. That's how good you are."

Suddenly, I was awash with an emotion I hadn't anticipated. "Gar, do you really mean that?"

"Hell yeah. Echo, you're a really thoughtful, courageous person, and your team believes in you enough to do some crazy shit."

"Could you?"

He squinted. "Could I what?"

"Believe in me enough to do some crazy shit?"

He laughed. "Already have, haven't I? Hell, crazy is my birthname."

"I'm not being very clear, Gar. What I was wondering was if you'd like a job?"

This surprised him, and he sat back. "A job? Doing what?"

"Whatever needs to be done. Fly, drive, bodyguard. Kick the shit out of someone."

He laughed again. "Just when I think I understand you, you come at me with a surprise. It never occurred to me you'd want a guy like me around…you know…kids and all."

"Look, you're a great guy with a lot of skill in a lot of areas. We need people like you, and the kids need a good role model."

"Who is we, anyway? You and that hot woman in the limo?"

It didn't surprise me he thought Dani was hot. "Well, sort of. All the adults you met work for me. We run a school of sorts…a mentoring community for kids with special…talents."

He nodded. "You know, in the Middle East, they don't have

so much fear for the extraordinary. That's what we're talking about here, right? The extraordinary?"

I nodded. "Yes. And if you come work for us, I promise there will be full disclosure. We need good people, and you're good people, Gar, regardless of your demons."

His neck started turning red. "To be honest, Echo, I was trying to figure out some way of asking you if you might have a place for me in your organization."

"Then you'll stay?"

He laughed. "I could dig that, yeah. I'd like to go home first and grab some things, but if you've got a big enough bed, then I'm all in."

I nodded. "Come with us now…in the limo. You can leave in the morning and make your decision after you see the place."

Once everyone was in, we headed through the streets of San Francisco on our way to Marin and the chateau Danica had built as a place for me to train young supers. When we arrived, the kids all followed Cinder through the house, jaws gaping as they ran around checking everything out. The house truly was a modern marvel full of the all the latest technological gadgets and security systems. It had everything a kid could dream of including a stadium seating movie theater.

Danica showed Gar to his room before coming back downstairs and meeting me in the kitchen. I had already placed a saucer of milk down for my cat, Tripod, and was sitting on a stool at the enormous ten-person island, waiting for my tea to steep. I would have loved to say it was good to be home, but this place was simply too new to be considered home yet.

"Umm, Clark? That's the biggest human being I've ever seen. He must weigh close to four hundred pounds."

"Gar's a good egg, Dani. He saved our bacon. Do we have any place for him here? Is there something he could do for us?"

"We could ride him like a pony."

I nearly spit out my tea laughing.

"Sorry. Bodyguard comes to mind. I'll spend some time with him tomorrow and see what all he can do, but that guy is enormously scary. I mean like you read about."

"He can fly. He's a veteran."

"And he's fucking huge! I say good on ya, Clark. I'll find a place for him. Don't you worry."

"Excellent. Thank you. We also have some bills to pay for the damages done in Alaska."

"Send me a bill, Clark. I'll take care of it."

I briefed her on everything that had happened at the airport and gave her the lowdown on the gaggle of kids who'd tromped through the house on their way to the bedrooms. The triplets were in awe, but as tired as they were, they crashed as soon as they'd taken their showers.

When I'd gone in to check on Nika, I stood over her bed for a long time thinking about what all of this meant. Though I had never wanted any kids of my own, it appeared I was a mother several times over. I just didn't know how to feel about that.

"You look tired," Danica said, studying me through intense eyes.

I nodded, bone-weary. "I'm exhausted. This one took the wind out of my sails, I'll tell you."

"So, you think Kristy found your dad?"

Wrapping my hands around the tea mug, I shrugged, suddenly feeling completely drained. It felt as if I would never get warm again. "Honestly? I don't really care. Kristy has her own ax to grind. If she found him, I guess it was meant to be."

"And if not? If he is still working for Genesys tomorrow?"

I stared down into the mug as the steam rose and curled. That was all I had thought about in the plane. Had I left the dirty work up to my big sister by not killing my father myself? It was a question I was sure I would wrestle with for quite some time. "Then I'll take him down with everyone else when the time comes."

Danica leaned across the island, her gaze intense. "Is that what we're doing here, Clark? Making little soldiers to go after Genesys? Is that what you really want?"

Taken aback, I just stared at her.

"Right now, we have our hands full with Tack, Cinder and the triplets. Those kids need to be trained. They need guidance, love, support. They need to feel safe and secure. They won't feel any of that if you allow the shadow of Genesys to hover over this house. If you're going to go after them, take Delta and Connie and leave the teaching to someone else. If you're going to teach the kids, you need to shelve your vendetta. You can't have it both ways."

I stared at her. "It's not a vendetta, Dani."

"No? Well, whatever it is isn't *their* battle, yet. Not until they can understand who they are fighting and why. You need to remember that. We got lucky this time, you schlepping those poor kids through the wilderness..." She shook her head. "Amazing we didn't lose any of you, but those kids deserve time to get used to their surroundings...time to settle in. You need to focus on them now. Get your priorities straight."

I studied her carefully. "Who have you been talking to?"

"No one."

"Liar."

She averted her eyes. "Fine. Bishop called. She had a lot to say. I guess she's been doing damage control with the Others ever since you left training. I think she worries about you trying to do this alone."

"I'm not alone." Why did everyone keep saying that?

"You know what I mean. The Others could have come in handy in the outback of Alaska. If you're going to take Genesys on, I think you need to repair your relationship with the Others."

"I'm not sure that's something I care to do. They're old and set in their ways. They still believe in bygone ways. Did she say anything about Mel?"

"She said that she and Malecon have returned to Europe to see if they can find some way of saving her. She said they are getting along like they did as children, and that she hasn't heard that lilt in Melika's voice in forever."

"Thank God. But Tip really needs to see her."

"Screw her! She's being an ass and taking her pain out on you? Fuck that. Melika is feeling up to the challenge, Malecon is doing everything he can to save his sister, and even Bishop sounded rested."

I nodded. "I am so glad. I haven't had much time to worry about them."

"Well, everyone is doing great, but…Bishop wants you to get your priorities straight. She and I had a long talk and I agree with everything she said. Put Genesys on the shelf right now and give these kids the attention and energy they deserve. Genesys isn't going anywhere."

I slowly nodded. "When did you get so smart?"

"Yesterday. Maybe the day before." She grinned. "Actually, hanging around you has broadened my horizons a bit."

"I hear you, Dani, and you're right. I didn't take over for Melika so I could create an army. What I'll do differently is make sure young supers know all the inherent dangers, including Genesys. I'll even let them know about Kristy's group…but mostly, I just want them to be comfortable in their own skin."

She crossed her arms. "You really want me to buy that load of crap? You're obsessed with going after them. You know it. I know it. Hell, *they* know it. It's only a matter of time before you take these kids after them. All I'm asking is that you make sure they are ready when that day comes."

"You know I will."

"Perfect. So, how was Firefly?"

"Well now, I saw a few things I wasn't ready to see."

"Such as?"

"She spoke."

"No!"

"Yes!"

"What did she say?"

I put my hand over my mouth and said, "She trash-talked another pyro."

Danica's eyes grew wide. "Oh my God! Was she her badass superhero self?"

"Ask her yourself."

Cinder waltzed in and gave Dani a hug.

"Firefly, I hear you were badass."

Cinder beamed and nodded.

"Sit up here a second," I said, patting the stool next to me. "Cinder, when Sonja threw everything she had at you, you…you put your hands up and were unharmed. How was that?"

Hopping up on the stool, she frowned as she thought. *"Melika discovered I have the ability to absorb heat and fire. I am like a magnet drawing it to me. Never did it like that, though."*

"Like some kind of heat conductor?" Danica asked.

"I suppose. I absorb it and it increases my own power. It was risky, but I had to do something. She's very strong and would have fried me."

"You should have killed the bitch," Danica growled. "Working for Genesys, shooting at my girls. You should have put her down, Firefly."

"Actually, she was working for Kristy," I explained.

"Well, if your sister is all fired up to go after Genesys, let her. You have a greater purpose."

"Spoken like Bishop."

She shrugged and poured herself some tea. "The woman is wise."

"I think, for now, I will listen to my wise women. I have too much to do teaching these young punks." Messing up Cinder's hair, I hugged her. "Thank you, Cinder, for always having my back. You were pretty damn impressive there."

"Mel says it's what we do for each other."

"It is, and I appreciate you and your skills, but until I can find an established pyro to help teach you, I'm going to rely on you to help me with these kids."

"Sure thing. The kids are cool, and I really like Tack." Sliding off the stool, she hugged Danica goodnight. *"Tack says he'd like to meet whoever does the electronics. I told him Sal was super cool and would teach him whatever he wanted to know."*

"Tomorrow. They'll meet everyone tomorrow."

As she skipped out of the kitchen, Danica shook her head. "They grow up so fast."

"Never thought I'd hear you say that."

We both laughed.

"Where *is* everyone else?"

"I sent them to an expensive dinner and a movie. We've been monitoring you around the clock. The troops are spent. Besides, I wanted the kids to have the run of the house. You know, not feel like people were staring or watching them."

Laying my hand on hers, I gave it a quick squeeze. "You're going to make a great den mother."

She pulled her hand quickly away. "Oh hell, no. No mother here. Uh-uh. No way."

"Daddy?"

She glared at me. "Don't make me hurt you."

Sipping my tea, I hid my grin behind my mug. "First thing we'll need is an English tutor for the triplets. They know a little English, but not much."

"That little girl is adorable. What is she?"

I shrugged. "Not sure yet. We'll get them acclimated first, say a week off, and then we can run them through a battery of tests and see who has what. Then we hit the books and the—" I stopped short.

Danica cocked her head. "And what?"

"Oh, nothing. I was going to say the river, you know, like…"

"Like home?"

I nodded, feeling terrible that I did not yet consider this my home.

"BOB, show me river photos one, two and five, please." Turning away from me, Danica approached a console on the refrigerator and pressed a large button. On the kitchen island, a television set slowly rose and turned on.

"You're kidding me."

"Sal likes to watch the news with her breakfast."

When the television reached its zenith, BOB, which stood for Bot on Board, and was the computer artificial intelligence-savvy software Sal had designed to run the chateau, said, "River photos one, two and five."

Looking at the screen, I saw a gorgeous river surrounded by grapevines and oak trees. The river wound around and through…vineyards?

"Oh my God, is that—"

The next photo was of a firepit almost exactly like the one we used to spend hours at on the bayou.

"It is. You made a river on the property!" I couldn't see photo number five because my eyes were all teary. "Oh, Dani. It's gorgeous."

"It was the last piece we were working on finishing when you left. And to be honest, Clark, I did it as much for me as I did for you. Some of our best times happened around those nightly fireside moments. I just had to create something as close to the bayou as I could for all of us."

I stared up at her and realized her eyes were teary as well. "I know how much you miss Jacob, the bayou, Melika. I just... I just wanted you to be happy here. I want you to call this place home."

I hugged Danica for a long time, before she pulled away and wiped her eyes. "We've got one more thing to show you. BOB, show the label please."

The television screen flickered, and a wine bottle appeared with a label I'd never seen. The top of the label showed two figures drawn like people on bathroom doors. One was black, the other white, and they were holding hands. The label said, "Friends Estate. Merlot."

"Oh, Dani. It's..."

"Perfect."

I nodded.

"The boys came up with hundreds of over-the-top super cool labels, but in the end, we decided that wasn't us. Simple, yet elegant, something uniquely us."

"I love it."

"Good. Welcome home, Clark."

I went to bed that night feeling calm and settled. Danica had my back, she grounded me in ways I'd never imagined. It was good to be...home.

Friends Estate?

Perfect.

After having coffee and calling Finn for a coffee date later in the afternoon, I made my rounds of the chateau. It was an amazing piece of property. Over one hundred and seventy acres of lush vineyards on rolling hills that would turn emerald green in the first wave of showers toward the end of October. The river was a man-made marvel that appeared anything but artificial. It had all the true marks of Mother Nature—from huge moss-covered boulders to stretches of silty banks, all it was missing were the alligators and Spanish moss, but it was amazing nonetheless.

Sitting at the firepit, I played at not overanalyzing Finn's less-than-enthusiastic voice on the phone. After all, in her world, I'd been MIA for a couple of days, not there when she was released from the hospital, and basically an absentee girlfriend.

In short, I sucked.

So instead of dwelling, I thought about all I needed to do to get ready for mentoring. Truth was, I hadn't the foggiest idea where to begin. It felt insurmountable. I needed real tutors for their natural schooling, super tutors for their power training. I needed a schedule, a plan, an idea of how to—

"I'm not even telepathic with people and I can feel you all nutted up all the way across the property." Bailey sat down and handed me a leaf of some kind. "Chew this. You really need to chill, E."

Taking the leaf, I chewed for a minute, the bitterness dissipating as I did. "Is it that obvious?"

"If it's any consolation, I'd be freaking if I were you, too. This is a huge undertaking we're doing here, E, but the operative word is *we*. You've done the one thing every good leader does—you delegated to people who are great at what they do. You have an exceptional team behind you, E. Trust that. Trust us."

"I do, but—"

"No buts. Let me run through the list." Bailey pulled out an actual list. "I've got animal telepathy, biology, zoology and botany. Roger has maths and statistics."

"Roger?"

She nodded. "Danica's got you covered for all the natural learning for the kids. Roger, math; Carl, computer science; Franklin, physics and chemistry. Connie, Spanish; Megan, history."

"History?"

Bailey chuckled. "Go figure. Taylor will do escapism and lock-picking."

"Wait."

"Think about it, E. It could come in handy someday. You don't need to be a lowly natural to need to know how to escape from places."

I was already feeling better. "Wow. I...I didn't realize—"

"I know you didn't, but I'm not done. Dani will handle the books, accounting, et cetera...well, her people will. William will run the vineyard with some help from the kids. There's no reason they can't learn the business. Speaking of which, Danica has some classes set up for you both to learn about the business. When the kids get settled in, you two will have a great week in Napa, or Sonoma. I forget which."

"That sounds heavenly."

Bailey nodded. "You deserve a breather. You haven't had a moment's rest in forever. So, you see, we have it all covered. You have a team far superior to anything Melika had on the bayou."

Inhaling deeply, I shook my head. "We're missing a telepath and a mover. Those boys are going to need someone to put them through their paces."

"Don't sweat it for now. I'll get the word out and we'll have someone here in no time. Just breathe."

I spit out the chewed up leaf and felt my muscles relax. "Thank you for that."

"Works every time." She stood. "It's beautiful out here, E. Really. Dani's done an incredible job on this place."

"Yes, she has. I love it."

"Then relax into it. There are no bad guys around, and if they were, our team would snuff them out where they stood. Things are going to be great. You'll see."

"I guess I need to go with that, huh? I need to have a little more faith."

"Yes, you do. Look, I've gotta scoot. Taylor and I are going out and giving ourselves some well-deserved R and R."

"Thanks for the pep talk. I really do feel better."

"Good. You want to really feel well, stop by the winery. That William is a magician."

I turned toward her to ask why, but she was gone. Bailey could do that; move quietly like a cat. It was one of her tertiary powers.

"Thanks, Bailey," I said softly.

Something was quite clear now.

I had picked my second in command. Or was it that she had picked me?

Either way, I was finally ready to assume my new role.

When Finn slid into the seat of the booth across from me, she didn't look like herself. She'd lost a lot of weight while in the hospital, and had a look in her eye that just wasn't what I was expecting. She appeared almost suspicious.

Out of uniform, she appeared smaller, less threatening, and yet, there was an air about her that made me double my shields.

"How are you feeling?" I asked.

"Getting stronger every day." She waved the waitress over and ordered for us both two coffees and a couple of Danish pastries.

I didn't eat Danish pastries, but said nothing.

Leaning forward, she kept her hands folded on the table. "There's no way to ease into this, Echo, so I'll just come out and say it. I've had a long time to think about what I saw, what happened after I hit my head, what happened after we both got home from New Orleans. I've had time to really examine our relationship, and I've come to a conclusion...we don't have one."

The waitress brought the coffee and poured it, telling us the Danishes were on their way. When she left, I was still too shocked to say anything.

"I know how I feel about you, Echo, but those feelings have no place to go. I know that now. I'm not blaming you. We both have all-consuming jobs that suck our energy and our lives. It's no one's fault. It's just the way it is. We're married to our jobs and throw crumbs at our personal relationships and then wonder why they never work out."

My hand went to my mouth. "Oh my God. You're breaking up with me."

She poured cream and sugar into her coffee, staring down into it as if waiting for it to reveal some secret to her. "I would be if there had been an us to break up, but there hasn't been.

Not really. An *us* would have left New Orleans together. An us wouldn't have run off while the other was recovering from a head wound." Taking my hand, she squeezed it. "I'm crazy as hell about you, Echo, but we need to face the facts—we're too busy to have a real relationship. We may want to, we may even convince ourselves it's important to us, but if it was, we'd both try harder to carve out time for ourselves...and we don't. We can't have a relationship over vidbook." Finn took a moment to sip her coffee.

"I...I really don't know what to say."

Finn's eyes held a sadness that pierced my soul. "I know you care about me, Echo. Hell, you may even love me, but a relationship needs maintenance. Time. We haven't done either, and by the looks of things, we won't be getting any soon." She paused and studied me a moment, her eyes telling me more than her words. "Say something."

Staring into my coffee, I waited for the waitress to drop the Danish at our table. "I don't know what to say. I thought...I guess I thought..." Shaking my head, I left my thought hanging... whatever it was.

"I'm really sorry, Echo, but you've got a full plate and so do I. We give so many other things priority in our lives, that our fledgling relationship just sorta died of neglect. We both deserve more than what we were getting."

Yes, we did.

"So that's it? We're done?" I felt like someone had pulled the rug out. I was stunned—not by the words she said but by the weight of their truth.

"Yes, love. We're done."

So, without further ado, Finn tossed a twenty on the table, kissed my cheek, and left me sitting with two uneaten Danish and a lukewarm coffee.

In a little under forty-eight hours, I had been left by both women I loved. Now, I was sitting here, alone, in a diner, feeling the gaping holes left by both of them—and those holes were huge. I had thought that maybe Finn and I had a chance, that maybe if I trusted her enough with my truths, that we could give it a go.

The only thing to go was Finn, and she'd made it clear her leaving was not negotiable.

I couldn't blame her. After all, I'd been gone more than not. She wouldn't have been in danger if she hadn't hooked up with me. Maybe this was one of those instances when letting go was really the best for all involved.

It was what I needed to believe, anyway. If I didn't believe that, the pain of her breaking up with me would have left me sobbing. As it was, I was simply too tired and too blown away to know how to feel.

In the end, it wasn't my secret that cost me my relationship—it was it was my lifestyle—my supernatural, paranormal lifestyle.

I had been planning on driving down to Santa Cruz to see my mother anyway, but now, it felt imperative. It really rocked me when Finn left me at the diner, and I needed the kind of hug only a mother can give.

Finn dumping me blindsided me big time. I suppose I should have been expecting it, but when she said the words, my heart buckled, but I understood. She deserved more. Better. She deserved someone without huge secrets who risked her life to help younger supernaturals. I shouldn't have been stunned, but I was, and for the first time in my life, I had my real mother to turn to.

Like most mothers, when Trish opened the door she knew just by looking in my eyes that my heart was aching. She threw her arms around me and hugged me tightly.

"Come on in, hon. You look like you've lost your best friend."

"Not quite, but close enough," I said.

She showed me into the comfortable family room, where we sat on a leopard print sofa that looked out over the ocean. I'd only known my mother was alive for four months, when I had employed Delta Stevens' detective agency to find her. Delta had not only found her and my grandmother, she also found the childhood that had been erased from my memory. Slowly but surely, I'd begun replacing blank pages in the scrapbook of my memory with photos of Charlie Hayward, little empath. It helped knowing who I was and how my life had been. I needed that. I needed to know where I'd been before I could firmly and with confidence move forward with my life. And though with those new memories came some shards of pain, I did not regret them for a moment.

"You look tired," Trish said, "Can I get you something? Coffee? Water?"

"No, no. I'm good. It's been a long couple of weeks. I lost one of my best friends, Melika shared she has an inoperable brain tumor, and I was dumped by not one, but two women. I've had better weeks."

Trish's motherly response was to fold me in her arms and hold me. It was from that safe zone I pulled out a shard of my pain and stabbed her with it.

"My father works for Genesys."

Trish slowly pulled away and stared at me, her eyes unblinking in their disbelief. "No. Oh please, Charlie, tell me you're joking."

I shook my head. "They call him the Professor, and he's very high up in their organization."

"How do you know this?"

"I met him."

Looking away, Trish didn't brush away the tears that slowly rolled down both cheeks.

"I wish I didn't have to hurt you with this, Trish, but I'm not one to let the truth hide in a shadow anymore."

She stared out at the ocean for a long time before saying softly, "How...how could he? After all he—" Her voice trailed off and she could only shake her head.

"I'm so sorry, Trish."

I remained silent for a moment, letting her process all she was experiencing. I could only imagine the anger, resentment and sense of betrayal that was soon to follow.

"Nine years..."

I reached over and held her hand.

"Did you...did you kill him?"

"I wanted to, but no. I dropped him off in the wilderness and left the killing up to Kristy."

Her head jerked toward me. "You were with your sister?"

"Not with, per se. Let's just say we were shopping at the same store."

I explained everything I had been through in the last couple of weeks, until she put her hand up for me to stop.

"So, you just left Alaska not knowing if he was dead or alive?"

"It doesn't matter. Either way, he is dead to me. What he did to Kristy...to you...if anyone deserves the right to take him out, it's her."

"Could she...I mean..."

"Kill him? Oh hell, yeah. Hate runs through that girl's veins. She is a very powerful super whose life was not only altered by Genesys, it also drives it. She *will* destroy Genesys or *it* will destroy what's left of her humanity. Either way, they are locked in a death embrace no one can unlock."

"My poor babies. All he's done to us." She let more tears fall. "I hope she killed him."

Nodding, I grabbed a box of Kleenex off an end table and handed it to her, saying, "It will be the final irony that he is killed by the daughter he handed over to them. Maybe doing so will alleviate the bloodlust that drives her."

"How...how bad is it?"

"Pretty bad. She doesn't really recognize us as family—though I don't blame her for that. She is single-minded in her pursuit of them. She will stop at nothing to destroy Genesys."

"And what then, Charlie? What drives her if she succeeds?"

"I've wondered that myself." I shrugged. "But I can't be concerned about my vigilante sister or demented father. I almost let her poison swim in my veins, but that's not me. Not now. I have a greater responsibility first, and that's to live up to Melika's expectations as a leader, and not put my people in harm's way."

Pulling out a Kleenex, she dabbed her eyes. "There will always be a Genesys in one form or another. You can either run around putting out fires, or you can live your life to the fullest. My hope is that you choose your life."

"Exactly. I understand now why Mel never told us. She wanted us to live...to be free. Kristy isn't free. She's trapped in a steel ball of revenge. That's no way to live a life. I don't want that for me *or* my kids."

She smiled softly. "Your kids, eh?"

I nodded, suddenly feeling this immense pride and incredible clarity. "Yeah," I nodded. "Mine."

We visited for another half hour before I felt the pull to go home.

"Thank you for letting me know," she said, walking me to my car.

"I'm sorry it still hurts. I know I'm leaving you with a black bag of emotions, but at least you can put a period at the end of that chapter of your life."

"Oh yes. I'm sure I'll run the gamut of emotions once the sadness dissipates, but at least now I know."

I held her tightly. "I'm really sorry."

Pulling away, she looked me hard in the eyes. "No Charlie, don't be. He was just an absentee husband to me. What he did to you girls was unconscionable. I'll be fine. I promise."

I left Trish feeling mixed emotions of my own, but knowing that she deserved the truth. The truth is like going to the dentist: We need it, and sometimes it hurts like hell, while other times, we walk away with a painless smile.

Right now, Trish Hayward was hurting like hell, but she'd get over it. I was pretty certain Kristy never would, and would one day discover that killing Hayward didn't free her of that pain, but, quite possibly would only add to it.

Picking up my vidbook, I called Bailey. "Hey, it's me. Do me a favor and gather everyone together at the dinner table in about two hours."

"Uh. Sure. Everyone?"

"Everyone."

"You okay?"

"I will be." Hanging up, I drove home.

Home.

It really is where your heart is.

When I arrived at the chateau, I realized Danica had changed the wrought iron signage to Friends Winery. I warmed inside thinking about all of the things she had done to make all of this possible.

When I entered the kitchen, everyone was seated around the large wooden dining table, chatting and laughing, and enjoying each other's company. There were the triplets, Cinder, Tack, Bailey, Taylor, Danica, William, Gar and Sal.

As I stood there watching everyone laughing and having a wonderful time, it filled me from within and radiated out to my fingertips.

These were my people. My family. My friends. These were the people I would commit my life to, that I would die for if need be. These people were the gift, the legacy given to me by a man who, whether alive or dead, had placed me on the path I was currently standing on. I needed no vengeance for this blessing of a life, no revenge. He had, in his own way, done me a favor. He had created me.

And I was okay with that.

As my eyes moved from face to face, my heart swelled with love.

They say you can pick your friends but not your family.

They couldn't be more wrong. *This* was my family, and I was their matriarch.

Suddenly, Melika's shoes fit just fine.

Publications from
Bella Books, Inc.
Women. Books. Even Better Together.
P.O. Box 10543
Tallahassee, FL 32302
Phone: 800-729-4992
www.bellabooks.com

CALM BEFORE THE STORM by Peggy J. Herring. Colonel Marcel Robicheaux doesn't tell and so far no one official has asked, but the amorous pursuit by Jordan McGowen has her worried for both her career and her honor.
978-0-9677753-1-9

THE WILD ONE by Lyn Denison. Rachel Weston is busy keeping home and head together after the death of her husband. Her kids need her and what she doesn't need is the confusion that Quinn Farrelly creates in her body and heart.
978-0-9677753-4-0

LESSONS IN MURDER by Claire McNab. There's a corpse in the school with a neat hole in the head and a Black & Decker drill alongside. Which teacher should Inspector Carol Ashton suspect? Unfortunately, the alluring Sybil Quade is at the top of the list. First in this highly lauded series.
978-1-931513-65-4

WHEN AN ECHO RETURNS by Linda Kay Silva. The bayou where Echo Branson found her sanity has been swept clean by a hurricane—or at least they thought. Then an evil washed up by the storm comes looking for them all, one-by-one. Second in series.
978-1-59493-225-0

DEADLY INTERSECTIONS by Ann Roberts. Everyone is lying, including her own father and her girlfriend. Leaving matters to the professionals is supposed to be easier! Third in series with *PAID IN FULL* and *WHITE OFFERINGS*.
978-1-59493-224-3

SUBSTITUTE FOR LOVE by Karin Kallmaker. No substitutes, ever again! But then Holly's heart, body and soul are captured by Reyna... Reyna with no last name and a secret life that hides a terrible bargain, one written in family blood.
978-1-931513-62-3

MAKING UP FOR LOST TIME by Karin Kallmaker. Take one Next Home Network Star and add one Little White Lie to equal mayhem in little Mendocino and a recipe for sizzling romance. This lighthearted, steamy story is a feast for the senses in a kitchen that is way too hot.
978-1-931513-61-6

2ND FIDDLE by Kate Calloway. Cassidy James's first case left her with a broken heart. At least this new case is fighting the good fight, and she can throw all her passion and energy into it.
978-1-59493-200-7

HUNTING THE WITCH by Ellen Hart. The woman she loves — used to love — offers her help, and Jane Lawless finds it hard to say no. She needs TLC for recent injuries and who better than a doctor? But Julia's jittery demeanor awakens Jane's curiosity. And Jane has never been able to resist a mystery. #9 in series and Lammy-winner.
978-1-59493-206-9

FAÇADES by Alex Marcoux. Everything Anastasia ever wanted — she has it. Sidney is the woman who helped her get it. But keeping it will require a price — the unnamed passion that simmers between them.
978-1-59493-239-7